Praise for *STRIPPED*

"Tantalizing . . . Their chemistry is intense."
—*The New York Times*

"A witty, wonderful romance that speaks to who we are, who we are meant to be, and who we are meant to be with."
—*The Washington Post*

"Vivid and naughty." —*Entertainment Weekly*

"Much like *Magic Mike, Stripped* is swoony, exciting and an all-around entertaining ride." —*Booklist*

"A sweet and sexy story that shows how life-changing—and gratifying—it can be to step outside of your comfort zone and question expectations." —*Shondaland*

"A perfect read for fans of *Magic Mike*."
—Smart Bitches, Trashy Books

"A sexy, funny contemporary romance . . . devilishly fun."
—NPR

"Castile delivers genuine chemistry . . . thoroughly entertaining."
—*Publishers Weekly*

"Take one sexy stripper hero, add one wild, witty school teacher heroine, and watch the fireworks. This book is my cherry pie!" —Ann Aguirre, *New York Times* bestselling author

"Castile's writing sparkles with wit. Readers will swoon for Robyn and Fallon's love story."
—Alexis Daria, author of *Take the Lead*

"In a perfect mix of sexy attraction that sizzles on the page and enchanting romance between characters you fall in love with, Castile's novel hits all the right notes!"
—Priscilla Oliveras, author of *Her Perfect Affair*

"Zoey Castile is a fresh and fun new voice, and the characters in *Stripped* will capture your heart (and possibly your dollar bills)." —Alisha Rai, author of *Hurts to Love You*

Books by Zoey Castile

Stripped

Hired

Flashed

Published by Kensington Publishing Corporation

FLASHED

A HAPPY ENDINGS NOVEL

ZOEY CASTILE

KENSINGTON BOOKS
www.kensingtonbooks.com

KENSINGTON BOOKS are published by

Kensington Publishing Corp.
119 West 40th Street
New York, NY 10018

Copyright © 2019 by Zoey Castile

All Kensington titles, imprints, and distributed lines are available at special quantity discounts for bulk purchases for sales promotion, premiums, fundraising, educational, or institutional use.

Special book excerpts or customized printings can also be created to fit specific needs. For details, write or phone the office of the Kensington Sales Manager: Kensington Publishing Corp., 119 West 40th Street, New York, NY 10018. Attn. Sales Department. Phone: 1-800-221-2647.

Kensington and the K logo Reg. U.S. Pat. & TM Off.
ISBN-13: 978-1-4967-1529-6 (ebook)
ISBN-10: 1-4967-1529-2 (ebook)
Kensington Electronic Edition: September 2019

ISBN-13: 978-1-4967-1528-9
ISBN-10: 1-4967-1528-4
First Kensington Trade Paperback Edition: September 2019

10 9 8 7 6 5 4 3 2 1
Printed in the United States of America

For Christine Higgins, sláinte and salud

PAT

December

Thirty-five was my lucky number.

I was thirty-five when I got my big break. A year before that I modeled on the cover of a book for a friend. That book went on to sell thirty-five thousand copies the first month it was out. My face was plastered all over airports, check-out counters, bookstores. Wherever books were sold, my mostly naked body was there—even a 350-foot billboard lighting up Times Square across three sides of a building.

I got picked up by *the* top agency covering LA, New York, and London. Signed my name away on a 3.5-million-dollar contract to star in the biggest summer blockbuster since *Avatar*. Matchmaking agencies were off the hook trying to get me to be photographed with or date starlets that my teenage self would never even have dreamed of, models from every corner of the world, even one duchess looking to get on the front pages of whatever gossip magazine would catch us in dimly lit Parisian bars. How many of them? That's right. Thirty-five women.

I had the life I'd hoped for, dreamed of, *prayed* for between shitty jobs and endless nights. I had the life I thought I'd earned. No. The life I deserved.

I'd yet to learn that no one deserves anything.

It took thirty-five seconds to change my life, too.

To get in that car with my brother and our dates for the premiere of my breakout movie. Sure, it was ten seconds to win the drag race, speeding at over ninety miles per hour across a quarter mile of empty, glittering LA streets with fans waiting at the finish line. I should have done a lot of things that night. Hell, before that night while I'm at it.

Thirty-five bottles of champagne at the pre- and after-parties for just my friends, probably more. But all I can think about is the moments after the accident. The guys on the losing side trying to take my brother out of the passenger seat to pick a fight. My fists flying, knuckles on skin, crunching on bone. Blood down my nose and face. Then, it was over. The fight was squashed for some reason I can't remember. We were okay for thirty-five seconds after that. I'm sure of it, even if it's impossible.

"Get in the car, Jack," I shouted at him.

I should have said more. I should have—

Ten seconds to rev the engine and get away from the nut job with a gun. Five seconds to get to the next intersection, screaming, laughing, slapping the dashboard at how fucking lucky we were. How alive.

Twenty seconds that the truck driver fell asleep at the wheel and T-boned my car and the world spun like a whirling firework on the Fourth of July, all brilliant sparks and red and blue lights on the spray of shattered glass.

"Jack?" I shouted only a single time before my luck ran out.

1
Go Your Own Way

LENA

June

My red 2005 Honda Civic wheezes and jostles its way up the dirt road to the McMansion. After half an hour of getting lost on Hyalite Canyon Road because I mistook the old ranch's entryway for a dead end, I'm praying to all the gods that this is the right place. I can feel every single rock and pebble that my busted shock absorbers fail to—well—*absorb*. You'd think that a place looking for a live-in housekeeper could afford to, I don't know, pave their driveway. If I get the job, I'm going to have to find a smoother back road that won't shake my car apart.

I clutch the wheel, my shoulders tight and my head leaning forward. "Hold on, baby. You can do it." But after a mile, I don't see the house, only the bright green landscape just south of Bozeman, Montana, I've grown accustomed to.

Right now, I'm 75 percent sure that I'm still lost. Even if I know I took the right turn, this pothole-marked road feels more like an entrance to a haunted house than anything else. I groan as the path slopes up and my motor makes the same sound I make when I'm coughing up phlegm. I shift gears and my car bucks.

"Come on, Selena, my darling," I beg. I turn off the CD player (yes, my car still has a CD player) and hit the gas, leaning forward as if I can push this thing up the hill with my sheer willpower.

Then, I'm up at the top of the hill. Bright-green trees in the distance make the view practically a postcard. It rained a lot this spring, and out here, there's a wildness to the surrounding lawn, overgrown in a way that looks almost forgotten.

"Okay," I say, this time to the Porg hanging from my rearview mirror. "Do you think I have a chance at the job, Leia?"

The stuffed animal my ex-boyfriend won for me at a movie theater does not respond, which I'm sure is good considering my state of being. Leia Porgana, as I instantly named her, is a gift I've kept as a token of home. Sure, that same ex sat through the movie screening clutching his soda angrily because I'd just told him I was leaving New York to go back to art school all the way across the country. The movie is a blur. I don't know why I didn't wait until after it was over. I just had this tingly sensation the second he captured the porg with the metal claw. He handed it to me and he was going to tell me he loved me. I felt it in my bones. He said, "Lena, I l—" That unfinished *L* haunted me across my entire trip here. He might have been ready to say, "I love spending time with you or I *like* crowded theaters with arcades for public declarations of romance." It wasn't right on my part to do that, but it was better to rip off the Band-Aid and break up in person instead of over the phone. Still, this tiny stuffed porg kept me company in that theater while my ex was spilling Coca-Cola on his lap, neither of us paying attention to the exploding cars and chase scenes on the big screen.

I know I made the right decision to leave. At least, I thought I did. I've been in Bozeman for six months and it's scary how little I miss from my life back home. I can count those things on one hand and they go as follows—my little sister, Ariana, pizza (real New York Italian pizza), hearing seven different languages at any given time on the way to work, having a twenty-four-hour pharmacy open for when I get a serious cookie craving and also realize I ran out of tampons at two in the morning, and the Colombian restaurant at the corner of my block. So, family, food, and convenience?

Before I can analyze my levels and limits of human connection and attachment, I breathe a sigh of relief when the McMansion finally comes into view. Having spent all of my twenty-six years of life in Queens, New York, and only Queens, New York, I don't know the difference between a working ranch or a ranch mansion or what the locals like to call Darned-Californian-Tax-Evaders. This is definitely not the rustic wooden house I'm used to seeing atop green hills. It's modern in a way that looks alien to this landscape, all clean metal lines and glass walls on the entire second floor. It has the sleek exterior of a possible serial killer's lair, gray and white and devoid of color. I pull up on the unfinished gravel lane near the front door. What might have been spiral topiary trees line the perimeter of the house, but they've outgrown their shape and weeds sprout all over the grounds.

To my right is a huge lawn equipped with a metal firepit and beyond that, a thicket of woods that goes on for miles . . . or acres. I honestly don't know the conversion. The point is, there's more property here than the square of backyard I grew up with. Practically a million times more. That's the thing I love about Montana. I can feel the outdoors here even when I'm in someone's backyard.

I put my car in park and grab the wheel to steady my nerves. *I can do this.* Yesterday, I answered a Craigslist post for a job. For hours I grappled with whether or not to call. The job was, after all, for a live-in housekeeper. My mom was a maid for a service on the Upper East Side and my aunt was a hotel maid. It was good, constant work. For years they toiled hard and put food on the table. But when my mom died, I knew that I didn't want to work myself to death. I didn't want to let some rich assholes bleed me dry. My mother was Mexican and my dad Puerto Rican, and I'm as New York as you get. But that also means—as a twenty-six-year-old Latina college dropout—cleaning houses is about where my college advisors thought I'd end up. It's honest work and yet, I still turned my nose up at the posting because when people who look like you are only seen in one dimension, one role, one type of job, you start to forget that you're more than a punch line. That maybe you have your own dreams and aspirations.

I should blame my stepmother for forcing me into a financial deficit, but I don't have time to dwell on that, thankfully, as a short, plump woman in a red plaid shirt walks out of the house. She gives me a concerned look as she makes a beeline for me.

"Heya, I'm Scarlett." Her voice is bright and friendly. Up close I can see the fine age lines around light-brown eyes and the smatter of burnt-red freckles over her nose. She scratches at the spot under her wedding ring with short sparkly nails. "Glad you found the place. You must be Magdalena Martel."

I inwardly cringe at the pronunciation of my full name. Only my dad used to call me Magdalena. Ariana calls me by my whole government name—Magdalena Luz Martel San Sebastián. But it never sounded right during roll-call periods where old teachers said my name like they were coughing up furballs.

"Everyone calls me Lena," I say, and smile as I shake her hand.

"Thanks for coming at such short notice."

I really need this job because my stepmother ruined my credit is probably not the correct response, so I pivot. "Your home is—lovely."

She barks out a rough laugh. "Oh, honey, this piece of modern manure, pardon my French, isn't mine. The house belongs to a friend. It's a long story, but the short of it is he needs someone to keep the place clean, prepare meals, do the laundry, the works."

"Is he, like, a millionaire recluse?" I ask, then instantly regret it. "I'm sorry, I didn't mean—"

Scarlett's too busy laughing and cuts off my apology with a wave of her hands. "You're absolutely right he is. He's a pain in the ass, but he's been through a lot and he means well. At least he might mean well if I could get him to leave the property once in a while. But that's neither here nor there."

Scarlett doesn't elaborate, and I know enough to not ask. She walks back to the house and I follow behind, leaving my car unlocked. Ariana was shocked when I told her people here don't lock their cars or home doors.

The foyer is pretty clean. I'm not exactly sure what kind of mess she might mean until we enter the living room. First, there's the beautiful parts of it. The high ceilings and exposed beams of pale wood, the place feels like a dome. Floor-to-ceiling windows give a startling view of the surrounding area, including the hill I crested with nothing but cheap gas and fairy dust. You know, I feel like maybe it's better I don't get this job because the idea of having to repeat this drive might shatter my car into hundreds of pieces.

I ignore my self-sabotaging thoughts and turn to a fireplace big enough to fit three people inside—I mean, if this was the witch from "Hansel and Gretel" and you were into that sort of thing. The walls are still unfinished, but there is nothing I love more than a blank canvas. A very empty bookcase flanks the entire main wall. A *wall*. For *books*. Then there's the stuff that's not so beautiful—dozens and dozens of boxes in various stages of unpacked, broken bits of wood from what could have been a coffee table. When I bump into one of the boxes labeled FRAGILE, the unmistakable sound of broken glass rattles.

"I can't tell if he's moving out or just moving in," I say, only half joking.

Despite the layer of dust on the fireplace mantel and the general disarray, I can see the promise of the space. It's a little more modern than I like, but I'm about fifty years away from being able to own my own house at the rate that I'm going, so what does it matter?

"The place was finished eight months ago," Scarlet says. "The Donatello Ranch was all but falling apart so Pat, as the oldest living son, made the tough call and built something over nothing."

For the first time since our introduction, she isn't cracking her warm smile or boisterous laugh and I take that as a sign that there's more to this story.

"Let me give you the tour," she says, and loops her arm through mine.

The gesture takes me by surprise. It's friendly, warm, and damn, it's been so long since I've had human contact like this that part of me wants to give her a hug. Growing up, I've always been used to physical contact. When I'd sit on the couch and do my homework, my mom used to brush my hair or plait it in two braids. When we walked in the mall, my mom and aunt and myself would walk hand in hand. Before I went to bed, I kissed Ariana on the top of her head even though all she'd say was, "You'll see me in the morning, *ugh*."

But what if I didn't? What if something happened? I wanted to make sure she knew that I loved her. Here, on my own for the first time in my life, I've forgotten how much I miss that.

I clear my throat and let Scarlett lead me out of the living room and down a wide hallway. My skin is chilled at how cold it is in here. The black wood panels are so sleek it almost looks like oil. I wish I'd taken off my boots because I'm tracking dirt and gravel on the gray marble floors. Scarlett shows me four empty bedrooms like this, two of them with bathrooms. Bed frames and side tables are still in their boxes waiting to get built. Light fixtures tucked in corners have collected dust.

"This is so much space for one person and we haven't even been upstairs yet," I say.

"I know what you're thinking." Scarlett steps over a packing tube in the bedroom at the farthest end of the house. It might belong to an expensive art print or a rug and I'm curious enough that I want to find out. "And no, he didn't get left at the altar."

"That's not what I was thinking at all, but I guess it's good to know about the person I'll be cleaning for. Uhm—the ad said I'd have to live here?"

The ad *didn't* mention anything about a man living alone near the woods but then again, it's Montana.

"I'll show you where you'd stay around back," she says, returning down the way we came. "It used to be a bunkhouse before the Donatello boys turned it into a place to work on their cars. Now it's the pool house. And you have the option of living there or at my place. I live just two miles through the woods between our properties. Now, this is the kitchen."

I nearly gasp. I'm not about to win an episode of *Chopped* but I love to cook. The oven is huge, with thick iron grills and more buttons than I know to push. There's a red stand mixer, a microwave that looks more high-tech than the burnt-spaghetti-covered mess at the house I live in now.

"I wonder if this is what Ina Garten's heaven looks like," I say.

"She'd probably get halfway to heaven if she saw the lonely box of Old Bay in the pantry," she says with a wink. "The microwave also heats up frozen dinners in thirty seconds flat."

I make a face. "Frozen dinners when you have all of this?"

Scarlett shrugs dramatically. "Some men seem to be able to survive on it."

"Not my dad," I say jokingly, but the swell of emotion that comes at the memory is both wonderful and terrible. It's been years since he passed and I still feel his absence. Talking about him makes it better, like a calming balm on a burn. "Are there more rooms?"

"Downstairs is the home gym." Scarlett's light-brown eyes flick up to the ceiling. "Upstairs is a little more *lived* in. Follow me."

We get to the stairs that run up and down the center of the house. The moment we get to the top floor, there's the slam of a door and something like a bear growling.

Scarlett puts on a tight smile. "Don't mind the little lord of the house."

I clear my throat and pace around the empty living room, from one of the glass walls to the other. When I was applying to schools, I remembered a brochure of a small art department at Bozeman University. The picture showed scenery like this—trees and green and the outline of mountains in the background. This sight still steals my breath. The sun is low in the sky, behind clouds that are big and fluffy enough to want to take a bite out of.

"Ain't it something?" Scarlett asks beside me.

"It really is."

"So that's the house," Scarlett says. She turns around and points to a dark hall with missing ceiling lightbulbs. "You wouldn't have to do anything up here. Just the main level and kitchen. Now, tell me about yourself?"

I practiced this speech in my dinky shared house off campus filled with ten people just to keep the rent at under three hundred dollars a month. It is similar to every introduction I've uttered at the first day of my classes in January. Teachers looked me up and down and plastered a surprised smile on their faces before asking, "Magda-leeeeena, tell us about yourself." I give Scarlett the same spiel I've given everyone, including the TSA guy at JFK.

"Well, I'm twenty-six. I'm enrolled at the university. Art major. I'm originally from New York City." I pause for the usual and inevitable arch of her brow and *wow, New York City? You're a long way from home.* "Yep. I have one little sister. She's almost fifteen and a handful and a half, but she lives with my stepmom. I was working up at Higgins Cafe but—"

"Gosh, sorry to hear about it closing down. Things get quiet during the summer but never quite like this. Have you ever worked in housekeeping?"

I shake my head. "I'm a fast learner. I got my first job when I was fifteen, bagging groceries, then a year later I was a cashier at a clothing chain. I got promoted to manager by the time I was eighteen. My mother and my aunt worked in housekeeping all my life. I know it's not the same, but—" This is where I get to the part where I start rambling about responsibility and how I've been entrusted at so many things.

As I take out the résumé letter from the inside of my jacket pocket, what I don't say is that I have to pay for school by the end of the summer or else I can't return in the fall. I don't tell her that the loan I had was canceled because my stepmother has been stealing my identity for the past six months. There's ten thousand dollars of unpaid credit cards with *my* name on them, and, while I could get her arrested, I wouldn't be able to do that to my little sister's mother. Who would give *me* guardianship over Ariana when I'm still paying off my dad's hospital bills? I couldn't let my little sister go to a stranger's home knowing I put her mom in jail. My chest feels hot with humiliation, with fear and panic at the uncertainty of my future. Scarlett has no idea of the anxious thoughts racing through my mind. Her eyes scan my résumé, nodding while she bites her lower lip. I'm seconds from throwing myself at her feet, but Scarlett puts her hand up.

She isn't shooing me out the door. She rests a hand on my shoulder. "Look, hon, I can tell you're a hard worker. You're also overqualified for this."

I brace myself for the "but—you're not right for the job."

Part of me has never been right for something. The first time I was in college, my first art teacher told me I wasn't quite right for the field and then didn't elaborate. The time I applied for regional director after being the manager with the highest-grossing store in the tristate area, I was told I wasn't right for the job.

"But tell me about *you*."

"Me?"

"Yeah, you're going to be here all summer and I'll be seeing a lot of you. Besides, Pat's not exactly a kitten. More like a grumpy old lion. Have you worked with kids at all?"

I laugh. "If my sister, Ariana, counts. When she was seven, my dad got sick. My stepmom—she really didn't know how to deal with it—so I dropped out of school to take care of her full time. Most of the time I had no idea what I was doing, but I learned and she's a good kid. Does, uh, Pat have children?"

Scarlett looks panicked at the thought. "No, but it's how I measure the required level of patience. I think you'd be perfect for this job, Lena."

"Really? It's not because you feel sorry for me, is it?" I ask. *Shut up, stupid, and take the job!*

She laughs that infectious laugh of hers. "What I need is someone with life experience. Anyone can sweep and mop."

"You've never lived with nine college kids," I mumble.

"Nine?" Her eyes go even bigger. "Oh, honey, no. Now, this is the setup. If you're comfortable, you can live on the grounds, but if not, I have a bunkhouse, too. We had it converted for an Airbnb. You'd have your own space there as well, you'd just be driving over for meals."

I glance around the empty space and that chill returns. Who needs the air conditioner blasting like this when the day is perfect outside? I suppose, it wouldn't matter if I have my own mini-house to keep myself company.

"I don't think my car could take going up that hill three times a day," I chuckle. "This almost seems too good to be true."

"Well." She tilts her head to the side, like she's weighing the next thing she's going to tell me. "Remember when you asked if the owner is an eccentric millionaire?"

"Is he like Jay Gatsby?"

"Sort of. Only without the parties and we're in the middle of nowhere Montana instead of New York."

"Okay . . ."

"Point is, there are some house rules. You have the run of the place except for times that will be listed. After today, the second floor is off limits. You can clean this living area, but as there's nothing but wooden floorboards to sweep, you'd just be in and out. Under *no* circumstance are you to enter the room at the end of the upstairs hall. That's Pat's space."

"Okay," I say, like this is the most reasonable thing I've ever heard. I desperately want to ask why everything is off limits. I've watched enough telenovelas to have a myriad of scenarios in my head. Everything from secret werewolf to rare disease that won't let him be around people or the outdoors.

"You will have to sign a nondisclosure."

I narrow my eyes at her. "As long as he's not in there because he's a serial killer, I'm fine."

"Definitely not a serial killer. I'll be the one cutting your checks and we like our privacy around here. Pat would sure appreciate it, too."

I'm sure someone who built a house they never finished decorating appreciates privacy. Though I can feel there's part of the story I'm not being told. I decide it isn't my business as long as I get the work done and keep to the pool house.

When I just keep nodding, Scarlett follows up with, "Can you cook?"

"Yes," I say. "But I'm going to need some salt and I always thought Old Bay was a kind of deodorant."

She laughs. "I'll make sure you have the groceries stipend in cash."

"Wait, I got the job?"

"Of course, you got the job." Scarlett is already walking ahead of me back downstairs. I start to follow when I see a shadow move at the end of the hall. The door I'm not supposed to enter closes quickly. He's right behind that door. I almost wonder if he's going to come out and meet me. I know that I'd want to see the person who's going to be living in my house for the next three months.

Rich people are so weird.

Scarlett shows me the area around back complete with a babbling brook, a hot tub, and a long crystal-blue pool. She tells me she's a romance writer and I tell her I've never read any before. She's practically brimming with book suggestions for me, and for the first time in so long, I feel at ease. This job pays more than I've ever made an hour in my whole life.

I don't know much about Pat Donatello. I don't care if I can't lay eyes on him. Recluse billionaire, secret werewolf, whatever he is, right now, he's my guardian angel.

PAT

The minute that tiny red hunk of junk starts jostling up my driveway, I try to picture the woman that's going to pop out of that front seat. Even from this distance, I know those aren't Montana State license plates. Probably some college student who's unfortunate enough to stay in town during summer break, fast food and receipts littering the seats and floor, and dozens of air-fresheners hanging from the rearview mirror. I stomp to the kitchen to face Scarlett West.

"I don't want to do this anymore," I say.

She's on her laptop going through applications. This is our last interview. It hasn't been a long process since there were only four people who want the job. The locals already know me. They know all about the accident, all about my name in the papers. If they're not new to town, then they know about my family, too. The Donatellos. Even though we lived in a dilapidated ranch inherited from Grandpa Donatello, my dad made his trade as a steel worker and my brothers smoke jumpers. Rough hands and rougher attitudes—well—as far as I'm concerned. Ronan was the funny one, the one anyone could be friends with, and Jack was the kind one, the sweet one, the one everyone loved. I was the one you didn't want your daughter bringing home. I can't quite remember why I got that reputation, but it's a small town. The reputation I have now? I suppose I deserve that one.

Those four applications on Scarlett's computer know nothing about what I did to my little brother. My friends. Myself.

"Let's forget it," I say, this time breathless despite the hours of cardio I've put in this week.

Scarlett finally takes her warm light-brown eyes off the screen and levels them with mine. She's about the only person other than my old boss Rick who can get me to shut the hell up. When they mean business, they show it.

"You sit your ass down, Patrick Halloran. You and I both know that you're not going to get these boxes unpacked and you're not going to clean out the mess of spider webs infesting every corner of this house. I'm too short to reach your confounded high ceilings and I've got a book to finish, so I can't be making sure you feed yourself *and* keep this place livable."

This house. This house that I had built on the foundation of my family's old ranch. Jack hated the idea of it, but I always thought he'd come around to it when he returned home. The second my check cleared from the agency last summer, I had bulldozers turn the ranch to splinters. Some of the neighbors who knew my family didn't voice their disapproval of my design, but back then, I didn't care what they thought anyway. I was thinking I could give my brother something to be proud of, something our parents couldn't provide no matter how hard they tried. Now, it just feels like a giant container made of glass and steel and wood. Sometimes, when I walk past the boxes of designer fucking pillows and unbuilt furniture, the only thing I want to do is carry everything out the damn door and set it on fire. And every day I can't. So, I settled for breaking one of the tables yesterday.

It didn't help.

"This will just be like the others," I say, and hear how ungrateful I sound.

Shaking her head as she pinches the bridge of her nose, Scarlett asks, "How do you know that? Did you suddenly develop psychic powers from staring at the same five walls every day?"

"Because. There's no one in this town during the summer and I don't need someone coming in here to gawk at me like the fucking freak show I am."

I don't look at her, but I know she's staring at me. She does this when she doesn't want me to feel self-conscious about the angry red scars zigzagging across my palm, up my forearm, my face. She looks at me like she's trying to prove a point and that makes it worse.

"You're not a freak show and no one is gawking at you, Pat."

I grip the edge of the kitchen island, a strange pressure building at the center of my chest. Am I really that nervous? Of course, I should be. Scarlett's the only person, other than the nurses and doctors, who has seen the rest of the scars on my torso and my legs. I rub a hand across my face. The thought of a stranger looking at me now makes the nerves in my chest fritz even worse. "You're gawking right now."

"I'm looking at you, Pat," she says softly. "We're having a conversation and I'm looking at you. I thought you agreed with me that this was for the best."

I wish I had something to throw on the floor, but if I make a mess of her paperwork she'll kill me. "Maybe I'm changing my mind."

Scarlett shuts her laptop and pulls her auburn hair into a messy bun. I go to the living room window and keep an eye on the car. Whoever is in there must be gunning that thing, but it's barely making it up the hill while going about ten miles per hour. At this rate it'll be sunset before the interview starts, which is fine by me.

"Let's talk about this," she says, and continues despite my groaning and moaning. "You need help around here. We agreed it would be my gift to you. We agreed on an NDA. She can't take pictures or go into your rooms. What has you changing your mind?"

I take a deep breath. Ball my hands into fists. "The first guy who walked in here was stoned out of his mind and I wouldn't trust him to take care of my goldfish—"

"You don't have a goldfish."

"If I had a goldfish, I wouldn't trust him to remember to change the water. The second was my math teacher from junior high and I hated that bastard. He failed me for taking his daughter to the movies even though we didn't even make out."

"I'm sure you called that nice girl back."

I sidestepped that verbal land mine. "The *third* one was a sixty-five-year-old woman who worked with my mother and wouldn't stop asking questions about Jack, and Ronan like he's still alive. I don't want people in my space. I don't want people turning me into a fucking joke—or worse. Another fucking tragedy."

"Okay, honey," she says, stretching to place her palms on my shoulders and rubbing slow circles. Scarlett's only five years older than me, and though she looks youthful, she's got the kind of motherly presence that calms me down. She takes care of me. She's the only person allowed in here because I trust her. "I don't want you to do anything you don't want to do. But if you take a moment to think about it, really think about it, you have to know that you need some help around here. Whoever we end up hiring is going to have a schedule. They can stay with me if you really want that. But you won't even notice she's here. I mean, look at this place. It's big enough for a dozen and *then* some. You'll barely know anyone's here."

I shake my head and peer out the window. The car finally pulls up out front. I start to turn to Scarlett. I want to tell her that I don't deserve anyone's help. I don't even deserve Scarlett.

But I can't say anything because when she steps out of the car, she is nothing like the person I had thought of. Even from here, I can see her high cheekbones, her full lips. Long brown hair whips in the early summer breeze. She shoves her hands in her jeans as she turns to look at the trees out back. Something inside of me rips the breath from my chest. She is heart-stoppingly stunning.

"I'll go greet her," Scarlett says, with a curious glint in her eye. "You'd better make yourself scarce so you don't have any-one *gawking* at you."

I growl at that, but even as she leaves me for the front door, I find myself following. A part of me says to keep going. To take a step over the threshold where there is nothing but ten acres of my land, filled with green hills and woods. It would just be me, Scarlett, and her. I try to think of the names of the applications but can't. Why didn't I look at them when Scarlett forwarded them to me?

But when I stand two yards from the door, I get a sick feeling in my gut and I turn around. I go back to the window that faces the red hunk of junk, the woman standing in front of Scarlett. That sick feeling doesn't quite go away, but it moves around.

She's taller than Scarlett, but then again, so is everyone. Her light-tan skin looks golden in the early afternoon sun. I only get one more glimpse of her face before Scarlett leads her inside. Beautiful is the first and last word that comes to mind because I shut that shit down. I run the hell upstairs.

This isn't going to work.

*   *   *

"You can't hire her," I say.

Lena. She said her name was Lena and she spoke at about a thousand miles per hour, which is faster than her car at least. I bet if I got under the hood, I could at least make the 2005 model run like a 2015 model. I shake my head and something angry and hot runs through me. There's the spark of a flash. The sting of glass.

"Pat?" Scarlett asks.

I shake my head. "What?"

"I asked why. She's professional, I can tell she's a fast learner, and she's in town for a while. She's going to school."

"I thought she was twenty-six?" I ask.

Scarlett raises an eyebrow. "I *thought* I heard you creeping about. You could have said hi."

I think about the nurse who unwrapped my head the first day I was fully conscious after the accident, after the surgery that got a piece of metal out of my chest and a hundred pieces of glass out of the left side of my face. I was swollen and red and sedated, but I remember the sheer horror in her eyes. I remember the glistening tears and the perfect circle of her mouth.

Ever since the accident, I've gotten variations of the same facial expression followed by pity and grimaces and apologies, as if they were the ones driving the car that night instead of me. I don't need that. It's been six months and I don't want to feel that way again.

"Give me one good reason why I can't hire her and I won't."

I suck in a breath and look at Scarlett dead in the face. She's barely five foot two but Scarlett Johnson, better known as Scarlett West, has a way of making even me shrink under the challenge in her eyes.

I think of the way Lena spoke of her little sister. The way she ticked off the times she wasn't right for the job. Mostly, I keep wondering why a girl like her, a girl who could be anywhere for the summer, would choose to be here. Then, I remember she said she was living in a house with nine other people.

"What if she brings people over? She'll turn the place into a frat house," I grumble.

"That is a bullshit reason and you know it. She told me she spends most of her time studying and painting. She's back at school to work and she needs this job. You need to eat something that isn't microwaved and to see your overpriced rug instead of dozens of boxes. It's a match made in heaven. Unless—"

I cross my arms over my chest. She's got this sparkle in her eye. I've seen it before she locks herself away in her house for two weeks at a time banging away at her laptop keyboard with the dozens of romance novel ideas she dreams up. "Unless what?"

"Unless you think there's another reason why you don't want her around. She *is* incredibly beautiful. You should see the cute little beauty marks on her cheeks."

"Okay, enough," I say and turn around because even if I didn't get close enough to see the beauty marks, I definitely noticed the rest of her. "Your line of work is a hazard in my life. Take two seconds to get your mind out of the gutter."

"Some of us like living in the gutter every now and then." Scarlett smirks, but I can already tell she's glowing because she knows she's won.

Scarlett is the reason my life changed over a year ago. She'd been my babysitter when Jack and I were kids. I hadn't seen her in years until she was in Vegas for a bachelorette party and recognized me even half-naked on a stage. It was only a little awkward at first. I hadn't seen someone from my life here in so long and I didn't expect to see her there of all places. She didn't know I was going by my mom's surname, Halloran. She just so happened to be in search of a cover model for her first romance novel and I fit the part. Then, the book was an international success overnight. Well, seemingly overnight. Scarlett gave me a new start and I destroyed it. Now, she's trying to help me even though she doesn't owe me a single thing. Even when I was a drunken mess, and even when I was rude and loud and *trying* to fall apart, she stood by me.

I'm such a fucking dick. She's hiring help because she needs time for her work. She can't take care of me forever and I've been using her as a crutch. I know I have.

"Did you tell her the rules?" I ask.

"Yep. Every single one of them. She's not allowed in your Vampire Den and she's not allowed in the house when she isn't cleaning or cooking. Though, is that really necessary?"

"The pool house is practically big enough to fit a whole family," I shout.

She purses her lips and I lower my voice. "I gave her the option of staying with me. Though I don't want her getting lost through those woods out back. You know how city folks are."

Scarlett isn't the kind of person to pass judgment, so I know she's laying it on thick. "Fine," I say. "But if she doesn't listen. She's out."

"Yes, yes, she'll follow your rules. She's going to bring her things here later tonight and I'll be back for when she does. Go work on your abs or whatever you do until dinner. You can be your grumpy old self at midnight, Groucharella."

"Groucharella is a new one," I grumble. "I don't like it."

She laughs and nudges my arm. "I'll be back."

She's halfway out the back door when I realize something. "What time is she going to be here? *When* are you coming back?"

My heart is racing, and I palm my left hand against my chest to stop myself from trembling.

"About five. But call me if you need anything, you hear?"

Relief washes over me. Maybe—maybe this can work. "Thank you, Tiny."

She walks back to squeeze my free hand. "Don't mention it, Stretch."

When she's gone, I glance at the clock. I have about five hours before this Lena comes back. I should make the most of my solitude, but I crawl back into bed. My room is the only part of the house that is fully furnished and even then, there's just my king-size bed, deep-blue painted walls, a mahogany dresser, and a reading lamp atop a bedside table. I pick up my copy of Scarlett's latest romance but, instead of reading, the lack of sleep from last night catches up to me.

I start to dream of a tiny red car, a narrow road, a girl with waterfalls of dark hair and beauty marks.

As always, the dream changes, and I relive the accident one more time.

2
Maldita Sea Mi Suerte

LENA

"Hey, Ari, I've tried calling a few times. I know you're mad at me for not being able to go home this summer like I promised, but I got a new job. I'm packing things up as we speak. No more cochinitos leaving their dirty boxers all over the place. Call me. Love you, nena."

I pocket my phone and finish throwing my things into the same black suitcase and duffle bags I moved to town with.

"Lena!" Mariana shouts from somewhere in the hall. "What is this business about moving out?"

Her head of black curls pops out from the hallway door. Her catlike green eyes narrow in my direction. Her bottom lip juts out in an exaggerated way.

"I told you," I say. "The job means I have to live there."

"Live there? Is it like a nanny for an adult?" She glides past me and throws herself on my bed, preventing me from getting the clothes into my bags. "Because they have a name for that. Someone's spouse."

I roll my eyes. "You're too young to be so jaded, darling."

Mariana's twenty-one, but despite being five years my junior, she's the one person in the house and in my classes that feels like an old soul. When I first got here, she was my first friend. There's a camaraderie that comes with *looking* like we're not from around here. She's an art history and archaeology double major, and when she isn't buried under stacks of books or in the studio with me, she's hiking in the wilderness. Like, for fun.

"Whatever. Who is going to feed us? Who is going to make sure we don't run out of toilet paper for a whole twenty-four hours? Where's this magical job, anyway?"

"It's off Hyalite Canyon Road. Used to be called Donatello Ranch but now it's a giant glass box."

"You're working for a Teenage Mutant Ninja Turtle?"

I tug at the hoodie she's crushing with her ass. She rolls to the side and I nearly stumble back when it comes free. "I'm actually working for a friend of the property."

"What?" she asks. "Okay, explain. I think I'm still dehydrated from yesterday."

"No one told you to forget your water bladder on a twelve-mile hike."

"*Anyway,* you were saying."

I give Mari the rundown of the situation. Every time I bring up a new detail like "recluse," "room I'm not allowed to go into," and "cook" she gets more and more bewildered.

"He's a serial killer," she says, nodding gravely. "Definitely."

I sigh and give up on packing while she's on my bed and sit down next to her. The twin bed isn't big enough for the two of us, so I end up slinging my legs over hers. I think of Ariana and how she's been avoiding my calls. When I was her age, I wouldn't even *look* at my dad for days when I was mad, so I foresee this being a long silent treatment.

"He's not a serial killer. He's just—odd. But I'm from New York. Odd is the normal."

"And I'm from New Jersey, bitch. And when you show up at a house and there's a man locked inside, you better run."

"You can come visit," I say. "There's a pool and some woods."

She perks up a little and rests her head on her propped-up arm. "I'm happy for you. Even if—"

"Don't do it."

"You—" She sucks in a deep breath and makes a crying face. "You wanna leave me!!!"

She puts on her best Greek accent. On our first ever hangout, we were both pretty homesick and ordered in the neighborhood pizza and even two snobs like us thought it was delicious and watched *My Big Fat Greek Wedding*.

"You sound like your dad," I tell her.

"Papa Tsamis would definitely not approve of this decision."

Mari's dad is her best friend in a way I've never seen before. It's not as if my dad and I weren't friends. It's just all my life there was a distance there and I was never sure if it was because that's who he was, or if it was because he never had a son like he wanted to, or because his illness just never allowed him to get close to anyone after a while. I guess I'll never really know.

"Don't tell your dad."

"He's very worried about your well-being. You haven't come to the studio in like two weeks. You aren't still moping over your B minus in Abstract Expressionism, are you? Because even I barely got a B."

That's not it at all, but I don't tell her it's because I can't afford any paint or canvas and I'm too stubborn or proud to ask for a loan, even if she'd give it to me. I pick at the pills on the comforter and settle for a truth I can handle.

"I've been uninspired."

"Maybe you should come and hike with me and you'll get some inspiration. Or at least, the guys in the hiking groups are really hot in that haven't-showered-in-two-days-pine-needles-and-beard kind of way."

I make a face. "That's strangely not arousing, thank you. Besides, me and nature aren't simpatico."

"My mom's like that," she says. "My whole Persian side. They're too bougie. My aunts blame my dad sending me to Greek camp in the summer and also for the reason I didn't want to go to business school."

"You in business school? You'd eat everyone alive."

"See? I can't be left unchecked and unsupervised. I'm about to tell Timothy about himself if he keeps leaving the upstairs toilet seat up."

"Wow, I'm really loving this convincing speech to get me to stay. But, I have to finish packing. I told Scarlett that I'd be over by five."

"That's like four hours away and everything you own can fit in the back of your car."

I don't know why, but that reminder bothers me. Growing up, we didn't have much, but I had *stuff*. Posters and collages I'd make from ripping up magazine cast-offs from the local salon. My mom would buy me books from the liquidator centers in New Hyde Park. I had a giant collection of Nancy Drew for that exact reason. Here, I have clothes and school books. A knife that one of my teachers helped me build in a mill at the beginning of the year. A very soft sheep's wool blanket from a local shop. If I could count Selena and Leia Porgana, that's it. That's my whole existence in a single car.

"Then come with me to the studio so I can get my easel and things. I'll even buy you lunch with the deposit I'm getting back from Landlord Louis."

"Giant souvlaki or bust," Mari says, and kicks into high gear packing up the remaining clothes on my bed.

After Mari and I pack up my car with my bag of brushes and paint tubes rolled up like toothpaste trying to squeeze the last little bit, we grab lunch. She runs through her latest crushes—a musician girl from Seattle and a surfer dude from California. Listening to Mari talk about her love life is better than most of the telenovelas I've grown up with. She always finds something scandalous about the person she's with. The exchange student she dated over the beginning of the year turned out to have been kicked out of the program because he was assuming his brother's identity to shirk family duties in Rome. A girl she was dating over Christmas was a famous winemaker's daughter and took her on their private jet. Why do I even need Netflix when I have lunch with her?

At about four o'clock, I have nowhere to go but to my new job. I head back to the Donatello Ranch and this time have no problem finding the rickety road. I'm pretty certain my car is going to fall apart with me still sitting at the wheel one of these days.

I notice the detached garage has one of the three doors left open. There's a shiny black pickup truck and another car covered by a tarp. I would expect the man who lives in this house would have something flashy and shiny and vaguely resembling an erect penis on wheels. I dial Scarlett's number but it goes to voicemail.

I sling my duffle bag over my shoulder and drag my suitcase across the gravel. I walk the blue-tiled path around the pool. A dead dragonfly floats on the surface, but other than that, it is pristine. There aren't any lounge chairs, but I imagine they're probably boxed up somewhere like everything else. Unsurprisingly, the pool house is not locked.

I let myself in, taking in the cozy living room. It has the same open feel and actual furniture. I can see Scarlett's touches. Plaid blankets and fuzzy pillows on the couch facing a wooden coffee table and entertainment unit. In the back there's a sink, a microwave, a fridge, but nowhere to actually cook, which means I'll have to go to the main house to do all of those things. I follow the wooden stairwell to the loft upstairs.

There's a little welcome note on the white comforter and a basket of goodies. A stuffed Montana State bobcat, a couple of bottles of wine, a jar of huckleberry jam, huckleberry chocolates, a small bag of Béquet salted caramels, and three paperback romances. The name Scarlett West jumps out at me right away because it takes up more space than the actual title. The guys on the cover are equal parts sultry and outdoorsy with cowboy boots and big belt buckles.

"Nice," I chuckle to the room.

I leave the paperbacks on my new bed and mosey over to the window. I take a deep, calming breath. More than anything, I can *breathe* again. Relief washes over me for the first time in a month. I don't have to drop out of college again. I can pay the medical bills. I can keep on going. But what about when the next three months are over?

You should go home, I think to myself.

What's waiting for me there? Daily fights with my step-mother. Isn't that why I left in the first place? I could have moved out, but New York is unlivable on your own if you're working middle class or less. I could share a place with a dozen people like I do here. I could make something work so that I could be close to Ariana. I could try harder. But that doesn't change that I needed to get away. I think of the conversation I had with my little sister before I left.

"Why do you have to go all the way to the *other* side of the country?" she asked.

"Because I got a partial scholarship and the loans will cover the rest," I tried to explain.

"Mom says you already *have* a job and you don't need to go back to school. She says you just don't want to be with us any-more."

I remember the rage that lit up my face and I thanked what-ever higher power is out there that Sonia wasn't home because I would have ripped her to shreds. "That's *not* true. You are the most important person in my life."

Ari pulled a giant unicorn plushie on her lap and hugged it. "Then why are you going?"

"Because if I get a degree, I can get a real job at a museum or at a gallery. School is important, no matter what your mom says. I don't want you slipping in your grades while I'm gone. You promise?"

"I promise."

I feel a tightness in my chest at the thought of her. I know that I'm doing the right thing. I just hope that I'm not too late.

I take a much-needed shower after running around all day, and slip into a pair of lightweight sweats and a tank top. Despite it being June, Montana isn't hot the way summers in New York are. I can't complain about perfect weather, though. The crisp air wraps around me. It isn't quite five yet, but I let myself into the house through the kitchen door to see if there are any instructions and instantly halt as something glass smashes on the floor.

"What are you doing here?" A deep baritone shouts.

I have one foot in the kitchen and one outside as I catch the blur of someone darting behind the door. Adrenaline zooms in my veins and my heart tries to jump out of my throat. "I'm sorry—I—I'm Lena. Are you Pat?"

"Don't call me that—" I can hear the frustration in his voice. He makes a deep guttural sound on the other side of the door. The glass of water he dropped is shattered on the floor, and I can see the liquid trickling this way. "It's Patrick. You're not supposed to be here yet."

"Sorry, Scarlett said—"

"I don't *care* what Scarlett said. Your one job is to only come in here during the times I specified."

I don't dare move from where I'm standing. But I know that he's just around the door. Maybe it's the adrenaline or maybe it's that he scared the crap out of me, but I say, "I thought my one job was to *clean*."

There's that deep grumble again. I'm pretty sure my car made the same sound while I was trying to get it up that damn hill.

"If you're going to be here, you have to follow the rules."

I bite my tongue. That's what my mother would have done. How many times did some wealthy boss talk to her like she was the grease splattered on the stove? How many times did she put on an accent because she knew it would appease the housewives she spent time cleaning up after? Servile. Humble. "*Always be humble*," she would tell me. In my heart, I know my mother was right about some things. But there's a difference between being humble and knowing your worth.

"Then I won't *be* here," I say and pull the door shut.

Tears flood my eyes. Angry, miserable, regrettable tears. I hate crying. I hate it more than anything. Between losing both my parents in the last fifteen years, I've shed enough of them. Hell, I was so angry at Sonia that I cried after a few rounds of beers with my roommates while we watched *Thor: Ragnarok*. "Llorona," my dad used to call me—*crybaby*.

I swallow that ache in my throat and ignore the faint "wait" that Patrick mutters. I pretend I didn't hear him. I don't even see Scarlett until I've bumped into her.

"Whoa, where's the fire?" she asks. Then she gets a look at me and I'm so mad at myself for crying that I cry even harder. "What happened?"

Somehow, I manage a broken, "I. Just. *Quit.*"

Scarlett stomps her feet and balls her fists as she goes into the house. The sight of her, so small and mad, warms my heart and gets a snotty wheeze out of me. I don't follow her, but I hover at the open door.

"Patrick Anthony Donatello—"

"Don't middle name me, Scarlett."

"What did you say to that poor girl to have her running out before she even starts?"

I can't see much of him but a bare right shoulder. Golden-blond hair. Maybe I walked in on him while he was naked and he was embarrassed? I would be. But then he comes around the kitchen island, his back to me, and I see the long gym shorts. He walks out of my line of sight, but I can still hear them talk. Someone is sweeping the glass away.

"I thought we had an agreement," Scarlett says.

"We did. Clearly listening isn't one of the things she's quick to learn."

I suck in a breath, straining to stay put. I remind myself that I need this job. I also remind myself that I gave up my room and have bills to pay, and if that wasn't enough, I have *nowhere* to go.

"I told her to come here at five. She's punctual. She's responsible. You're the one looking for excuses because you just want to be miserable and alone. It isn't good for you, Pat."

He sighs loudly. I don't know what's going on between them but there's the shuffle of feet. Glass going into a garbage can. "I just—this is new for me."

"I know. But you have to try, okay? Just try. And don't be a giant dick."

He does that growling thing again, and I don't know whether or not to be a little turned on by it. *Not,* my mind scolds me.

"Fine. Tell her I'm sorry and ask her to stay."

I can practically hear Scarlett shake her head. "Tell her yourself. She's outside. Probably listening. Right, Lena?"

I gasp and freeze like a mouse caught feasting in the middle of the night. "Uh—yeah. Hi."

"I'm sorry, Lena. Please stay."

Yeah, I need the job. But am I desperate enough to put myself around someone with so much—baggage? Anger?—I'm not sure what the right word is for him. There's something there that gets under my skin because when he says "stay" I can hear a deep hurt in his words.

"You can't scare me again," I say with a warning.

"You scared me first," he says, then a muttered, "*ouch*."

"Well, now that we've got that sorted out, you can go back to your hovel, Groucharella. Lena and I are having dinner and you're not invited."

Scarlett closes the door and I take a deep breath. "Are you okay?"

"I am." I begin walking away from the house to the steel firepit. "I'll be fine. I don't usually cry. I just got so mad."

Scarlett sighs, exhaustion and something like worry crosses her features. "I understand. I'm sorry, too. I'm the one hiring you, technically. His attitude is not part of the job and if he does give you a hard time, send me a text or call me."

"Maybe there's some other way for me and Patrick to communicate."

"You can leave each other notes on the fridge—"

I laugh. "Or we can text. Unless he's one of those people who hates technology for no reason."

"Believe me, he loves his little toys." She gives my shoulder a tap with her fist. We head over to a shed and drag two Adirondack chairs to the firepit. "I hope you like pizza and wine because that's what we're having for dinner tonight. I can answer any questions you might have about the area or what to do on your downtime this summer. Whatever you need."

"What happened to him?" I ask. I can't help but glance over my shoulder to the glass house reflecting the sun like a rough-cut gem.

"Except that." Scarlett takes a seat and grips the armrests. "It's not my story to tell. Just know that the Pat I knew was full of life. He was the life of the party. All I will say is that he went through something that changed him. I still have hope that he'll come through it a better man."

"He could start by getting rid of his boxes." It's a shitty thing to say because can't I relate? The last fifteen years haven't been a fairy tale. Or maybe they have been since everything goes wrong at first, plus there's the evil stepmother. Isn't it about time I get to the good part? "But I get it. If he doesn't mind, maybe that's something I can do. I'm not an interior designer but I can put my in-progress art degree to some sort of use."

"That would be great! Yes, definitely." She gets up and dusts her hands. "I'm going to bring out the wine. What do you want on your pizza?"

"Mushrooms and extra cheese," I say.

"Do you know how to build a fire?" She eyes the empty pit in front of us and then me, a wry smile lights up her face.

"I might be from the city, but I can light a match," I say, a little too much confidence in my words considering I have, in fact, never built a fire before. Scarlett leaves me to my devices and I go to the garage where there's a row of neatly stacked chopped wood. I wonder who does the chopping if Pat—Patrick—never leaves the house. I would put my money on Scarlett. But the wood has cobwebs on the top layer. I brush them away and haul a stack in my arms. Thank goodness for CrossFit.

I drop the wood and stare at it. I pull out my phone and find instructions. I can do this. I just have to do what I've always done. Keep my head down and figure out the job. This paycheck will help dig me out of debt and pay for school. I can even see Ari for Christmas.

Nothing, not even a recluse millionaire jerk, is going to get in my way.

PAT

She has no idea what she's doing.

Lena. I can't even bring myself to say it out loud in case I like the sound of her name coming from my lips.

She's stacking the logs on top of each other, not letting any room for the fire to catch. Then she tries using a match. A single match. *Go down there and help you ijit,* something inside of me says. But there's a knot right at the center of my chest. I press my palm over it where my ribs meet. Ribs that were broken six months ago. My heart rate picks up and I peel myself away from the sight of Lena trying (and failing) to build a fire. I glance back at the window one last time and she's restacking the logs, her toned arms flexing in the slim black tank top.

Don't look at her, I reprimand myself.

I go straight to the home gym. There's every kind of machine I could think of. There are no mirrors or windows here. I start with running on the treadmill for fifteen minutes. I kick up the incline and the speed until my heart feels like it'll run faster than my legs. I wipe the sweat from my face and jump off and to the weighted cables. I adjust the weights and swap out the grips and pull. Pull. Pull.

"Find something you can control," the doctor said. "Find something that makes you feel good."

"Nothing can make me feel good," I snapped. "Look at me. Fucking look at me!"

"I am looking at you, Patrick. Are you?"

That was the last time I saw a shrink, but I think of her words often. Does ripping my muscles to shreds make me feel good? It used to. Nothing gave me as much pleasure as working up a sweat at the gym and under the covers. I used to like a lot of things. I used to be a different person. I never would have been the kind of guy who yelled at Lena that way. I made her cry.

I drop the weights and they make a pinging, slamming echo in the room. I grab my phone from the pocket of my sweats and flip through the numbers in the contacts. I had to get a new number after the accident, so if I call my friends, they won't even know it's me. That might mean they'd actually pick up. I sit on a bench and lie back, a metal bar with a hundred pounds worth of plates on either side rests behind me. I used to be able to bench more but my left arm still gives me trouble. It's nothing compared to the people who were hurt. It's nothing compared to Jack.

I thumb the screen until I see Aiden's name. Fallon. Rick. I shut my eyes and think of the last time I saw them before the accident.

We were in my hotel suite waiting for my Los Angeles movie premiere. The makeup crew and stylists had just left. Miriam, my agent, was on her phone yelling at someone about a picture of me that had gone viral. I'll admit, it wasn't my finest moment—public displays of nudity would get most people arrested, especially if you're in the middle of the Metropolitan Museum of Art trying your best to imitate the sculptures in the Greek exhibit. At least it wasn't when there were families around. It was after-hours during some charity for the whales. I care about the whales as much as the next guy but hey. I was bored and all the recent attention was getting to me, inflating me like fucking Snoopy at the Thanksgiving Day Parade.

"I like that picture actually," Aiden had said. He was going through the suits on the rack that had been sent over. It was the first time I'd seen any of them since I took one weekend off the promotion tour. We'd gone on vacation for his birthday when he showed us the rings he was looking at for his fiancée, then girlfriend, Faith. I was the first one to tell him not to do it because they'd only been together for eleven months, but the other boys waved me off. "With that shamrock tattoo on your ass, you look like a six-foot-tall leprechaun."

"I'm six three!" I shouted.

Fallon almost snorted in his drink. Rick was flirting with some of the women that were there. I don't remember who those girls were, but someone called them in. Was it me? My agent? I just remember saying that I wanted to start the party right, and someone made women appear. For a few months it felt like the world was my magic lamp, granting whatever wish I asked for. I asked for something and it materialized at my feet, at my hands. I never questioned it and I should have.

Everything came too easily and that's why it went wrong just as fast.

"Shouldn't we get going?" Jack had said. He looked polished as hell but kept fiddling with his tie. He sat quietly on the leather couch sipping one drink. He was never like me. He was the good Donatello kid.

"Relax, little bro," I said.

"You guys are related?" One of the girls asked. I don't remember her name.

A second one curled up on the couch beside Jack and he went from still to petrified. He tried to get out from under the hand she rested on his chest, but the girl didn't seem to notice he was uncomfortable. "You don't look alike."

"I look like our mom," I said to her. "He takes after our Da. Italian stock."

They seemed to like this little detail.

"Where's the tequila?" someone asked.

"No tequila here," I said. "Just whiskey."

The first girl flipped her brown waves over her shoulder and grabbed the bottle of whiskey from the table. This is where the memory always gets splotchy. I remember Fallon saying something like, "Perhaps you don't want to be doing belly button shots before you have to walk a straight line on a red carpet."

But I shoved my tongue on that girl's belly button and suctioned my lips around her soft brown skin and I drank like I was being fed from the cornucopia of the gods.

"You're going to get your suit dirty, mate," Rick said.

"Your turn, Jack," I said and stood.

My brother shook his head and said, "I'm good."

"*Now,* Jack."

"It'll be fun," the second brunette encouraged him with a wink.

"You don't have to do anything you don't want," Aiden said.

"The fuck, Aiden?" I said, my tongue loose. Someone should have done me the favor and chopped it the fuck off. "Like none of you have never done things you didn't want to do. Fucked old ladies, got played by a twenty-year-old, and you got robbed by your house mom."

"Patrick!" Jack yelled at me. Jack never yelled. But suddenly everyone was yelling. The girls were screaming and recording themselves as they made an exit out of the suite. I don't remember them doing that, but I remember watching the footage of Rick shoving me into the bathroom. I might have five inches on him but he's strong as fuck.

"What are you doing?" I shouted. "Come on, can't you take a joke?"

Rick's face was as red as the suit he was wearing. His blond beard was threaded with white but it was hardly noticeable unless you were facing him in close quarters like I was.

"You weren't joking, kid," Rick said, eyes bulging out of his face. "What's gotten into you, Pat? You get a little money and all of a sudden you turn into some Hollywood douchebag?"

"Why can't you just be happy for me, Ricky?" I shouted. "Do you know how long I've worked for this?"

Rick got real quiet. I was ready for him to throw a punch. I was ready for him to walk out and not come back. But instead he said, "I know how hard you've worked. You've put your everything into whatever job you've had. If you keep going down this road, you're going to lose all of it. Maybe not right away, but you will. Believe me. I was the king of pushing people away."

"But you're fine! Everything is going to be fine, bro!"

"Why do you think I left Sydney? Why do you think I had to start over with nothing to my name?"

"I'm not going to do that."

"I don't want you to make my mistakes. Look, the money, the women, the clothes, it's not going to mean anything if you're alone."

"Whatever, Rick. You're not my fucking father."

That night is a blur for the most part, but if I want to see it, there are plenty of videos of me on Twitter and Instagram. Videos of me stumbling on top of a reporter. Videos of me tripping on my co-star Daisy's dress because I was so drunk before the show even started. I stepped on the train and ripped it and whatever chemistry we had going on was gone because I embarrassed her. I embarrassed everyone. I have videos of that entire night but none of what went down in that bathroom. I don't need them. I remember the look on his face when I said those words to him, and the moment he walked out.

Now, I hold my breath and tap Rick's number.

Before the second ring chimes, I hit the red button to hang up. It took six months, but this was the first time I've actually made the call.

What would I even say? "I'm sorry" doesn't feel like enough. There will never be enough to take back what I did to my friends.

Ricky was right. I'm alone. I didn't think that he would have been so right so quickly.

I grab the metal bar and lift it. My muscles tremble and I get in five reps before I have to stop.

When I head back upstairs, there's something on the kitchen island. Half a pizza pie and a glass of wine. My first thought is Scarlett, but the note on the scrap of paper isn't her big, bubbly handwriting. It's small, neat, meticulous. *Truce. Hope you're hungry. This is my number. Give me a heads-up with your preferred time tables.*

I carry the paper to the window. The sun is setting. Lena and Scarlett are sitting around the fire drinking wine. The pizza boxes are burning in the middle of the pit.

I'll be. She got the thing started after all.

3

Bidi Bidi Bom Bom

LENA

Everything I learned about cleaning a house, I learned from my mother. When I was a little girl she used to say, *We might be poor but we're clean.* She was so meticulous with everything, polishing things with a lemon mixture she'd make herself. She used Q-tips to get behind hard to reach places around the water knobs and the caps on the toilet seat.

She also used to play her favorite salsa songs. I used to hate it. I wanted to listen to Britney Spears and Destiny's Child. I told her everyone in the building could hear her. But she'd only smile with her perfect, straight teeth and say, *That's the whole point of music, nena. To be heard.*

They say that you become your parents, no matter how hard you try to avoid it. I did everything I could to delay that. I was top of my class and obsessed with getting straight As. I didn't date, no matter how hard the boys in the neighborhood tried to mack on me. I didn't go to parties with my girls, except for one time I let my friend persuade me to go to an all-ages day jam on Lefferts Boulevard where old men would wind up behind girls young enough to be their daughters. Hard pass.

Point is, I worked so that I could get into a good school, and I did all of that. I got into SUNY Purchase for art. By then, I wanted to honor my mother's memory and make something of myself while also doing what I loved. It changed after my dad got sick, and no matter how hard I tried, I pushed myself to the point of exhaustion and the world pushed back harder. Turns out, no one cares about your grief and your art when there are bills to pay.

I never wanted to be my mother, and here I am, swiffering the home of a rude-ass millionaire who hasn't left his house in who knows how long.

Patrick texted me last night at two in the morning. He was sorry about yesterday. *Thanks for the pizza,* he wrote.

If I were back home and a guy was trying to text me at two in the morning with some bullshit apology, under no circumstance would I ever text him back. But it's *not* a normal circumstance, and even if Scarlett is my boss, I'm staying on his property and have to make the best out of this situation. There was no way I was sleeping, so I saw no reason to not respond.

I replied: *Not NY pizza but good.*

I saw him starting to type. Then stop. Type. Stop. Whatever he was trying to say ended up as: *I'll be in my study all day tomorrow.*

Me: *What do you want for breakfast?*

Patrick: *Don't worry about breakfast or lunch.*

Me: *Scarlett told me you have to eat.*

Patrick: *Dinner is fine.*

Me: *Any allergies?*

Patrick: *No.*

Patrick: *I don't like weird flavors.*

Me: *Define weird.*

Patrick: *I don't know. Just make meat and potatoes.*

Me: *Keep it basic, got it. Are you allergic to salt?*

Patrick: *What? No.*

Patrick: *Feel free to use the grounds.*

Me: *Okay.*

Patrick: *Okay.*

Me: *Good night, Patrick.*

Patrick: *Good night, Lena.*

* * *

I ended up having strange dreams about a grumbling voice that yelled at me from the shadows, then followed to the fire I ended up making with instruction from Scarlett. As I finish with the kitchen and downstairs living room, I move on to the room at the farthest end of the house.

I've spent so much time assembling furniture for friends that I should probably get a job at IKEA. His stuff is a little more high-end, but I can imagine the delivery trucks arriving and Patrick scaring them away before they could even get to work. I find a box cutter and tear everything open. Packing peanuts litter the floor as I get started on a small bedside table in a distressed white wood.

For a while, I work with nothing but the sound of screws twisting into wood. Then, when I accidentally apply a piece backward and there's the sound of that screw being cranked out and removed. I don't dare touch the central air in case it sends Patrick into another screaming frenzy, but it's hot and I'm sweating. I use a bathroom hand towel around my neck and tie my hair into a ponytail.

As the hours pass, the silence unnerves me. I usually work to music or the background noise of *Friends* reruns. I grab my phone and search for a playlist. Because I'm particularly homesick, I pull up a playlist of old-school salsa songs. I sing along to the lyrics about men longing for women that left them, men longing for a kiss by the most beautiful girl they've ever seen, men longing for youth and their dead moms and their country.

Wow, I never realized salsa songs were basically about men longing for things they can't have. But I still sing along because these are the songs I grew up with. They're the ones that remind me of my parents dancing at weddings and quinces and backyard barbecues.

I dust my hands and stand to turn the table over and examine my work. One thing finished and only an entire house to go.

I head to the kitchen to make a list of the things that need to be done and realize I have a text from Patrick.

Patrick: *Do you have to sing so loudly?*

I march to the bottom of the stairs but I think twice before taking a step. For a second, I consider complaining to Scarlett, but this is something I have to deal with on my own. Whatever this man went through changed him. That's what Scarlett said. But aren't tragedies supposed to bring out the best in people? Or have I watched too many Hallmark movies?

I growl to myself and decide to reply in text instead of shouting.

Me: *If you can hear me singing then you know I'm still on my shift. That means you stay in your corner and I stay in mine.*

Patrick types and stops. Types and stops. It's infuriating watching and waiting to see what he might say. It stitches anxious little knots on my skin. Maybe I was too brash in what I wrote. Maybe I'm about to get fired for a second day in a row.

Patrick: *Can you at least sing something in English?*

I don't bother texting this time. I simply shout, "No!"

With my heart rattling in my chest like a single coin in a glass jar, I return to the bedroom I was working on.

Patrick: *I'm saying you could change it up a bit. Don't you know any Kenny Chesney?*

Me: *What?*

Patrick: *Country.*

Me: *The only country I know is mariachi and banda.*

Patrick: *That's not country.*

Me: *That's country music in MEXICO.*

Patrick types and stops. Types and stops. Four more times.

Me: *Oh my god spit it out.*

Patrick: *Never mind. I'm going to work out and put my headphones on.*

Me: *Fine.*

Patrick: *Fine.*

Patrick: *Where are you in the house?*

Me: *Room in the far end downstairs.*

I hear his heavy footsteps stomp down to the first floor and stop. I wonder if he's testing me. I wonder if he half expects that I'm going to stick my head out that door to try to get a look at him. After all, part of the NDA says that I can't take pictures *of* or inside the house, and it says I can't go into his room or gym, but it says nothing about getting a peek. That's the NDA. But test or no, if he doesn't want me to see him, I won't. I'll respect his space even if he doesn't respect my music choices.

He keeps going downstairs.

I can't help but wonder aloud, "What happened to you, Patrick?"

I open the box with the bed frame in pieces. I search for an Allen wrench and get to work.

PAT

"Hey, Jack," I say.

There's silence on the other end of the phone line and there's a heartbeat when I think that maybe he isn't going to answer. Maybe he's not done hating me.

"Hey, Pat. How's it going?"

"Just, you know, the same."

"Lies." He chuckles. How can he laugh? The accident left him nearly dead. After the surgery that saved his life, he was transferred to the Kessel Institute for Rehabilitation on the Upper East Side of New York City. It's the least I could do to help my brother's recovery. At first, he needed 'round the clock care, and now he's learning how to walk again. And yet, he's laughing.

That slick, hot feeling spreads across my chest again and I just let him laugh and keep talking. "Scarlett said she hired you a babysitter."

"Scarlett called you?"

"She calls me once a week," he says. Silence spreads and fills in the blank, *unlike you.*

"So, she's ratting me out now?" I say, trying for light but ending up somewhere in disgruntled.

"Oh, you know. Something about an incredibly gorgeous art student who quit on her first day because you made her cry."

"I did not—" Did not what? Make her cry? I did. I heard the way her voice choked up when I yelled. But the thought of her walking in and looking at me made my body react violently against my own impulses. I wanted to scream and run away from her. I didn't mean to scare her, to drop the glass I was holding, to say those things. "I didn't know she was so sensitive."

"People generally are that way. It's a people thing. Human reactions. Even *I* know that and I'm a newborn calf." His words drip with self-deprecation.

"Jack . . ."

"Look who's getting all *sensitive*," he says. "When am I going to see you?"

My mouth is suddenly dry. I can barely swallow each and every excuse that comes to my mind. Because I'm out of excuses. I don't have anything to do except run and lift weights and listen to my new housekeeper sing off-key in Spanish.

"What is that sound?" Jack asks.

"See? She sings *so* loud," I say.

"It's kind of nice. What song is that?"

"I don't know. Some Latin music."

"Better brush up on your high school Spanish."

"She's from New York." I don't know why that's relevant, but all I know about her comes from her application. Going to school in Bozeman. Had a ton of jobs that don't quite make sense. Likes to yell at me. Has legs muscular enough they could crush a man's head. I clear my throat. "Maybe that's why she's so *rude*."

Jack laughs. "Sounds to me like the only person being rude here is you. At least you're not alone in that big old glass box you call a house."

"That's our house, too, Jack."

"I know."

"No one has been here except for Scarlett."

"Don't you think it's about time you change that?" I can hear Jack moving around, the sound of sheets and bedcovers. Maybe he's trying to sit up. He could barely move for two months straight with an entire body cast encasing him. "I mean, look at me."

I'm sorry, Jack. I should say that. I should apologize for not being strong enough to walk out that door and onto a plane. I should apologize for not going to his side. For burying myself so deep that I can't dig myself back out. I just can't.

"I'm going to leave her alone to do her work," I say. "That's why Scarlett hired her."

"That doesn't mean you pretend like she doesn't exist. She's not a faceless body walking around your house."

"I know."

"No, you don't. You say you do but you don't. It's been six months, Pat. You're not the one laid up in bed. Instead, you're the one who pushes every single person away. Your boys. Even me."

"I didn't push you away."

"Do you know when the last time you called me was?" he asks, his voice wound up so tight I'm waiting for the snap.

There's the crackle of dead air as I don't answer.

"A month ago," he says. "I remember because that's the day I took my first fucking step."

I'm sorry, Jack. I should say it. I want to say it. But it isn't enough.

"I'll get better at it," I say.

"I'm sorry, Pat," he replies. "I know it's not easy, believe me."

How is it so simple for Jack to apologize to *me?* Why can't I ever say the words without feeling a great strain coming from every part of my body, like trying to move in a weighted gravity ride at a carnival?

"Go easy on her, okay? Maybe you'll make a friend," Jack says. "My PT is here. I gotta go."

He hangs up and I sit on my workout bench staring at my phone for a long time. I listen to the sound of Lena's voice for what feels like hours. I swallow the knot in my throat and take the stairs one by one.

I have to prove to my brother that I'm going to try for him. I can walk into that room and look into her eyes and introduce myself properly. *Hello, I'm Patrick Halloran.* This used to come so easily to me. Not just the part about talking to women but talking to people in general. My mother used to tell me that I had a gift for making people laugh. That ever since I was in elementary school I wanted to be an actor. I'd put on skits for her and use Jack as a prop. That was so long ago it might as well have happened in another life to a different person.

I get to the first-floor landing. Lena is singing and I recognize a single word from her off-key song—*corazón*. I don't know what it means but I know I've heard it before.

I press my hand over my chest because there's a gurgling feeling right there. Is that normal? Is that heartburn from the two hundredth frozen sausage egg and cheese sandwich I've microwaved since January?

The bottom stair wheezes beneath me and Lena stops singing.

I can speak to her like a normal guy. I can make this living situation better for the both of us. But when my feet won't move forward, I know that I can't keep going. Instead, I freeze with the memory of waking up in the hospital, my head covered in bandages and a searing pain slashing across my face, my chest, my legs. I remember trying to move and not being able to. I remember being alone for hours in a dark room with no one there to answer me as I shouted, "Hello?" Over and over again without a reply.

I remember.

"Patrick?" Lena says my name like the wrong note on an otherwise perfect song.

I can see her shadow elongating, spilling out into the hall.

And I do the bravest thing imaginable. I turn and run back upstairs.

LENA

I take a quick trip to the supermarket to get the basics. Scarlet left me cash for incidentals in an envelope. It feels a little sketchy, like money passed under the table, but it's easier than having to handle someone else's credit card or front money I don't have. I get a couple of chickens, ground beef, veggies, and some snacks. When I moved to Bozeman, I brought five supersize bottles of Adobo Goya with me. Ariana said it was an excessive amount of seasoning considering I barely cooked on my own now. Mari told me that it was unreasonable that I own more condiments than I do lingerie, but we all make tough choices.

I clean the place out of its sea salt, pepper, paprika, and all kinds of herbs. Despite everything that's happened in the last couple of months, the single thing that's been reliable in my life is cooking. Where painting has failed me, chopping onions never does. Plus, I can blame the crying on the vegetables.

When I pull up back at the ranch, I notice Pat's shadow at one of the top windows. I'd be lying if I say I'm not curious about his situation. What would it take for me to lock myself away for six months? This house has no pictures of other people. No family. Not even friends. Other than a box of Scarlett's books I came across, it's haunted in the most chilling way because the owner is very much still alive.

My phone beeps, and I grab for it after I park in the garage. Because we've been trading texts back and forth, I instantly frown and wait to see what Patrick has waiting for me. Maybe I'm parking my car too loudly.

But it isn't Patrick. It's Ariana.

Ari: *I'm not mad just disappointed. Mom's turning this place into a nail salon party at night. I can't even concentrate and the fumes are* terrible.

Me: *Want to vid chat?*

Ari: *No, I have to do homework and I wouldn't be able to HEAR YOU ANYWAY.*

I grip the steering wheel and let the flash of anger run through me. It's like a wave crashing over my head. It pins me in place. For a moment, I can't even breathe. The thought of my stepmother is enough to get me to turn on this car and hit the gas until I'm all the way in New York. I take deep breaths, each one like swimming to shore in bright, clear water. I remember that Selena wouldn't make the trip across the state of Montana after the mileage I've put in her. Besides, what would I do to my stepmom? Smack her in front of her own daughter? What would my mom think of me? What would my dad? There's something heavy in my chest that settles like an unmovable stone, a mountain that somehow gets bigger every day.

My phone buzzes again.

This time it's my *boss.*

Patrick: *Something wrong with your door lock?*

I type furiously. Me: *It's a little creepy that you can watch me and I can't see you.*

He types and stops. Types and stops. Patrick: *I was closing the curtain and noticed you struggling to make the drive up. Wasn't sure you were going to make it.*

Me: *This car is a piece of crap but it's a piece of crap I bought with my very first paycheck. Be nice to Selena.*

Patrick: *You named your car Selena? Is your bicycle named Justin Bieber?*

It's my turn to type and stop because what I really want to say is HOW DARE YOU?! And you know what? I do.

Me: *HOW DARE YOU? It's Selena Quintanilla as in Bidi Bidi Bom Bom.*

Patrick: *I have no idea what you're talking about.*

Me: *I guess I know what playlist we're listening to tonight.*

Patrick: *Great   :/*

I get out of the car and carry the groceries inside. I'm still startled by how *new* the house smells. Is it like that with all houses? The apartment we lived in when I was little was a relic from the 1960s in New York City complete with thick white walls, each coat of paint just rolled one on top of the other as families came and went. The floors were hardwood and glossy but still scuffed. A great, giant radiator hissed in the corner of the living room and there were thick iron bars on the windows for safety. It wasn't much, but it was home. Even when I'd go over to a friend's house, decorated by Pottery Barn or IKEA or West Elm, they smelled *lived* in. Patrick's house has no traces of the old ranch that it was built on top of.

Is that something that just happens when people move through a house? When people pick out paintings and rugs and vases to fill with flowers. When people burn scented or prayer candles and cook and track in dirt and leave fingerprints on every surface. I wonder.

Before I get to work on dinner, I plug my phone into the fancy kitchen speaker system and turn the volume at a medium.

Me: *Warning you, I'm about to play music and start cooking if you want to hide in your torture den or whatever it is.*

Patrick: *It's a home gym.*

Me: *Exactly.*

Me: *Do you happen to have any punching bags?*

Patrick: *Yeah, why? You box?*

Me: *I used to. My dad did. He taught me.*

He types and stops. Types and stops. I head to the bottom of the stairs and take one step before my belly is gripped with a tightening sensation. He has boundaries, but how can he have me live in his house and avoid me like this?

Patrick: *The bags are in the garage. I never set them up.*

Me: *No worries. Dinner will be ready in an hour, then I'll go back to the pool house.*

Pat: *Okay.*

"Would it kill you to say thank you every now and then?" I mutter out loud before I hit play on my music.

I set everything up on the counter. As I listen to the soundtrack of my childhood, I chop onions and garlic and sauté them in oil. There's something about the hiss of searing vegetables that soothes me, a combination of heat and transformation. I drain the ground beef and season liberally with fresh black pepper and coarse sea salt. I dance around the kitchen island, singing my way through the song.

My mother's favorite songs were in Spanish and I never really understood why she couldn't be one of those moms who just cooked in silence like our neighbors. But my mom was herself—always too big, too loud. At least, that's what she was like when she was at home. It was different at work, in houses and apartments that could fit our whole world in their living rooms. She'd change into the humble, demure, quiet foreign woman who would clean toilets and kitchen sinks and ignore the couples fighting. She worked.

When I think of Patrick in this house by himself, I can almost understand the need to hide. The need to be a *different* person than the one you might be elsewhere. Isn't that what everyone is doing anyway? We walk through the day putting on a brave face, going through the motions until we can get to the safety of our homes. We're just trying to get home.

Maybe Patrick is already in his safe place. He is literally in *his* home, after all. I feel guilty for trying to get him to move out of that just because I was hired to make sure his house is clean and he stops eating like a college kid. Though to be fair, his frozen meals were way better than what I was shoveling into my face before trying to get to classes every morning.

I slide across the kitchen in my socks to stir the tomato sauce. This beef Bolognese is a recipe my mother taught me. I still rolled my eyes when he asked me to not make anything with "weird" flavors. But the minute I was walking through the greens of the grocery story I felt a strange melancholy I haven't in a while. I'm starting to wonder if maybe being out here isn't as good for me as I initially wanted it to be. Maybe I shouldn't be alone, either.

The timer dings, and I make a plate for Patrick and take some in Tupperware for me.

But before I leave the kitchen, I find a Post-it Note and leave it next to the dish.

PAT

Bon appétit! Lena   :)
She has the kind of handwriting that reminds me of old-fashioned calligraphy. Each letter is elegant and clear, but the ink pressed down hard enough leave an imprint in the paper. It's the kind of handwriting that can't be rushed.

This is the problem with having someone in the house. It smells like onions and garlic. The last time my house smelled like this was when my parents were still alive and my brothers and I were little. It's going to fuck with me and make me feel things I don't want to feel. Before I can wallow in those memories, I pull up a barstool and eat.

I have to shut my eyes because this might be the best thing I've ever put in my mouth. I burn my tongue, but I keep eating until the plate is clean. There's more in the fridge, arranged in three Tupperware containers. I heat up two more before I'm disgustingly full.

I pull out my phone and do the familiar dance of scrolling through the numbers. Aiden. Fallon. Jack. Ricky. I feel like a fucking reject waiting for a phone call on a Friday night.

Just call them, you big ijit.

But I don't.

I click on my messages and find Lena's name.

Me: *This is good. Too spicy but good.*

I regret it the instant I hit send. Why couldn't I just have left it at "good"? Why couldn't I have said what I wanted to, which is, "This is almost as good as how my dad used to make it"?

Lena: *I guess coming from you that's as much of a compliment as I'm going to get.*

Me: *I guess.*

I groan and slap my own damn forehead. She thinks I'm an asshole and I haven't done much to discourage her. From the moment I saw her shitty little car making its way up the road, I wanted her gone. Part of me still does. Scarlett is wrong. I'm not ready to be around others.

Try.

Me: *Where'd you learn to cook?*

Shit, maybe she's pissed because she hasn't even read it. Half an hour passes as I scroll through the news—everything is terrible—and Google search my name—everything is still terrible but at least all the information is outdated. I'm a has-been, a never-was.

I walk to the back of the kitchen and look out the window. The pool house windows are all lit. She could be in the bathroom. She could just not want to talk to me and I'm being a fucking creep. I pull the blinds shut.

My phone dings.

Lena: *My mom. She worked for this Italian family for a year and the grandma that lived there taught my mom her favorite recipes.*

Me: *My dad's family was Italian.*

Lena: *LOL I figured.*

The left side of my face hurts right over my cheekbone. I shut my eyes and see the beams of a car, the glitter of broken glass. My face hasn't hurt in a while, but I ignore the feeling for now.

Me: *Right. The name gives it away.*

Me: *My dad was the one who liked to cook. My mom was great, too, but there's only so many casseroles we could eat.*

Lena: *I've never had a casserole. What's in it?*

My face hurts again. Worry drives into my chest and I move on to the bathroom down the hall she was working on earlier. I don't think I'll ever be used to the guy staring back at me. For an infernal second, I blink enough times that maybe the next time I see myself I'll go back to the way I used to be. The scar tissue is a mess over the entire right side of my face. When Jack saw me, he was so hopped up on pain drugs that he laughed and said I looked like I'd gone two rounds with Edward Scissorhands and I said, "At least I can fucking walk."

I shake my head. I am not a good guy. A good guy would never have said that to his baby brother.

I touch the mound of my cheek, but it doesn't hurt when I put pressure on it. What the fuck? The last thing I want to do is call my doctor, but what if there's something wrong with my scars?

I can hear my phone beeping from the kitchen, and honestly, I can't keep staring at this reflection. This is the face of a stranger. This can't be my face. I ball my fingers into a fist and it's all I can do to stop from smashing it into the glass.

Lena: *Any preferences for breakfast?*

Me: *No whatever you feel like.*

Lena: *Good night Patrick.*

Tell her she can call you Pat. Tell her thank you for making a meal that you had three servings of. Tell her something more.

Words are meaningless. I've known that for years. People lie.

People tell you what they want you to hear. How many times did I do that? How many times did I tell a woman I'd call her back just to spare her feelings? How many times did I tell myself everything would be all right?

Lena is going to leave here at the end of August. But that's over two months from now. Until then? She has enough in this house to keep her busy. She doesn't need to actually pretend to be my friend. What would Scarlett tell me in this moment? She'd tell me to do something nice. But Scarlett writes about the kind of men that don't exist.

Lena needs to keep busy. That's the idea. She mentioned she liked boxing. I guess I could let her use the gym when I'm not in there. The problem is that the punching bags are in the garage. The plan was to turn the garage into my own gym but that didn't work out, did it? I had the movers bring everything inside. All I'd have to do is lift a hundred-pound bag and hook it up to the metal rings in the ceiling.

That's it.

That's fucking doable as a thank-you for this meal, isn't it? Keep her out of my hair and maybe she'll be too tired to sing off-key inside the house. It's a win-win situation.

I slip on a pair of sandals in the foyer and open the front door.

The evening air is chilly, the sun bleeds orange over the tree line. I gulp down the crisp, clean air. I grew up running down these slopes, back when the ranch was a piece of shit that was falling apart because my dad made some bad investments and we never really recovered even if, in the end, we were happy. My mother loved us and my brothers and I grew tall and strong, and then there was Ronan . . .

"I can do this," I say out loud.

For the first ten steps, I keep my eyes shut, but I make it outside. When was the last time I even opened a window? I don't look back at my house because I know if I do, I'm going to want to run inside, like when you're climbing a great distance and they tell you not to look down. I shouldn't look.

"Keep walking," I say, and my words get lost in the sweep of cold air.

The garage is perhaps one hundred feet away, give or take, but it feels like it isn't getting any closer, like I'm in one of those optical illusions where the road beneath me widens and elongates at the same time. I get about halfway before I look back.

I stop and get on my knees. My pulse has multiplied to every part of my body, so much that I'm vibrating, shaking until I press my hands on the gravel and lower my face down. I shiver as I close my eyes because I'm positive I'm dying. A numbness runs across my shoulder blades and moves to my chest, my arms. Is this a heart attack? Memories are flashing across my mind faster than I want them to.

There was the night of the accident. The grill of that truck smashing into Jack's side of the car. We spun so many times that the only thing that stopped us was a metal post, shattering my window right against my face.

There was the ambulance. My throat hoarse because I was screaming for my brother, who wasn't moving beside me. They put me under and I woke up in the dark to voices, to people touching my chest, stitching me up like a stuffed toy split down the middle.

Sometimes when I wake up, it's because I can hear the heart rate monitor beeping as if it's right in my room. Other times, I wake up because I dream of the last time I saw my brother six months ago at the rehab clinic in New York, and it's his voice that wakes me. "I fucking hate you, Pat. I hate you so much."

It was my boys who drove me all the way back to Montana. Two thousand, one hundred and ninety-five miles over two days. Two days of me cursing their names, their wives, their loved ones. Two days of me asking them to leave me the fuck alone, to drop me off in the middle of a highway in North Dakota. For the life of me, I don't know why they didn't do it. When we got here, I locked myself in the house for a week and they went to get Scarlett. I didn't even say goodbye the day they left.

When I open my eyes, it's only to vomit in the grass. Everything comes out painfully, violently until I'm exhausted. But at least I'm not shaking.

Lights come on from somewhere, and every part of me is an alarm. She can't see me like this. Somehow, I crawl all the way back inside. Drag myself up the steps and into my shower.

I sit there for a long time, shame burning my skin despite the handle being turned all the way up to the cold side.

When I go to sleep, I don't dream.

4

Dime Store Cowgirl

LENA

"I have emerged from my writing cave!" Scarlett says when she walks into the room I'm working in. Her auburn hair is in her usual messy bun, and she's wearing a white blouse with tiny red roses printed all over. She gives the room a once-over and her eyes widen. "Now, I know I parked in front of the right house, but you wouldn't know it from this. The guest rooms almost look like they should be in one of those coffee table magazines in Massachusetts."

I laugh hard. A surprising sense of pride settles over me when she says that. Sure, it isn't painting, but I can call it interior design to make myself feel better. "I'm just arranging things around. It would be nice if all the walls weren't stark white."

"You know, that *would* be nice. I just have to talk to Pat about some paperwork," she says, letting her hair down in waves that come up just below her shoulders, "but I'm sure he won't mind."

"Really?" I ask, arching an eyebrow. As if thinking the same thing, we both look up at the ceiling where Patrick is doing—well whatever he does up there during my hours in the house. "Won't he want to pick the colors?"

"Tell you what, I'll run it by him right now and if he says no, then the walls will stay White Walker white. You go get your stuff just in case."

I don't really have any "stuff" to get, but there's a chill in the air. It's *summer* for Christ's sake and the end of June. Mari told me that during her freshman year it snowed right up until the end of June. I go to my little pool house, retracing the steps I take at least six times a day, then wait for Scarlett by her mud-splattered silver truck.

"No complaints from Groucharella. He said as long as it's not pink or orange he doesn't, ahem, give a rat's ass."

I snort. "Do you think rat's ass comes in a swatch color?"

"I happen to like a guest room in a nice shade of salmon." She hops in the truck, and it's almost comical seeing her sling herself up in the giant truck.

I follow suit and, then we're driving down the Damn Hill that gives me so much trouble. It's quite a different experience in Scarlett's metal behemoth. "Holy shit, is this what it feels like to drive on this road when your shock absorbers are working?"

Scarlett's big belly laugh fills the car. "So, tell me, just between us girls. How's my boy doing? He treating you okay?"

It's such a loaded question because everything is okay on paper. It's been two weeks since I've arrived and the last time Patrick had an outburst was the day that I quit. Maybe Scarlett can give me an insight on the subtle change in Patrick. I tell her about cooking and singing. I say nothing about our texting for some reason I can't quite explain to her or myself.

"He did mention he has to listen to his music at eardrum-shattering volumes when you're around, but I know he doesn't mind."

"It was like, for a minute, I thought we could be friends. He liked my food and he's been eating everything without complaining. At least, not to me." With the windows halfway down, I can't help but turn my head toward the sun and breeze.

"Seems like a prince." Scarlett turns onto the empty highway. "But you think something's wrong?"

"Did he say anything about me?" I ask, and instantly regret it because I sound like I'm in high school. "Like if I did something wrong. Or is he always just surly and doesn't say please or thank you?"

Scarlett sighs and purses her lips together in a defeated sort of way. "I'm going to be honest with you, Lena. Patrick has a lot of healing to do. Not in his body but in his mind."

"You still wouldn't be able to tell me what happened, right?"

"I can't."

I nod, understanding.

"Just know that it isn't you," she says. "When I went there to have him sign some checks, he grunted his way through a conversation, but he's always like that."

"His texts were kind of funny for a couple of days," I say and laugh. Then realize my slip.

"He was texting you?" Scarlett takes her eyes off the road to glance at me. "Like the schedule?"

"No, just asking me to play country music, which I don't have. He asked me about casseroles, which I've never eaten before. Like I said, it almost felt like we were starting to be friends."

Scarlett taps her chin. "Interesting."

"What's interesting?" I ask.

"Well, I just know that Patrick hasn't been very chatty with anyone. Except Jack, his brother. And even then, he's done a fine job of shutting people out."

"Six months is a long time to be alone," I say, but feel a tug at my heart because that's right about the amount of time that I've been here.

"Sounds like you miss home," she says. "I don't mean to pry. Who am I kidding? I actually can't help myself. I know you're here for school, but why Bozeman? New York City seems like the perfect place for art."

I give her a kind smile. "It is. I was working at the Met for a little while actually but at the coat check. When my dad got sick, I had to help around the house. My sister, Ari, she was so little and my stepmom was *no* help."

"You're just a Cinderella story, aren't you?" she asks, turning into the hardware store parking lot.

At that, I have to chuckle sarcastically. "Maybe just the step-mother part and dead parents. Instead of cute mice, I just had big old subway rats and pigeons at my window. This job will help me get to see my sister for Christmas. That's the plan at least."

Scarlett puts the car in park and looks at me, her light-brown eyes joyful and full of mischief. "Maybe there's a fancy ball waiting for you after all. As in, there's a July Fourth party in town. We should go together. Might as well have a little fun since you'll be stuck in the house all summer."

July Fourth back home was always my favorite holiday. My friend's parents threw a huge party with a pig roast and illegal fireworks. Her dad even built a tiki bar from the shack his Harley used to be parked in. At the end of the night, only the mosquito torches would be lit while all fifty cousins gathered around to do shots and eat cake.

Maybe it's the overwhelming longing for a past that feels just out of reach, or maybe it's because Scarlett is the kindest person I've met while I've been out here, but I say, "I'd love that."

PAT

"What's changed in your routine?" Kayli asks, her voice is bright and there's curiosity in the flecks of gold in her blue eyes. She hangs her stethoscope back around her neck.

We're in the room that was meant to be my office, adjacent to my bedroom. There's a desk and a swivel chair that still smells like it came out of the box. She takes a seat on the chair while I tug my shirt back on.

She's got a practice in Big Sky, and I trust her enough to let her see me, but thankfully she'll make the trip to my house instead. My older brother went to school with her sister, so there's family history there, even if it's ancient. Still, I remember a time when she used to run in our yard with arm floaties, so I feel a little weird referring to her as Doctor Maffei.

She clicks off her tiny silver flashlight and pockets it, knitting thick brown eyebrows while she waits for an answer.

"I do the same thing every day that I've done in the last six months."

She smirks like she's used to patients withholding truths from her. "Why do I get the feeling that's not true?"

"It's part of the truth," I mutter.

"Patrick," she says. Just my name, like that's enough to get me to be the sort of man that's rational. None of this is rational. Not the way I live and not the way I've been feeling, like there's something lodged in my chest, like there's still a chunk of glass they never fished out right beneath my skin.

"My diet's different," I say.

Kayli tents her fingers like a villain in a spy movie. "I'm glad your sodium intake will decrease."

"Not the way Lena's been cooking."

"Lena?"

I roll my eyes. "Don't play cute. I'm sure Scarlett has already filled you in on what she's done here."

"Actually, I haven't spoken to Scarlett since she went into her 'writing cave.'" Kayli uses air quotes for the last couple of words. "Why do writers call their offices that? I mean, imagine if doctors did that? Be right back, I'm going into my surgery cave. Doesn't have the same ring. Anyway, go on."

"Is that what you think about?" I ask, running my fingers through my hair. The scar tissue on my scalp is becoming more and more familiar to me as my locks get longer. I let out a slow breath. "Scarlett hired a housekeeper for the summer."

Kayli does that doctor thing, where she cocks her head but makes no facial expression. "What's she like?"

"She's loud and talks too much. Doesn't listen. She broke the first rule of the job the minute she got here."

"Is this like Fight Club?"

"Kayli—"

"How's the food?"

"It's good. Really good."

"I'm not understanding, Pat. Everything sounds normal. Your house is spotless, though it always was when Scarlett was the one doing things. Why did you call me? Your checkup isn't for another two weeks."

I bury my face in my hands and let out an exasperated sigh. "I just know that something is wrong."

"The pain in your face?"

I nod. "What if there's still glass under there? What if—"

Kayli clears her throat. "What happened each time this pain occurred?"

"I don't know, I think—" I run my hand over my forehead, then back. I need a haircut and I can't exactly get a barber to come see me. I let Scarlett chop my hair off once, but it looked like I'd let a kindergarten class use me for a craft project. Maybe Lena knows know to cut hair in addition to everything else she knows how to do. *Lena.* All of my thoughts keep going back to either her or the accident and it makes everything in my head a clusterfuck of confusion. "I was texting."

"With?"

"With Lena." I set my face into a deep frown. "It's nothing really. Why, why are you looking at me like that?"

Kayli gets up, her shoes make hushed sounds as she closes the space between us and takes my face into her hands. I hold on to the sides of my desk and tilt my head back.

"What the hell are you doing?"

"Pat," she says, tracing her thumb across the right side of my face where the skin is smooth and unblemished. The half of me that seems to be the only proof I have of the man I used to look like if all the other evidence was burned. "There is nothing wrong with you other than your sudden amnesia to manners. Your blood pressure is a little high but still lower than it's been the last few months."

I huff into her hold. "Then what's happening to me?"

"Well, cheekbones tend to hurt from *smiling.*"

I swat her hand away and get up. "That's your medical, your *professional* opinion?"

Kayli's laugh is like the chime of bells and I'm glad the women in my life seem to think my misery is hilarious. "Next time it happens, really think about what's going on. Your muscles recuperate in different ways and I'm going to go out on a limb and say that you have absolutely not smiled since the accident."

I hate doctors. Even Kayli, whom I've known practically her whole life. They have this coldness, which I don't always think is intentional. But when she just says "the accident" like she's saying "since the baseball game," I feel that familiar heat at the center of my chest. I still haven't forgotten about the panic attack I had when I tried to leave the house. I utterly failed to make it a hundred feet to my garage all because of *her*. Everything Lena related is bad for me, clearly.

"If you truly think it isn't your face learning to smile again, then I'm happy to get some X-rays done but you know what that means, don't you?"

I cross my arms and turn to the window. Out on the road, Scarlett's truck is kicking up dust. They're going to paint my house. I'm not exactly thrilled, but the more Lena's busy, the less she'll be in my hair.

"I know," I say, acknowledging that in order to get an X-ray, I have to leave the house and I can't bring myself to tell her that it's getting worse. That I fucking puked and crawled back inside and blacked out in the shower. "Thanks, Doc."

"Pat, have you thought about what I suggested last time?"

I walk to the door and hold it open, the universal symbol for "get out."

"The shrink? I haven't really . . . I don't know."

"Take your time." She pats my arm and leaves.

Doesn't she realize, while I'm in here, I've got nothing but time?

LENA

A gorgeous woman in a hip-length white coat is walking down the stairs when I walk in the house. She's strikingly beautiful with a strong jaw and bright blue eyes. When she sees me, she pauses, coming down slowly. I can imagine the questions that must be forming in her head. Who are you? What are you doing here? At least, that's what I think until she gets to the last step and approaches me with her hand extended.

"You must be Lena," the woman says. "I'm Doctor Maffei."

A dozen questions run through my mind, but the one I settle on is, "Is Patrick all right?"

She looks over my shoulder at where Scarlett is bringing in the second box of sample paints. "Kayli! You're not due here for another two weeks." Her face blanks and her voice drops the excited. "What's wrong?"

I look back and forth between them. Kayli inhales as she smiles, settling her blue stare on me. "He's fine, I promise. He had a few concerns, but I've hopefully given him peace of mind."

I blow a steady breath, then scoff. "Maybe that's why he's been extra quiet lately."

"There's definitely something different," Kayli says, arching a perfectly trim brow. "But it doesn't have to be a bad thing. Anyway, I should get going."

"Aw, come on," Scarlett says, beckoning the doctor toward the kitchen. "Between my deadline and the influx of Californians coming in for dehydration treatment, I never get to see you anymore."

"Whatcha having?" Kayli asks curiously.

"How do you feel about burgers?" I ask.

"I feel I very much love them," the pretty doctor says.

"Let's go out back," Scarlett says. "I'll help you with the spread."

We get the burgers going after I take the paint swatches into the separate guest rooms. This is shaping up to be the strangest job I've ever had. Scarlett chops up the fixings while I dust the burger patties with Adobo and salt. My mom would have made a sofrito, but I'm not as good as she was. I take the tray of patties and Kayli helps me out with the grill. While the girls bring out local beers around the fire pit, I make a burger for Patrick, with the lettuce, tomato, and cheese on the side because I don't know how he takes it.

I text him.

Me: *Soup's on.*

Patrick: *I thought you were making burgers.*

Patrick: *I could see you all from the window.*

Patrick: *I wasn't watching you all.*

Me: *LOL. You're welcome to join.*

Patrick types and stops. Types and stops. I shake my head and pocket my phone. What is up with this man? I shouldn't keep thinking about it, but the more I see glimpses of his life and the people in it, the less I understand what's happening.

It's not your business, I think to myself. Do the work. Get paid. Move on. Go see your sister.

I check my phone and he still hasn't replied.

When I step outside, I look up, but the windows of his bedroom are dark. Even though I can't be sure that he's looking at us right now, I wave.

I take a seat around the fire, which Scarlett has already gotten started. Kayli has swapped her jacket for a wine-colored Grizzlies hoodie.

"So, Lena," Kayli says, balancing a paper plate on her lap. She doesn't seem concerned that she might get her jeans dirty with ketchup. "Scarlett says you're studying over at Bozeman. You a Bobcat yet?"

I laugh. "I suppose I have to be, right? The colleges in New York don't have a strong rivalry, so I never used to think about it."

"Rivalry only about half covers it," Scarlett says, twisting the cap off a Moose Drool beer. "I've seen couples divorce over lost games."

"That's why I'm not married," Kayli says.

"Cheers to that," Scarlett answers, and the women kiss the tips of their beers together.

"Didn't you just spend the last two weeks writing a book about true love?" I ask.

Scarlett nods vigorously and waits to chew her food before answering. A bolt of sadness crosses her brow, and I know whatever she's going to say next is going to be deeply personal.

"I believe in true love," Scarlett says softly, touching her bare ring finger with her thumb. The day I met her it was still there. She sees me notice. "I finally got rid of it. The ring, I mean. I had a hard time over it. You know, I always believed that when it's right, so right that vows and words *mean* something, love is the best thing a person can have in their lives. But when it's wrong, well, I haven't felt that kind of hurt over anything else."

"I'm so sorry, Scarlett. I didn't know," I say, and she brushes my comment away with her good-natured smile.

"We were together since we were fifteen. High school sweethearts and all that. That's twenty-three years together. Didn't seem to matter, in the end. I couldn't have kids but his secretary could." She makes a raspberry with her lips. "Even *I* couldn't write that cliché. So, I started writing about happily-ever-afters because I couldn't have one. It gives me a little bit of hope that there are still good men out there even though you have to wade through garbage-fires first."

"I'm sorry," I say again. "I've never been good at relationships. When I was in high school, I broke up with my first boyfriend after a week. He cried. Then I dated another guy. I don't know what it was, but I couldn't seem to connect and so I broke up with him. The third one called me a cold-hearted robot. That one stuck. Robot Girl was my nickname until I graduated."

Kayli makes a guttural sound of disapproval. "I grew up with the Donatello boys. *Every* girl was in love with them. Jack Donatello was my prom date."

"Really?" I ask, curling up on the Adirondack chair with my beer in hand. "Does everyone around here know each other?"

"No," Kayli and Scarlett say at the same time.

"Anyway," Kayli says. "Jack and I went our separate ways. He went and became a smoke jumper like his big brother, bless his soul, and I went away to school in Seattle to become a doctor." She looks down at her bottle and a sad smile tugs on her lips. "Doesn't matter since he's in New York now."

"Jack is in New York?" I ask.

The two women, the *only* women that Patrick seems to let close in his life, exchange a knowing glance.

"I feel like I'm in the middle of some Jane Austen novel set in Montana," I say and laugh. "I figured you were close since you were allowed in to see the Wizard."

"What did you guys go into town to get?" Kayli asks, taking a hard left on the conversation.

I glance over my shoulder. Is Patrick standing there? I have the sensation that I'm being watched. Or maybe it's that as the afternoon passes, the temperature cools and I'm just shivering. I throw another log on the fire and listen to Scarlett recount our adventure in the hardware store. We picked outrageous colors, and Kayli finds it hilarious.

"Can I be here when you tell Pat that his guest room is going to be pink?" Kayli asks.

"It's *salmon*," I say, pinching the bridge of my nose. "No sense for colors."

The girls laugh, and I feel something inside of me soar at this sensation. Of course, I've had Mari as a housemate, but I have missed *this*. Sitting around with a group of girls and just talking.

"Now I *really* should be going," Kayli says, checking her watch. "Today I had three people come in after attempting to hike around Mt. Ellis without bringing an ounce of water with them."

"I didn't know hydration therapy was a thing," I say.

"It's mostly a Vegas thing," Scarlett says, then raises her beer to her lips. "Or so I've heard."

"One word of advice if you decide to go into the woods," Kayli says. "Be prepared. All the trails out here look the same."

"I'll stick to my car," I assure her.

"Though if you ever want to take a long walk," Scarlett says, pointing to the woods in front of us, "the trail through here takes you out all the way to my house. Just a quick left, and you're there in two miles."

They laugh at the face I'm making.

"See you on the Fourth," Scarlett waves at Kayli.

"Good to meet you, Lena. You're exactly what this place needed," she says, and then with a final wave, she's gone.

Scarlett and I settle into a comfortable silence, but I can't help but feel bothered at what I said to her before.

"Hey, Scarlett, I'm really sorry about the romance comment. I didn't mean to bring up any bad memories or anything. I'm terrible when it comes to this stuff. Robot Girl, remember? I swear, this is why I'm single."

"First of all, there is nothing wrong with you and don't let anyone tell you otherwise." Scarlett points a finger at me. "Secondly, it's fine. It's the best thing that happened to me. I choose to see it as a blessing. If I had never gotten divorced, I never would have started writing again, and I never would have gone to Vegas for my divorce party, and I never would have seen Pat again."

"You know," I say, "I'm trying really hard not to pry, but I grew up with some of the gossipiest aunts in the world and that might have rubbed off on me."

"I don't need to tell you anything about Pat he wouldn't tell you himself," she says. "Lord knows I want what's best for that boy. But I swear, he's talked more to you than he has to anyone else in his life and I see that as progress. Whatever you're doing, keep doing it. You're a goddamn miracle."

We have such a different way of seeing things, but it's nice to be appreciated.

"I don't know about that, but I *am* going to play with some paint," I say, and take the empty plate to throw into the trash.

When I take out my phone to put on my playlist, I have a message from Patrick waiting.

Patrick: *Thank you for lunch.*

Hot damn, maybe there are miracles happening around here after all.

5
Pink

LENA

The smell of paint is intoxicating. I've missed this, even if it's just the feeling of dipping a sponge brush into the can of salmon-pink wall paint. I streak an X on the main wall, and then repeat the same with a slightly brighter coral. When Patrick said he doesn't like pink, I took that to mean that he doesn't like the color he associates with Barbies or Pepto-Bismol. Most people don't.

But there's something about the perfect pink that is soothing to look at, especially against the white furniture. Every day, I've worked on this room, sweeping up the kernels of Styrofoam peanuts and wood shavings, it's right around sunset. The light hits the walls from the wide windows and it feels like the embrace of the sun itself.

I snap a few pictures of the colors and send them to Patrick with a smiley face.

Me: *What do you think?*

Patrick: *I think I said no pink.*

Me: *The one on the left is salmon. The right is coral.*

Patrick: *Those are uppity ways of saying pink.*

Me: *Correctly identifying a color is not uppity. It's my line of work.*

Patrick types and stops.

I grumble, and take the opportunity to change the music from

Selena to the latest Enrique Iglesias songs. I've had a love affair with Enrique since I first heard "Bailamos" on the *Wild Wild West* soundtrack and all of my friends made fun of me for it. But when it comes to my music, I am faithful. Then, I get a better idea and pull up an Aerosmith song I think Patrick will enjoy.

Me: *This song is dedicated to you.*

"Pink" by Aerosmith blasts from the Bluetooth speakers in the kitchen and I paint a few more swatches. One is a little paler, like the bottom of a blush rose starting to bloom. Now that one I will admit is pink. Another color dries too dark, like the shade of rust over metal.

Patrick: *Seriously?*

Patrick: *Last time I checked, this was my house.*

Me: *I'll paint it white again if you want.*

Me: *But why did you say it was okay to paint if you were going to be like this?*

Patrick: *It's not the painting part. It's the COLOR.*

Me: *Will you trust me? I'm about to make dinner. Just give it a chance.*

Me: *Please?*

Patrick types and stops. I wonder what are the words that are lost every time he deletes a potential text. How many of his thoughts go unsaid?

Patrick: *Fine.*

Patrick: *Isn't it a little early for dinner?*

Me: *Deliciousness takes time. Trust me.*

Patrick: *I'm wary of people who ask me to trust them twice in the span of ten minutes.*

Me: *I'm wary of people I've never seen face-to-face, but . . .*

Me: *I'm sorry, that didn't come out right.*

He doesn't answer and the song ends and I feel a nervous coil in the pit of my stomach as I take out the pork shoulder from the fridge. I mix the condiments in a bowl, the cumin and pepper making my nose itch from their delightfully pungent aromas. I grind two heads of garlic, cilantro, and olive oil, then rub the mixture all over the beautiful cut of meat. I dance along to a fast merengue jam that's popular at all the sweet sixteens and quinces in my old neighborhood. When the oven timer dings, it's finally hot enough to put the pork in. I set a new timer, wash my hands, and because I can't exactly start painting a room all four swatch colors, I head into the living room.

Standing in the middle of all these boxes makes me feel like a giant in a city made of cardboard. Each one is stacked like a toy high-rise and spaced for enough room to walk, like a labyrinth, or midtown Manhattan. When I told Scarlett I could do this, I wasn't really aware of what it entailed. It isn't just a couple of things that Patrick has here. It's an entire life. It's everything from house warming gifts to things he must have picked out himself when he thought he'd be moving in to *live* and not haunt the place.

I moved to Bozeman with a single suitcase and two duffles stuffed with more brushes than shoes, more pencils and charcoal sticks than jeans, more sketchbooks than I own hair products. And yet, aren't they all in the back of my car this very moment? Those swatches were the first brushstrokes I've made since the semester ended, when I couldn't bring myself to imagine anything because I was sure, I was *so* sure that my stepmother had ruined my life and I was going to have to drive all the way back home with my tail tucked between my legs.

I've unpacked the start of an entertainment set. I built a mini fort to give myself enough room, and at the end of it, I'm sticky and smelly with sweat. The oven dings and I wash my hands before turning the pork so the skin gets nice and crispy. Pernil was my mother's specialty, even though everything she made was delicious. I only hope I can do justice to her recipe, which she learned to make for my dad's Puerto Rican side of the family. I make the sides—greens beans, a tomato and onion salsa with lemon and salt, and white rice.

At the end of the night, I leave Patrick another note. This time I draw a fish and hope he understands it means it's a salmon.

"This is so weird," I sigh to myself as I walk back to my place. I don't know why it hadn't occurred to me to dip my hands and feet in the pool before. But tonight, I stop, and rake my fingers across the water. It *is* heated and it's kind of a waste that no one uses it. I almost feel a little guilty using Patrick's property when he can't do it himself. That guilt is outweighed by the temptation to *swim*.

It's been months since I've been in a pool or body of water. The rivers and lakes here are *too cold* for my liking. I change into my swimsuit—a red and blue number covered in white stars that I got for last year's July Fourth party—and dive right in.

The water envelops me, and I swim laps over and over, relishing in the resistance of the water. Maybe I've said a lot of wrong things today to Scarlett and Patrick, and maybe I'm away from my sister, but I've done one thing right. I know that pernil is going to taste amazing. When I get out of the pool, heart slamming against my ribs, I see his name light up my phone.

I scroll up, an eager spark in the pit of my stomach as I read his text.

He says: *The salmon.*

PAT

I eat the food Lena made for me like a starving man at an all-you-can-eat buffet. When I was in Vegas, I used to wonder how the people there could eat that much, that quickly. The body I've carved out for myself has come with more than hard work. It has come with deprivation, with sweat, with anguish. When I played soccer in college, I didn't always worry about what I ate as long as it included so much lean meat I can't look at a grilled chicken cutlet without cringing.

Then I got injured and my professional career was over before I finished my first season. I turned to acting, and fell so flat on my face that I never quite recovered. Then, I met Ricky and the boys and Mayhem City became my home for years. I tried one more time, going to LA to model. After a couple of bland gigs, I joined up with the boys again in Vegas. I pushed my body into the best shape of my life. My set always got the most screams from the crowd, and I drank in that adoration. It was sweeter than champagne, sometimes it was better than sex. I was *wanted*.

Meeting Scarlett again was destiny. I didn't recognize her at first, but she remembered me. Funny how she rescued me in a way I didn't know I needed then. Then, the movie happened after Miriam signed me to her agency. It was all so fast that I didn't feel ready. I trained and ran and pushed my body even harder. I went without sugar for six months to squeeze every ounce of fat out of my body for the semi-nude scenes. I had a major *movie*. I had a *life*. I could take a step outside the house without feeling paralyzed or worse.

Now, I eat the dinner Lena spent hours making. I hold the Post-it and stare at the fish drawn in marker. After the accident, it took me a while to want to move my body again. To lift weights and run for my heart health. It took me months to want to eat food that wasn't frozen. God knows, Scarlett tried. But when Lena leaves food on the kitchen island, I feel a hunger that is so deep it terrifies me.

I set the Post-it on the marble when I catch the sound of a splash outside. I go to the kitchen window where I have a view of the pool. Lena is swimming laps as the sun sets. She's fast, moving like there's something, somewhere she's trying to get to. Or get away from.

I used to love to swim.

I used to love a lot of things.

I go to the guest room and find the furniture covered in plastic. Lena did this. She took this room and assembled it. To my right, the sun sinks behind a hill, filling the room with a warm light. I shut my eyes against the brightness of it and swear under my breath.

When I pull up her name in my phone, I reread that last message she sent. "I'm wary of people I haven't seen face-to-face but . . ."

Would she be less wary of me if she could see me now? I know I can't leave the house, but she doesn't have to go anywhere to stand face-to-face with me. Scarlett does it. Kayli does it. Kayli touched my scars and she didn't grimace the way my first doctor did. She didn't gasp and recoil the way the nurses did when my bandages came off. She did have the same sadness in her eyes, though, but haven't they all? It's that *pity* that feels like salt in wounds I'm not sure will ever close.

I don't know Lena. Not truly.

I shouldn't care about what she would say if she looked at me. She doesn't seem like a shallow kind of person. I think of every girl I ever rejected because in my mind, she wasn't perfect. She wasn't my *bullshit* version of perfect. The twisted, sick, downright vile kind of man who could take someone who was beautiful and make her feel like she wasn't enough. That's the man I was.

That's the man you still are, I think.

And that's not the man who can stand face-to-face in front of Lena. That man can't ask not to be judged.

I find myself typing. *The salmon.*

Then I hit the gym and push myself until I'm drenched in sweat, until it rolls down my chest and arms like I've been standing in the middle of a fucking thunderstorm. I blast my music, but I keep picturing Lena swimming back and forth. I picture her turning around and looking up at me, the way she knew I was standing there watching the three of them sit around a fire pit, the only part of this land that is still the same as the original.

I think of the way my face hurt again and I cursed Kayli's name because I was smiling. I was fucking smiling at a girl who couldn't see me, but I could see her. I could see the broad strokes of her eyebrows, her wide brown inquisitive eyes. A mouth that quirked up. A mouth I keep wondering whether or not would gasp under my weight. Or scream if she saw me.

I turn around and punch the wall. I break the skin of my middle knuckle, then go to my closet for a towel but there are none there.

"Are you fucking kidding me?"

I grab my phone from my pocket.

Me: *What did you do with my towels?*

Lena: *They're in the closet with all the other towels in the laundry room.*

Me: *Why aren't they in the gym?*

Lena: *Because I didn't know they belonged there? And I didn't think I could go downstairs.*

Lena: *I'll put them back. I just thought it'd be easier.*

Me: *Well, it's not. I like grabbing my towel from the gym.*

Lena types and stops over and over. I wonder if this is what it's like when she talks to me.

Fuck, I'm being an asshole again. Am I really angry over goddamn towels?

All of a sudden, it is like the fog of anger dissipates and I can see my words clearly. I can imagine her face contorting with anger. That sweet, pouty mouth marred with a scowl.

"Fuck!" I shout at no one but myself.

I'm sorry, I type.

Lena says nothing.

I'm sorry, I type again. *That was out of line.*

Lena doesn't respond. I walk to the kitchen and put my plates in the dishwasher. Is this the first time I've done that since she got here? I shake my head, wishing I was brave enough to walk a hundred feet to hang my boxing bag because that's what I need. There is too much anger inside of me and she shouldn't be the one I take it out on.

Lena, I type.

I can see the lights of the pool house are still up. Every time I text her when I go to bed, she says good night before the lights go off. It is such a weird, random thing to notice but I can't *un*-notice it right now.

I take the stairs two at a time and go into the shower in the master bedroom. When I had the old house knocked down and remodeled, I wanted the kind of bathrooms I'd seen in five-star hotels I'd stayed at. Decked out with marble sinks and white mosaics fit for a Moroccan palace. Now, when I'm in here, I feel ridiculous. It's too big, too empty, like the rest of this house. At the very least, the water pressure is good. There's a modern tub big enough for three people on one end, but clearly, I've never used it. Instead, I head into the separate shower stall—big enough to fit at least *five* people comfortably with two sitting ledges and all—and two waterfall showerheads.

A warm sensation settles in the center of my throat, and I know enough about myself that it isn't anger. I *am* angry at myself, but this is different. I've regretted so many things over the last six months. This feeling is not regret, either. Why can't I put a name to it?

I turn off the water and barely wrap a towel around my waist before I go in search of my phone, dripping all the way into my bedroom.

She hasn't messaged me back. That's when I think I know what this feeling is in my throat—I'm sorry. I'm afraid.

I brush my hair away from my face, water seeping on my comforter as my heart slams in my chest. I touch Lena's name on the screen and an anxious rivet cleaves me in half because I'm calling her and, before I can hang up, she answers.

"Hello?" Her voice asks, sleepy. "Patrick?" Startled. I can hear the crush of fabric. Lena moving around on her bed. "Is everything okay?"

I clear my throat, and because I'm a fucking idiot, I say, "How can someone with such a beautiful speaking voice sound like a drowning cat when she sings?"

She barks out a laugh, then goes back to sounding like she just woke up. "Did you really call to insult me? Because you could have sent me some more rude text messages to read when I woke up."

"You were sleeping?" I ask, and the ache in my throat eases. This is weird. This is stupid. This is fucking wrong. What am I doing freaking out over a *good night* text? Is that really who I've become?

She makes a slight moaning sound, like she's stretching, and the vibration of her voice sends an ache down to my crotch. If my face hurt from stretching muscles into a smile, then my dick is feeling even worse.

"I fell asleep with the light on. Did you need something?"

"What would I need?" I ask.

Her voice is like licking honey off your fingertips. "Well, you've never called me before."

"I—" I wanted to make sure you weren't mad at me. I wanted you to accept my apology. I wanted you to tell me good night. I say none of those things. Instead, I go with, "I wanted to say I'm sorry about the towel thing. It was stupid. In case you haven't noticed, I'm fucked up."

I mean it to come out as self-deprecating. Being self-deprecating worked for my friend Fallon. Overconfidence was more my speed, but there isn't any kind of confidence to be found these days. Still, she doesn't laugh at me.

"You're not fucked up," she says softly. "I don't know what happened to you, but I know it must have been bad. I know that *you* can't be all bad."

"Not all bad," I say slowly, despite my hammering heart. "How could you know that?"

"You wouldn't have people like Scarlett or Kayli trying to take care of you if you were a complete lost cause. They haven't given up."

Emotion swells in my chest at her words, then floods to my groin. Fuck, this is not what I had in mind. It's almost painful to get hard at the sound of her voice. It's wrong. "You don't think I'm worth all this trouble?"

"Well, even if you don't believe it, *they* do."

But do you? I want to ask her. That alone is utterly ridiculous because how could she believe anything about me. "I should let you get back to bed."

The silence between us stretches as neither of us hangs up. I hold my breath until she makes a sighing sound again. "I'm awake now. And you're the only person around for *miles*."

"Except for Scarlett and this new couple that moved by the lake in the spring."

"Seriously?" she asks incredulously. "Is there like a newsletter out here? You haven't left the house in months and you know who's coming and going?"

"My newsletter is called Scarlett West."

"You should really get cable in here. I guess I could always read one of the books Scarlett gave me."

My heart spikes and my mouth gets dry. My hard-on quickly vanishes at the thought of her holding one of those books. I have *read* those books. "Which one did she give you?"

I can hear her move around. A door open and close. The refrigerator maybe. There's the hiss of a soda opening. Her voice is light and playful when she says, "*Save a Horse, Ride a Cowboy.*"

Part of me is relieved because I'm not on the cover of that one. Another part wants to laugh at that title for completely different reasons. I say, "Ah, that's the start of her new series."

"Can I ask you something personal?" Lena asks.

"Depends."

"On what?"

"On how personal." I sling my towel around my neck and move to the armoire for a pair of boxers. This time, my face hurts a lot less when I smirk at her words, though fear pools in anticipation of what she wants to know.

"The girls let it slip that your brother's in New York."

I make a grumbling sound. "What else did they say?"

"That they weren't going to tell me everything there is to know about you. I have to tell you that this is pretty—"

"Weird?" I offer.

"Unconventional," she says.

I sigh and sit on the side of my king-size bed that isn't covered in shower water. "I heard what you said on the first day here. I'm not a billionaire recluse."

"So just a recluse?"

There's something so playful in her voice that warms the skin of my chest. I take a deep breath and think of what Kayli suggested. Of what she has been suggesting for the last six months. That I need a professional to talk to. That I need *someone* to talk to. So here she is, a complete stranger who knows nothing of my life except fragments from Scarlett and Kayli.

"There was an accident," I say. Those four words feel like lead rolling off my tongue. I wait for some sort of reaction but she seems to just be waiting, the steady sound of her breathing is something to focus on. I clear my throat. Breathe again. "It was my fault. People got hurt. My brother got hurt."

"You don't have to tell me everything," she says, a voice so soft it's like feathers brushing across my arms, my face. "I just want you to know that I understand that you're going through something. I mean, I could never know everything about what you went through. But I understand wanting to be alone. I get being, I don't know, lost. That sounds stupid when I say it out loud." She laughs nervously, a rambling sound that makes me smile again.

"I suppose I did wonder how a girl from the big city chose to come all the way out here."

"The short version?"

"Mm-hmm."

She takes a long breath. "My mom died when I was little. My dad remarried. He had another daughter. I love my little sister more than anything. But then my dad had a stroke and never got better. I quit school to help take care of Ari because my step-mother wasn't dealing at all. And then one day, I couldn't take it anymore. I could see my life slipping away and I didn't want that. I wanted to try one more time to finish school. I thought of going overseas, but part of me was scared. I'd never left the state I was born in." There's that nervous laugh again and I wish I was strong enough to go down those stairs, around the pool, and knock on the house. And then what? Let her cry on my shoulder? Tell her it's okay? Be her friend?

Kiss her.

"Go on," I say.

"It's your turn."

"My turn?" It's my turn to chuckle my nerves out, that's for sure. "I told you about the accident."

"Not the accident. Your brother."

I think of Jack laying up in that recovery room. I remember the moment I opened my eyes and I saw him pinned against the door of the car, more blood than I'd ever seen in my life. I thought he was dead. "It used to be me and Jack and Ronan. Ronan was our big brother. We used to call him Hercules because he was so fucking tall and strong. He was a smoke jumper. There was a really bad fire down in California. Ronan didn't make it. Broke my mother's heart. My mom had an aneurism the same year. My dad followed soon after that at a work accident. Jack is all I had left and I almost killed him."

"I'm so sorry, Patrick."

I shut my eyes and lean my head back. It's the first time I could say all of that and get through it. "I shouldn't be telling you all of this."

"Well, too late. Between us, we can fill our own cemetery. Sorry, that's weird and morbid. Sometimes I don't think before I say things."

I laugh so hard it gets her going again. Laughing out loud with Lena is an outer body experience. I can see myself. I am floating out of my self and watching me sit in my boxers on a wet bed on the phone with a girl who is less than fifty feet away.

Go to her, a voice tells me.

"It's a good thing," I tell her. "I feel like I can be assured that you'll be honest with me at least."

"Yeah, I can do that."

"Thank you."

The silence returns and this time it's awkward. We've run out of things to say. She's bored. I've scared her.

"I should go to sleep," I say.

"Okay. Good night." I'm about to hang up when she says my name. My name on her lips is the last thing I want to hear before I go to sleep from now on. "It's nice to meet you, Patrick."

"You can call me Pat."

6
Party in the USA

LENA

July

It takes me two days to paint the salmon room and another to do the finishing touches. The boxes in the living room contain vases that I fill with wild flowers. There are matching bedsheets and Scarlett helps me find throw blankets as fluffy as white clouds. When it's done, I can finally feel Scarlett was right when she said it looked like something out of a coffee table magazine. I snap a couple of pictures for Pat to see and send them to him even though he's probably going to look at it in person the moment I leave.

After that weird conversation we had the other night, part of me gets a rush every time I see his name on my phone. It's a completely different feeling from the ire I felt before. It's like living with a new person versus the one I met on the first day and I'm not exactly sure how I feel about the change. Why is it easier to be angry at someone than feel some sort of empathy?

I don't let myself linger on that for too long because I might have told Scarlett that I don't know about love or relationships, but I know enough to recognize this feeling. Butterflies unfurling in my stomach when I hear him walking upstairs. Nerves rattling when he calls me before bed for the most random reason. Last night it was to ask me what I put into my food to make it taste so good, which is his way of a compliment. Eventually we ended up talking about our respective favorite summers as kids—him with his brothers running around these hills. Me on my block eating cherry snow cones with my friends on the way to Coney Island to sunbathe.

All morning I've heard him shuffling around in his gym downstairs. If I didn't know any better, I'd just think he was throwing things around. When I head to the laundry room, I think I hear him on the phone. I wonder if he's talking to Scarlett. I wonder if there's someone else he has to talk to aside from the few people I've met. Does he talk to his brother the way I talk to Ari? Whenever I bring it up, he changes the subject in that way of his, making a deep rumbling sound at the back of his throat. I shake my head, dispelling the memories of his voice and the tingling it sends down my spine.

I am not allowed to like him.

I am not allowed to like him.

I'm *not*.

I repeat that as I get ready for the Fourth of July party at the lake. I grab my clothes from the dryer. Had I known I was going to do this much swimming, I would have packed another bathing suit, but I'm relegated to the same one. At least it's thematic.

I leave Pat's lunch on the island counter and head to the bottom of the stairs, my small laundry bag slung over my shoulder.

"Pat?" I call out.

He opens the door to the gym and steps close enough that I can see his shadow. He runs a hand through his hair, and then stands still. My name is a quick gasp, his breath surely short from his workout. "Lena?"

"I'm going to the July Fourth party by Scarlett's."

"You don't need permission," he says, his words softening into humor. Being funny, or trying to be funny, is strange on him.

I make an *ugh* sound. "I know I don't need your *permission*. I just—I thought I might mention it in case you were thinking of going."

He's silent. Shifting his weight at the threshold. All he has to do is take a single step and he'll be at the bottom of the steps directly in my line of sight.

Come on, Pat, I think.

"That's not a good idea," he says.

"You can sit with me," I say playfully. "We can count the number of cutoff Carhartts we see."

That garners a chuckle at least. "You should go, Lena."

"Well, if you don't want to," I say, and I swear I've had this conversation with Ariana, trying to get my sister to put on her clothes to go to school in the mornings. *Well, if you don't want to be super smart and learn. Well, if you don't want to eat your vegetables to be as tall as me.* Only Ariana was a kid, and she didn't suffer the same trauma as Patrick.

"I want to," he says. The whisper is low, begrudging, but it's out there.

I take a step down the stairs where it's dark, and the wooden floorboards so new and tight that the only sound is the brush of my bare feet against the cool surface. I swallow the nerves in my throat. Why am I so nervous? It's Patrick. My rude, jerky, angry housemate. He's also my middle-of-the-night phone call, sweet, heartbroken friend.

I should leave him alone.

But he just said he wants to come. He doesn't *want* to be alone. That's different. Maybe what he needs is a little push, a bit of help to bring him out of his dark room and into the light.

I take a second step and I hold my breath when I take the third. His shadow is still, elongated against the opposite wall.

"Don't," he tells me.

I stop.

I take hard steps back so he knows that I'm not coming closer. "Okay, Pat. Take your time. You know where I'll be."

I drive to the lake around Scarlett's property. I could have taken one of the trails through the woods, but two miles in the dark on the way back would be a mistake even I don't think I can make. I park in the gravel lot stacked with cars facing the water.

The lake is, as Ariana would say, *poppin'*. Groups of the

younger locals are gathered around four large picnic tables. A rainbow of blankets line the lake shore, and thankfully, I'm glad to not be the only one wearing a themed swimsuit. I find Scarlett by a coal grill, a *Game of Thrones*–themed apron around her waist that says "Chef in the North."

On the way over, I take out my phone to send Ari some snaps. The only people I have on Snapchat are my fifteen-year-old sister and Mari. Mari's photos are filled with pristine blue waters and the portrait worthy vistas of the Greek seaside town Mykonos.

Ari sends me a selfie where she looks pensive. *I fail to see why you aren't here.*

I type back: *Christmas!*

Ari: *Fine. Is your weirdo boss there?*

Me: *He's not weird. And he's not my boss. Call you later.*

Ari: *Send me picssssss.*

I stow my phone in my back pocket so I can carry the box of beer I picked up on the way.

"Lena!" Scarlett shouts, flipping burgers over a grill pit. "Come over here and meet people."

I can't be shy after trying to persuade Pat to come out of his torture room, but meeting new people always gives me a queasy sensation. Small talk is boring and there are only so many times I can talk about the difference in weather between Montana and New York. When I had my first attempt at art school, my teachers would lose patience with me because I wouldn't communicate. I felt out of my element. I say the first thing that runs through my head and not everyone likes that. The problem with meeting new people is that you're being judged by how you look and what you say in the first sixty seconds of a conversation. What if you're in a bad mood? What if you have a headache? What if your home life is in shambles and you don't want to talk about the source of light in so-and-so's latest art exhibit?

Wow, all I have to do is say hi to Scarlett's friends, but my brain takes a hard left into Shy Town.

"You own a lake?" I ask Scarlett.

She barks out a laugh. "God, no. Though I did get the house in the divorce. Property line ends over on that tree line. This is just a state campground."

"Do you want a hand with that?" A tall, dark-haired guy with kind brown eyes asks. He's probably the most beautiful man I've seen in the last six months, with broad shoulders and a smile that is as genuine as it is hot.

"Sure," I say, handing over the twelve pack.

"Lena, this is Hutch and River," Scarlett says, pointing the metal spatula at a young woman with cornflower-blue eyes and blond curls that reach her bare midriff. She's like a punk rock Stevie Nicks. I shake both their hands.

River asks with a lift of her chin, "Where in New York are you from?"

"Sunnyside," I say.

"Forest Hills," she says, with a wink.

I let out a squeal and yank her into my arms. I feel her relax and laugh as she hugs me back. I definitely needed this tiny piece of home, even if it's from someone I've never met.

Scarlett turns to Hutch. "Do you think they're going to do some secret New York handshake?"

He musses his thick brown curls and shrugs. "I've seen it with my own eyes. They'll probably start talking about the best deli sandwiches next and something called *bagels*."

"Shut your filthy beautiful mouth, Hutcherson," River says, but she's all smiles, and a pink blush creeps around her cheeks when she stares at him.

"Make me, Thomas," he shoots back, playfully biting his lower lip.

They are definitely together and definitely madly in love. I don't know why, but couples in love make me happy. I know I'm the first person to say that I've never experienced it, but still. When I see it and it's real, it gives me hope that maybe I'll find something similar.

"Pass me that tray of hot dogs," Scarlett says, and Hutch volunteers as grill master junior for the afternoon.

Over by the lake, music blares from a speaker. Two guys are

lining up boxes and boxes of fireworks. The sun is bright and unobstructed by clouds, and bodies slick with oil brown (or at least turn different shades of red). I grab a beer and take a seat across from River at the picnic table designated for food prep.

"So, no bullshit, Sunnyside, what brings you out here?" River asks, offering me an open bag of chips that I gladly dive into.

"Well, Forest Hills. Second attempt at getting a degree and running away from my family," I say. There's something about River that makes me feel at ease. I sure as hell know I'm not talking about how perfect the weather is. "You?"

"Went to rehab a few towns north of here and fell for the wrong guy who turned out to be the perfect guy," she says, and pushes her curls away from her face. I follow her stare to where Hutch is bent over, checking the tank of gas attached to the portable grill.

"Why was he the wrong guy?"

"He was my counselor," she says. "Well, *a* counselor, not mine. But still. Very bad for all parties concerned. But it worked out in the end. Scarlett says you're working up at the Donatello Ranch? We just moved down from Missoula."

"What's down here?"

"Oh, you know, saving the world," River says, an easy grin on her lips. "I had to find myself someone with *dreams*."

I laugh at that. "How will you save the world?"

She shrugs a bit. "Hutch isn't going to be a shrink anymore. But I think about the way I grew up and I wonder if there's a way that we can help other kids, too. The goal is to start a youth center and get enough funding to bring kids here from all over the country. Sort of, disrupt the school to prison pipeline, among other things."

"Like a school for wayward kids?" I offer.

"Yes, minus the super powers," she says.

"Well, sounds to me like Hutch isn't the only one with dreams."

River peers over her shoulder, and the look of love and admiration that crosses her face is as plain and bright as the day.

How can someone love another that much? How can you give yourself over? Isn't that dangerous?

Thankfully, I don't have time to ruminate on that for too long because the music gets increasingly louder. Scarlett introduces me to her small writer's group, which consists of a lesbian couple writing cozy mysteries in their lake house twenty-five miles away, an old man who is on his fifth career and attempting his first gay erotic romance, and a librarian with blue hair working on her young adult novel.

"I've never met so many writers before," I whisper to Scarlett between beers.

"We are everywhere. You can't escape us." She winks.

"Don't look now," I say, though I think I'm too tipsy to be *cool*. I set my beer down. "But there's a guy over there who has been staring at you for hours."

She looks, and I have to fight myself to not fall over laughing. Right by the lake there is a *man*. He's tall as the trees surrounding us and thick, with a shaved head and full ginger beard.

"That's Jake Madison," she says, trying to suppress a smile. "They brought him up here as a trainer for the football team."

"And?" I ask.

"And he's about ten years too young for me." Scarlett looks at him, though, and I can feel the way she fidgets with her hair, the collar of her shirt.

"How old is Patrick?" I ask.

She lifts a brow suggestively. "Thirty-six. *Why?*"

That *feeling* of anxiousness swirls in my stomach. I can feel heat creep up on my neck. *I want to,* he said before I left the house. What would I have done if he took me up on my offer? Would we be swimming? Would we be staring at each other like River and Hutch?

"*Because,*" I squeak. "He sounds like a grumpy old man. Older than thirty-six. You know he referred to Snapchat as Slap-clap? We live in the modern world! You can't hate some tech and like others when it's convenient."

Scarlett holds her stomach laughing. Over in the lake, River has her arms wrapped around Hutch's neck as he does the swimming for both of them. I force myself to look away because it feels like I'm intruding in their private moment, even though we're surrounded by tons of people.

"Pat's a little bit old-fashioned and hates social media even though he loved attention as a kid."

I try to think of the man that belongs to the voice I hear before I go to sleep every night. Playful, self-conscious, sweet. He can be all of that as well as the things that made me want to hate him when I first met him. Those butterflies return and I hold my breath, like that'll squash them.

It doesn't completely work. I end up trying to call Ari, but she doesn't pick up. She texts she can't come to the phone, but I know she has to be at a neighborhood party.

"Come, my sister wants to see you," I tell Scarlett. "She asked if she can read your books."

I wrap my arm around Scarlett's neck and bring her close. It feels so nice to be able to have this kind of closeness with someone. We record a little video in which Scarlett tells Ari that she is far too young to read her book, but will gladly send her a list of teen novels.

Ari is extremely excited by this.

I haven't had this kind of day in a long time. I've drank enough beers that I don't care about how cold the lake will be. I float in the water for a few hours with a couple of guys who are getting their masters in forestry. I didn't realize that was something someone could study. I think about how I live in one of the biggest, most populated places in the entire country and still there is so much that I don't know about the world. I think about what Hutch and River are trying to do with their youth center and I wonder, after all of this is done, how am I supposed to give back to the community that raised me? The people that supported me through my mom's death and then my dad's. How am I supposed to make life better for Ari?

Suddenly, it feels like too much, so I submerge into the water, so clear and refreshingly cold. I find a sparkling blue stone and bring it back to the picnic table. I give Scarlett a wry smirk because she's talking to the hot football trainer. When the sun has set and everyone is good and drunk, the fireworks go off. I consider that it's a bad idea to mix booze and explosives, but at my family July Fourth two thousand miles away, we used to do the exact same thing.

I take pictures of the fireworks to send to my sister. Then, because I can't help it, I also send one to Pat. I'm sure he can see them from his bedroom. I wonder if he's lonely.

It's not your problem, I think. *It's not your job to coax him out of that shell.*

I know that it isn't, I truly do. But there's something that makes me want to try. Every part of today, I find myself wishing he were here. It's a strange thing to feel for someone I've never truly been around in person. Someone I've never seen.

After the long night, when the only light comes from the logs crackling in fire pits and the car headlights nearby, I get ready to go.

The thing is, my car won't start.

"Come on, Selena," I say to my ancient little darling. "We made it this far, just give me another ten miles."

"Having some trouble?" River asks, leaning against a giant red truck to my right.

I sigh, defeated. "Yes, please. I'd ask Scarlett, but I don't want to cock-block her."

Hutch comes around. I noticed neither of them were drinking today, so I feel comfortable getting in their car.

"We'd normally stay out late, but I'm sleepy," River says, scratching her eyes like a cute, fussy baby. "Get up in the front seat and I'll nap in the back."

"I've never met anyone who can sleep as much as you do, Thomas," Hutch says, and I can feel his smile even though he's in the shadows.

"And yet," she says, climbing into the truck and ducking her head, "you take me as I am."

Hutch and I follow, and he glances at River once to make sure she's fine. She's knocked out in seconds. We pull away from the lake party, smoke from the grill and fireworks clings to us all as Hutch backs out onto the main road.

"You're at the Donatello place, right?" Hutch asks.

"Home sweet home," I say dryly. I've avoided doing night-time driving while here because there are literally *no* lights. It is a dark tunnel illuminated by random headlights and the stars, perhaps the moon when it's out. Fireworks color the sky as we drive, a song I recognize as country by the reverberating lilt of the singer's voice is low on the radio.

"Does he still play?" Hutch asks.

I'm confused and think I missed something he said. "Who plays?"

"Donatello. When I was in high school, he'd just started playing for the US team. They were going to the World Cup but he got injured and fell off the face of the planet for years. We're new to the area so all we've heard is there was some family ac-cident and no one's around anymore. Can't really be a haunted ranch when it looks—well, the way it looks."

I have to laugh at that. I didn't know Pat was a soccer player. But what do I really know of him?

"McMansions can be haunted in other ways," I say.

"What's he like now?"

"He mostly keeps to himself." That's a very chill way of say-ing that I've lived in that house for a month and I have never seen the owner before. "Not what you'd call a people person."

Hutch nods methodically, brown eyes flicking to the rearview mirror where River is knocked out. "Everyone needs to go at their own pace."

"You're a therapist, River said?"

He nods, adjusting his hands around the wheel. "I should warn you, people usually do their best talking in cars."

"Why?"

"Because you've got a person's attention and sometimes it's easier to speak honestly when you don't have to look at them. For instance, you might feel comfortable asking me something personal, or a favor, because we're both staring straight ahead. Takes off some of the pressure."

"Okay," I say, thoughtfully. We're almost at the road to the house. Hutch puts on his blinker even though we're the only car seemingly for miles. "What would cause someone to be unable to leave the house?"

"There's the usual agoraphobia. There's the less common enochlophobia, which is closely related. It's a fear of crowds, but it's very specific. There's a deep trauma that has nothing to do with the exterior world but the internal."

"But, is it normal to not want people to—be around you or see you?"

Hutch glances at me for a second, his truck jostling so gingerly it momentarily makes me angry at my baby as we easily crest the Damn Hill. "You've never seen the person you live with?"

I shake my head. "I get the sense that he wants help, but other than his doctor, he doesn't talk to anyone."

"Look, I can't make any kind of professional diagnosis on a person I've never met. But it seems to me that you should keep a lookout when someone is asking for help. On a personal note, I know what it's like when someone wants help but doesn't know how to ask for it. I, for one, made a lot of mistakes because I was trying to do the right thing and failed. I'm glad I followed my heart, though."

We park at the end of the driveway. Pat's bedroom light is on and the sensors flick on in front of the house.

"But you wouldn't change anything for a bit, Hutcherson," River says sleepily.

Of course she's been listening. I would have. She sits up with a stretch and I chuckle.

"I don't want to push anyone who isn't ready," I say.

"Ask," River says. "Let him know that you're there. That you will be there. But don't do it if the offer isn't for real."

"I seem to remember someone being very stubborn at first," Hutch says, and River gently and playfully swats his shoulder. "But everyone heals at their own pace."

"As hippie-dippie as that sounds, he's not wrong," River says.

"Thanks for the ride," I tell them.

River puts her hand on my shoulder. "This better not be the last time we see you, Sunnyside."

"Definitely not," I say, and get out of the car.

Hutch gets out to tighten one of the headlights, and I accept the warm hug he offers, along with a friendly, "If you ever need to talk . . ."

I always thought that when people offered that, they weren't being genuine. But there's something about River and Hutch that makes me feel like perhaps, the rest of my time around here isn't going to be as lonely as I had imagined.

PAT

When I hear the truck come down the road, I know that it can't be Lena. I race downstairs with a staggering heartbeat and wait by the window. I don't turn on the lights. I remember the days that these floors would creak with the barest touch. Now, I can hear how silent my steps are.

The car stops in front of the house and the automatic lights come on. There's a good-looking guy at the wheel. His eyes look up at the house, but then he turns his attention to Lena. He steps out, and I feel like a ton of bricks slams into my gut when he hugs her, whispering something in her ear.

These feelings bearing down on me are irrational. They burrow under my skin. What does he feel with his face in her hair? What does he feel when he wraps his arms around her? I have dreamed about the way Lena smells and tastes and feels. They are dreams I'm not proud of, but I can't control my mind when I'm unconscious.

I should not feel this way, but I do.

I should not want her this way, but I do.

I have no right to her, no claim, nothing.

For a moment, I consider turning on the light and forcing myself to welcome her. Wouldn't I just end up scaring her again? Then, I remember that she isn't going to come in here. Her shift was done long ago. She's fed me and left me to my own devices like the feeble weakling I've become. So, I stand in the dark with jealousy running rivers across my skin.

When she left the house this morning, I opened the front door and stood there in the clear blue day. I took a step outside and then another and another. The point was to get to my car, to the garage. I did it. I didn't throw up and I only got sort of dizzy before my heart started racing. Before the crash flashed before my eyes. Before I recalled the first day I woke up in the hospital. I pushed through that dizziness and got behind the wheel, but when I put my seat belt on, I could feel the tug of the same seat belt that night, pinning me into the side door, the straps they had to use at the hospital to keep me calm before they pumped me full of sedatives.

Even now, my pulse thrums through me.

As I stalk back into my room, I tell myself that today I made some progress. It was because of Lena. All I could hear was her saying, *Okay, Pat. Take your time. You know where I'll be.*

I wanted to be where she was. Listening to her voice at night has set something loose within me, has set something free. It's terrifying because I'm starting to care.

She was at that lake and then she came home in someone else's car.

The need to know every detail about that guy burns me up. I get in my bed and lie back, the light from the pool house floods my window. This has become our way of communicating, signals that we've developed over the last few weeks. We only ever text when our lights are on.

Me: *Hey*

Lena: *Hi*

I groan and lean too hard on my headboard. I type: *How was the party?*

Lena: *I had a good time. Food. Fireworks. Scarlett might have a new boyfriend.*

I hit send before I can change my mind.

Me: *Just Scarlett?*

Lena: *Meaning?*

Me: *The guy who just dropped you off.*

Lena types and stops.

Me: *It's not my business I shouldn't have asked.*

Lena: *You're right.*

The ants under my skin feel like they're multiplying, burning so much that I scratch at the phantom sensation.

Lena: *But he's just a friend. Selena wouldn't start.*

Me: *You can use my truck if you need.*

Lena: *That's fine. Scarlett will give me a ride to pick her up tomorrow. How was your night?*

Me: *The usual.*

I should tell her that I made it all the way to the garage today, but I don't. What would come after that? Nothing because whatever I'm feeling needs to be buried so deep it can never resurface.

Me: *I wanted to be there.*

Lena: *I wanted you to be there, too.*

My fingers feel out of control as I type: *Who was the guy?*

Lena: *I didn't catch his first name. He's a counselor actually.*

Me: *Meaning?*

Lena: *Meaning if you need anyone to talk to . . .*

Me: *Don't talk to people about me Lena.*

Lena: *Copy that.*

And then she goes silent.

I scream into my pillow. Why is it that when it comes to Lena, I take two steps forward and five back? I want to call her and tell her that I don't know how to say the right things. That when it comes to her, I keep messing up. I was going to *go* to her because I knew where she was going to be. I could follow the strangling, wailing, shrill sound of her singing anywhere because when I hear it, this entire place doesn't feel as hollow anymore.

I don't say any of that.

The shitty part is that she isn't wrong. Kayli isn't wrong. Scarlett isn't wrong. I need help and I'm afraid to ask for it. The only one wrong and decrepit and twisted is me. Why can't they see that I'm beyond being pieced back together?

I rest the phone on my chest and stare at the dark ceiling. It is like being swallowed whole on all sides by her silence. Her, this girl ten years younger than me that keeps pushing and pushing in ways that may inevitably break me.

What was it that I used to tell my friends? There is no point in falling in love. There is no point in being with one person at a time. Women were a blur in my bed. Faceless. I do not deserve the women in my life because I don't know how to be a better man than the one I was.

How can I be better now?

I pick up the phone and hold it to my ear. I know it's going to go to voicemail but this time, after so many failed attempts, I don't hang up. "Hello, this is Pat. Patrick Halloran. Call me when you get this message."

When I hang up, my entire body lights up when I see her name.

Lena: *Goodnight, Pat.*

I drift off to sleep.

7

Wide Open Spaces

LENA

"Oh my gosh, he is *so* fine," Ari squeals on the phone after I send her a picture I found from Pat's soccer days.

After riding in the car with Hutch and River, my curiosity over Pat's former soccer career couldn't take it. I did what anyone would do. I Googled him. He didn't come up right away and there were a lot of other suggestions. *Did you mean* this other *Patrick instead?* No, Google Overlord, I didn't.

Pat's soccer stardom was short-lived, and the only real article I could pull up was archived from *The Bozeman Daily* seventeen years ago. While Patrick was undergoing knee replacement surgery and having his dreams crushed after the death of his older brother, I was a nine-year-old playing with my second-hand Barbie dolls. How could our lives have been so different and then, somehow, ended up in the exact same place—at least for a time?

I am not diminishing anything that I've ever been through because it's not a Sadness Race, but damn. It couldn't have been easy to go through so much tragedy back-to-back. My heart goes out to him in a way that is inexplicable. Or maybe it's not inexplicable at all. Maybe it's as easy as empathy.

Mari told me when she first met me that I would take care of every stray if I could, and she wasn't talking about the literal stray cats that I kept feeding in our yard. When people want something from me, I want to help. Yes, Ari and my stepmother, Sonia, were family duty. I am still doing everything I can for them even after what Sonia did to me. Mari and I became friends because I saw how we were both struggling with the workload. Didn't I turn myself into an unofficial mother hen in the house I was living in? Making giant meals that anyone could take as leftovers and eat properly. It's draining, and I know that's the reason it took me so long to go back to school, so long to see that no matter what I did, I would never have a good relationship with my stepmother. I would allow myself to break in two just to make sure Ari is happy and has everything she needs.

As I look into Patrick's face from this faded photograph, I wonder if I'm just collecting him the way I do to others. My job isn't to heal him or be his friend. It's to clean his house and cook. Why am I stressing this man?

Now that I've seen his face, I feel conflicted in a different way. The picture online was blurry, but there was a box I un-packed that had a better portrait. The box was labeled USMNT and I figured if he didn't want me opening it, he would have just hidden it in that basement of his. There was a jersey, cleats, the usual, and this magazine with a page on him earmarked. I try to match the deep, gruff voice to the boy kneeling on a green field with his arms behind his back. I've only seen his shadow, but I know that now he's bigger. His hair longer. Yes, Ari is right. He's Fine with a capital *F*. But the boy in this picture is not the man in the house across the pool.

"You need to tap that," says my fifteen-year-old sister.

"Uh, *esqueeze* me?" I ask. "What the hell do you know about that. Do we need to have a talk?"

"Please, Mom already had a *talk* with me. She was all, don't be like me. Keep your legs closed. Blah blah blah."

"Ari—"

"It's fine, Lena." I can practically see her roll her eyes. "My school has a sex ed class. I don't need this conversation from you, too. Plus, Mom has a new boyfriend and from what I can hear, I don't want to be doing any of that yet. You're just trying to change the subject. We were talking about how your boss is totally cute."

"First of all, he's not my boss. Scarlett is my boss. Secondly, this photo is old. Thirdly—"

"Oh, this is an interesting development, we never get to a third point."

"*Thirdly,* he's my friend. I want to help him."

"I know you want to take care of everyone," she says. "But maybe you should have some fun for yourself instead. It's the summertime! Even *I'm* having fun and I don't have an allowance."

"Send me your grades and I'll send you some cash when my check clears, but do not give it to your mom. I already paid the rent."

She sighs, like she's deflating, but then mutters a thank-you. Why is everyone around me so resistant to saying thank you? Seriously, being polite doesn't kill.

"I'm just worried about you being by yourself out there."

"I made some friends the other day. This girl River is actually from back home."

"Wow, another weirdo like you willingly living in the middle of nowhere."

"I'm not weird," I say, matching her shrill immaturity. "Your *face* is weird."

She cackles, having elicited the response from me she wants. "I miss you, Lena. I have to go. The cute firefighters across the street are letting the fire hydrant run for a little while because it's boiling outside."

"I miss you, too," I say, but she's already hung up.

Weeks pass in a blur of paint and boxes. I finish two more rooms in greens and blues and unearth some of Patrick's family memorabilia like black-and-white photos and porcelain Christmas decorations. I put all of the holiday things in one box that he can do what he wants with after I'm gone.

Patrick and I have talked less and less on the phone since that weird exchange on July Fourth. I really wish he hadn't asked me who the guy was in the car. There was something possessive in his questions. Almost like he was jealous. What does he have to be jealous about? Perhaps that's just me projecting. Didn't I feel the same way when I saw Kayli? The beautiful doctor's monthly visit came and went, and we actually spent the day together after she was done with Patrick.

Scarlett and Kayli had these wild stories about midnight barn parties and dirt bike racing guys in back roads for money. It goes to show that you never truly know someone by their appearance.

A week later, on a pristine July weekend, Hutch and River come pick me up for a trip to Flathead Lake. I don't invite Pat, but I leave him food in the fridge and a note with a smiling salmon. River and Hutch spend the drive telling me their whole story, and I only wish I had popcorn for some of it. In town, we eat more huckleberry ice-cream than I ever thought possible and then we find a campground. I have my first glamping experience. Hutch only asks about Patrick once, but since Pat shot down my suggestion, I realize it's not my place to push him into doing anything he doesn't want to. He'll go at his own pace. He isn't my project to fix.

And yet, the strangest part about the new distance from Patrick is that I find myself missing the sound of his voice. I've started to forget it, like a fading echo. Every time I want to call him, right before I get into bed, I run through the reasons why it's a bad idea. Sometimes, I dream about the boy in the soccer photo. Other nights, I dream of his voice asking me to come into his room. Those are usually the nights I wake up sweating, with an ache between my legs.

By the end of July, I've gone through every recipe I know and finished all five of the downstairs rooms. The living room is going to be next but that's a huge project to paint, and I have the perfect remedy.

"Hey, Pat?" I call out for him at the stair landing.

"Yeah?" He doesn't even hesitate. There's a clanking sound like metal falling on metal.

"Is it okay if my friend Mari comes to help with the living

room? It's a big job and since I'm leaving in a month, I want to make sure everything is finished."

His familiar silence drags on for a bit. I wonder if he's thinking about me leaving at the end of August or if he's wondering if he even wants another person here. Mari is a gem, but he doesn't know that.

"That's fine. Just let me know when she gets here."

I lift my eyebrows in surprise, but shoot Mari a text message to come on over before he can change his mind.

When she arrives, her usual olive tone skin is a deep bronze tan after nearly two months in Greece. She's in metal sunglasses, hair brushed neatly back. Her painting clothes are a lot more glamorous than my painting clothes, which include a raggedy pair of sweatpants and a tank top that I've washed so many times, it's nearly see-through.

"You got your nose pierced!" I shout as she runs to me from her car.

"It's my senior year look," she says, framing her nose with her hands. The little gem twinkles in the summer sun, and I usher her inside to get down to business.

After she's done inspecting the place, and after I tell her she has to keep to the first floor and only the first floor, she spends the entire time we paint telling me about the beautiful men she encountered across the Greek islands.

"Did you also have a musical montage," I say, then gasp, "which one is the father?"

"What are you talking about, My Lena?" she asks, dipping the roller in the storm-gray color I chose for the main wall.

"Please tell me you're old enough to know about *Mamma Mia*."

She deadpans confusion, then can't hold back her laughter. "I do, I'm just fucking with you. You are so easily tricked."

"It's my most annoying quality," I say.

"So." She takes on a flirty tone. "How's everything with Pynchon over there?"

"First of all, ew. Second of all, things are fine. We get along a lot better than we did at first."

"Is he cute?" she asks, wiggling her eyebrows as she rolls Xs on the wall.

I try to signal her with my eyes because Patrick might be able to hear us.

"*What?* I'm just saying it would be perfect if you fall in love and then stay in this house forever since you've basically done all the work to put it together. I can be your live-in friend and we can start a sitcom about our adventures!" She raises her roller so high she splatters paint on the floor. I'm glad I put down plastic everywhere.

"Oh my god, can you not?" I say. "Also, I already have enough of those love theories in the required reading Scarlett gave me."

"You could be the lady of the manor, painting away, and turn one of these *thousand* rooms into your studio."

I shake my head, but I know there isn't much I can do about Mari. I love her as she is, and Pat will just have to deal with this theorizing of hers. After we finish the main walls, there's only the area around the fireplace left, for which I picked a matte peacock blue.

"We've earned a break," I declare. "Are you hungry? There's still leftovers from lunch we can eat by the pool."

Mari is already ahead of me, out through the kitchen door and racing along the blue-tiled path that leads to the pool. I carry the bowl of watermelon and feta salad and two forks. We change into our swimsuits. She jumps in, but I hang back because my phone beeps.

It's Patrick. My heart feels like it's on an unbalanced weight.

Patrick: *I didn't think it was possible to have someone in the house louder than you.*

Me: *You wouldn't say that to my face.*

Pat: *Touché.*

I look up at the window of his room, blocked out by the sun. He's standing there, his shadow not moving.

Me: *Come down.*

Pat: *I don't think I want an audience for the first time we see each other.*

Me: *Are you planning on breaking your own rules?*
Pat: *I could.*
Me: *Don't tease me, Patrick.*
Pat: *Lena?*
Me: *Pat?*
Pat: *Thank you for lunch.*

Mari pops her head up from the water. Where did she find a pool floatie? "Magdalena Martel, who has you grinning like a fool?"

"No one," I say. "Where'd you get that?"

She swims over to me, a purple noodle under her arms. "Your pool house, duh. You were too busy texting. Would I be correct in assuming it's Soccer Star Patrick?"

She cranes her head toward my lap, but I raise the phone over my head. I don't want to explain this thing between me and Patrick because it feels fragile, breakable, too-thin glass testing the weight of iron. Something like that doesn't have a good foundation.

"It's my sister," I lie. I set my phone facedown on the poolside and dive into the warm water.

Whatever this is, I don't think I'm imagining it. Maybe Mari is right about the way I try to take care of people. But I think in this instance, maybe Patrick and I both are a little bit stray.

8
I Walk the Line

PAT

"How are you?" I ask Jack.

"You know, doing my best impression of a calf taking its first steps." He scoffs, but he seems in an okay mood.

"They treating you okay?"

"As best as they are able. It helps that I'm the handsome one in the family." We're both quiet. I know my brother isn't trying to be a dick. Between the two of us, that was always my reigning title. We've always had this joke, even when it was the three of us and it was clear that Ronan was the one that women went wild over. After the accident, it's different. "Fuck. I'm sorry. I didn't mean—"

I chuckle and remember when it was our father who would dust his calloused hands. We'd be having dinner or sitting out back in one of the few weekends he was home and Ronan and I would be fighting over who got to call some girl, who was taller, who was more attractive. Dad would say the same exact words Jack spit back at me and we'd all laugh it off because it didn't matter. Because we were family. "You're stealing all of Dad's best lines."

Still. I trace the scars along my left cheek.

Jack takes a deep breath, and even if what he said feels like a kick in the gut, I sidestep it and keep going. After all, I'm the one who put him in that recovery room and me in this glass box.

"How's it going with Lana?"

"*Lena*," I correct, and know the land mine I stepped on.

"Whoa, easy now. It was a simple mistake. How's *Lena?*"

"It's not like that, and she's fine. She's in the pool with her friend from school."

"How do you get that lucky even when you're a miserable old man?"

I shake my head, walking into the kitchen. I grab a glass of water but it's a shitty excuse because I have water bottles all over my gym and my room. Every part of me just wants to be closer to where she is. "I'm not watching them, you pervert."

But I can't lie. Seven months ago, the guy who drove that car, the guy who was doing shots out of a girl's belly button and trying to talk his best friend out of getting married, would have absolutely watched Lena and Mari sunbathing by the pool. When I danced with the guys of Mayhem City for the very first time, I didn't really understand the point of shaking your ass on a stage when you couldn't touch. I'd been to strip clubs with friends for all kinds of reasons, but I never liked them because I had always preferred physical interaction. The spark that comes with looking into her eyes and knowing that we want the same thing. Then, on her go, we'd get into bed or whatever location inspired us.

Ricky was the one who showed me how to loosen up on stage, to not be so stiff. It was just after my knee surgery, when I had wanted to be someone else. I even took my mom's last name instead. I didn't think Dad would mind because he was dead, but the guilt still dug its heels into me. It was before the days of truly invasive social media, so it was easier to leave my past as a failure behind. The Donatello name is a ghost around these parts, and that has saved my privacy. At least while I'm home. But with Mayhem City, up on that stage, I learned the instant attraction that comes with watching a body move. The instant want. Desire. Lust. All of it.

Lena is not on a stage, and she is not for me to ogle at when she isn't aware. But from the open window, I can see her and Mari sunbathing facedown, giggling to each other in a way I never hear Lena laugh when she's with me.

She isn't with you. She works in your house, ijit.

That realization alone gets me averting my eyes. Focusing on my brother's words.

"What?" I ask.

"I said, my doctor says I'm making an improvement. That maybe I'll be out of here by the holidays."

"Good. You'll be home soon."

"Can't wait to see what you've done with the place," he says sarcastically. "Hope you haven't stuck to the same chrome dome aesthetic you had going on."

"No," I say and clear my throat. "Lena's already finished the first floor. It's nice. Not what I imagined but it feels—" I want to finish that sentence. I want to say it feels like *home,* but I know the implications that come with that. "Better."

Jack sucks his teeth and mumbles something I can't quite make out.

"What was that?"

"I'm asking if she's going to still be there when I get back?"

I shake my head, a leaden feeling beneath my ribs. "She's out at the end of August."

"You shouldn't be alone, Pat." The worried change in his tone gives me whiplash.

"I'll be fine, little brother."

He takes a deep breath but doesn't fight with me about it. Instead, he tells me about the nurses who are the nicest to him and about what his career options look like after this. That Ricky had always wanted to hire him even before the accident. I was never sure why I didn't want Ricky hiring my little brother. It wasn't because I wanted to protect him. It's a good life with good pay and he's a grown-ass man. Was I jealous of my own little brother upstaging me?

I don't want to think about it anymore.

When we say goodbye, I want to tell him that I love him and that he's going to be all right, but the words are only half formed, and by then, he hangs up on me.

Lena's laugh draws my attention. Whatever her friend is saying has her rolling over on her back and clutching her stomach. Jealousy surfaces hot on my skin because I want to be the one eliciting that laugh. I want to coax more than a laugh from her pretty mouth. From the kitchen window, I see her eyes glance back.

She can't see me. I know that, because of the glare. But somehow, she knows that I'm right here. Her hair is a glorious tangle of black over a warm brown shoulder, and her eyes are squinting against the sun. Water drips from her skin and for a moment, I can't breathe when I imagine what my fingers would feel like running up and down her spine.

That sensation moves down my chest and settles around my crotch. It is safe to say that I haven't had this feeling since I got home. The first few months I just laid in bed. I didn't sleep. I didn't eat. I sure as hell didn't jerk off. I wanted to remove myself from this body, this thing that wasn't me.

For the first few months I thought there was something wrong with me because no matter how much porn I watched, I couldn't get my body to cooperate, my dick to move. It's not like I wanted to, either. But I grew increasingly fucking frustrated. I just wanted to know that I still could. It was one of those things I couldn't bring myself to tell my doctor in California or Kayli when it became clear I wasn't going to leave the house. At one point in March, I lost the ability to want to do anything, even get out of bed.

Thankfully, Scarlett came to my rescue in the form of books. Perhaps it speaks to my own ego that it was reading the series I modeled for that got part of me moving. Seven months is not a long time to go without sex. But for me, it is. I can't quite explain the reason I abstain from touching myself in this very moment, thinking of Lena.

It's almost wrong.

No, not almost. It *is* wrong.

Dirty in a way too fucked up even for me.

God, I'm already mortified as I take my painful erection upstairs. It is so fucking hot all of a sudden that I open the window I haven't opened in seven months. There's a breeze and it helps. For about ten seconds.

I throw myself facedown on my bed, but then I find myself grinding against my fucking mattress in a way that is even more painful.

Lena is laughing again, and I want to bottle that sound forever because it means that she's happy. She isn't stressed about putting the towels in the wrong place and she isn't tearing up because I have, yet again, snapped at her. I get up and go to my bathroom and turn on the shower.

Why are you like this? I ask the foggy, warped reflection that stares back at me in the glass. I turn the water as fucking cold as I can and gasp when I stand under the shower, raking trembling fingers through my wet hair.

Right, because pneumonia is the cure for a hard-on.

I don't bother with pajamas or even dinner. I jump into bed and take one of the Lunesta sleeping pills Kayli prescribed to me for my insomnia. I haven't taken any since I started talking to Lena on the phone or through text, but I need it now because I can't think clearly without envisioning her in that swimsuit, her long muscular legs powerful enough to crush my head between her thighs.

When I close my eyes, I see her swimming. I see her climbing out of the pool. I see her glistening in the sun, refracting water. I see her coming up the stairs to my house and walking slowly down the dark corridor leading to my room. She opens the door and stands at the threshold. She doesn't scream when she looks at me, and instead, she keeps walking. She crawls into my bed, under the covers, and climbs on top of me.

I try to touch her, but she shakes her head, biting her bottom lip, and says, "No hands."

So, I keep my arms pressed on my mattress, bunching the fabric in my fists. I feel the cold rush of water turn into hot, wet warmth as she takes my dick in her hands.

"Close your eyes," she says, and I do. I do whatever she wants me to do as long as she'll just keep touching me this way.

"Lena," I sigh as she sits on her knees, guiding the swollen tip of my cock into her slick, wet pussy. I can't breathe as she sinks down, sits deeper until she is all around me. She is everywhere, wholly consuming me, and I don't want her to stop.

I try to grab her hips, squeeze the muscles of her thighs. She presses her hands on my chest.

"No hands," she whispers, fucking my cock in bold, hungry swivels of her body.

"Lena," I say over and over until I open my eyes and a sharp, jerking sensation wakes me.

I sit up, my swollen dick in my fist.

But then, I hear a sweet cry come from outside my open window. It's dark out and Lena's singing. No, not singing. She's moaning.

When I rush down the hall to get a better look at the front of the house, I do not see any other car but hers. Lena is moaning alone in her apartment.

I return to my bed. The moment I turn on the bedside lamp the sound stops.

Fuck. I brush my hair back and instantly regret it.

I pick up my phone, my fingers possessed as I find our messages. She asked me if I had dinner. She asked if I was okay. She said good night and I wasn't there to answer her.

I can't be the only one imagining this feeling.

You up? I text.

Lena types and stops. Types and stops for the most torturous sixty seconds of my time with her.

Lena: *Couldn't sleep.*

Me: *Lies.*

Me: *I heard you.*

Then she's calling me. I don't realize she's calling me at first. But suddenly, I'm staring at her name lighting up my phone, my heart racing at a thousand miles per minute.

I slide my finger across the screen and answer.

"I heard you first," she says.

LENA

"Come on, Lena," Mari says, splashing water at me. "I lived with you for the better part of last semester and I know for a fact that you never brought a guy home. You're the hottest piece of ass in our class, except for me of course."

"What's your point?" I ask, laughing into my beer. Considering we've spent all day painting a living room, I don't feel so bad drinking Patrick's supply. He hardly touches the stuff anyway. I glance over my shoulder, my eyes flicking to the window of his room. *He isn't there, Lena.*

God, what's gotten into me? Is it just Mari's energy after not seeing her for months? Is it because a part of me misses talking to Patrick on the phone most nights? I wish I had an endless supply of patience, but mostly, I just want to face him. I want to know if this feeling he evokes is a figment of my imagination. I want to know if I get the same butterflies in person as I do when we're exchanging messages.

"My point is that summer is for flings and you are not flinging. Come with me to the Whiskey Tap tonight."

"You and my sister should be friends," I say. "Especially since the two of you are obsessed with my love life."

"*Lack* of love life."

I gasp and splash water at her. "The guys in school are too young for me."

That seems hypocritical since I've spent the last month convincing myself that I don't have feelings for Patrick who is, quite literally, a decade older than me. "Besides, I don't want to be someone's college hookup. I've never had anything serious and I'm not going to start when I'll leave in a year and a half."

"You know what I'm hearing, Martel?"

"A rational adult explanation?" I offer.

"Excuses, excuses, excuses!"

We both share a good laugh and then she floats on her back, recounting her new long-distance relationship. "I don't think it will last. I need to *see* my person. I want to be spoiled. I want to spoil them back. That's my love language."

"Greek?" I ask, only half joking.

She splashes me again. I check my phone to see if our laughter is bothering Pat, but so far, nothing.

"No, silly," Mari says. "Gifts. My love language is gifts. I think yours is touch. What do you think?"

"What do you mean by love language?"

"Like, the way you show people that you love them. It doesn't have to be romantic. It can be with your family or a lover."

"Please don't say the word *lover*."

She cackles in that way of hers, then swims up to me poolside. She picks up her beer and drinks it, though it must be warm now in the sun.

I think of her words. *I need to see my person.* Other than flashes of a shoulder, the movement of a shadow, I've never seen Patrick. There's a knot in my throat and I drink my beer to try to push it down.

"Why do you think mine is touch?" I ask.

"Because you give the *best* hugs ever. Seriously, it's a skill. You never give a half-assed, one-arm hug or pat me on the back. When we watch movies, you play with my hair in the non-creepiest way. When you're the *most* sad and homesick, I know I need to put my arm around you or lean against you and you seem to feel better. I get it. It's hard being away from home, and a place like this doesn't make it easy."

I think about the way I grew up. My mother braiding my hair before I went to sleep and my dad kissing my cheek ever morning and night. I used to hate his mustache, but now that it's gone, now that I'll never feel it again, I miss him terribly.

I remember how settled I felt when Scarlett offered me her hand, the ache that hit me when I watched Hutch and River finding ways to touch each other in the lake and by the picnic table. Sometimes, just before I go to sleep, I wonder what it would feel like to touch Patrick. Then I push the thought away because it's stupid, because it won't happen, because he won't be ready, and even if he was, I'm going to go back to school on September first and I won't be living here anymore.

"Maybe you're right," I say, draining my beer. "But I don't think any of the guys I've met at school feel right."

"How would you know if you don't give anyone a chance?"

"I give people chances."

"Case in point," she says with a finger pointed at the sky, "during the class exhibit there was a super-hot TA. He was really sweet and totally into you and you just ignored him and went to stand with Professor Galland to talk about color theory."

I remember the TA. He was beautiful, and sweet, and I can't even remember his name because when he talked to me, all I could think about was that I'd have to drop out and be a failure once again.

"It wasn't him. Really. I just had more things to worry about."

"I, for one, am worried for you. When was the last time you even painted?"

"We just painted a whole living room!"

"I mean, painted your own original work on a canvas. You said it yourself you've been having a hard time."

"My artistic capabilities have no relation to the last time I had sex."

She shakes her head. "That's not what I mean. Art is about passion. When was the last time you felt that passion? Not just sex, but with anything. With life. With cheese. With your mystery recluse boss even."

"Mari! He's not my—*ugh*." But then it devolves and we're talking about the usual things like the impending semester, and whether or not we'll have the dreaded Professor Meneses. Mari has to visit family in Chicago before she comes back for the semester, so I won't get to see her much after this.

When it's sunset and she's gone, my body is restless. I swim a couple of laps in the neon blue of the pool and then lay out in the perfect summer night to air dry.

Now that Mari's told me my love language is touch, I can't unthink it. All I want is to feel the weight of arms wrapped around me. Is this loneliness or something more? When I close my eyes, I picture Patrick. Not the old photo I have of him, but a figure just out of focus. He is the sensation I get when I'm near him in the house, on the other end of the phone. He is as invisible as the weight of the wind, but I can still feel him there.

As the night stills, revealing the sounds of nocturnal crickets, I hear something else—a deep guttural moan. My attention snaps up to the house.

I text Patrick a few times, but he seems to be asleep.

Then I realize, the window of Pat's room is open. Oh. Oh. *Oh!* Is that sound what I think it is? The moans deepen, and my body reacts with a flutter between my legs.

Oh no. I can't sit out here listening to him do—Do whatever he's doing. I grab my towel and shuffle a few paces to my pool house when I stop.

"Lena."

I only hear it once, clear as the night sky right now. Once is enough. I close my door behind me, tracking water upstairs to the bathroom. I slip out of my swimsuit and hang it out to dry, then rinse the chlorine water off my skin, lathering my hair until it's soft again.

My heart swells, a heavy feeling that heats up my skin with want. Want for a man I've never truly laid eyes on. A man who has yelled at me and been kind to me and made me confused all at the same time. A man who hurts the same way I do but is dealing with it in different ways.

I shut my eyes and Patrick's moan, though distant, reverberates from the apex of my heart to between my legs. I follow that feeling with my fingers, slipping them between wet folds and a swollen clit.

I bite my lip and, then, surprisingly find myself testing out Patrick's name on my tongue. Too bad this bathroom doesn't have a detachable showerhead.

I shut the water off and towel off, but that restlessness takes over, and though I'm wet in more ways than one, I climb naked into bed. I sink into my nest of pillows. I rub my palm back and forth between my legs, the friction sends warm shivers up my torso and down my thighs. I wonder what he feels like. I wonder if his voice could play me like a guitar. I wonder if I could come with his face squeezed between me.

My pleasure is interrupted by the vibration of my phone. I half want to ignore it and half want to see if it's him.

My heart jumps when I see that it is.

It is one in the morning and Patrick is saying that he can hear me moan.

"I heard you, too," I want to answer. It feels stupid to use my fingers, so I call him. My skin is hot enough to fry an egg.

The second he picks up, I think my voice will fail me. I whisper, "I heard you first."

His breath is a deep shudder. "Lena. What are you doing?"

My heart slows to a grind, full and ready to burst because I know the sound in his voice. Desire, ripe as low-hanging fruit. I want to pluck it, devour it, and lick the pit. I settle on my bed, lifting the cover around me.

"I think you know what I'm doing."

He curses in a whisper.

"Say that again," I voice low into the phone.

"*Fuck.*"

"Fuck what?"

"Fuck me."

I slip my fingers into my wetness and drag the finger back out around my clit. "I'm so wet thinking of you. I want to feel you inside me."

He growls deeply, and I can hear his breath pant, speed up. "I want you so badly, Lena."

"Come here," I sigh. "I'm right here."

"I want—"

"What do you want, Patrick?" I hear him hesitate. This is new for both of us and strange and right. A moan makes my voice hitch. "Tell me, *please?*"

"I want to bury my face in your sweet little cunt."

I gasp at the throb of pleasure that moves through me when he says that. "What else do you want to do to me?"

"I want to taste you and fuck you until you scream my name."

A shock travels from my clit to the pit of my stomach. I let out a little cry, then stroke my fingers faster. "Patrick."

"Like that. I only want my name in your mouth. Say it."

"Patrick." I feel the swell of the orgasm crash over me, my voice is tight, reaching new octaves as his lowers and moans his pleasure until we are both panting.

The realization of what we just did hits me hard and fast. Shit, what did we just do?

"Good night, Pat," I say quickly, and before he can answer, I hang up.

I stare at my ceiling and think, tomorrow is going to be the strangest walk of shame I've ever had.

PAT

"What the fuck was that?"

I ask that before I close my eyes and sleep like a fucking baby. I ask it again the second I wake up because I must have dreamed it.

Then, I make the mistake of rubbing my face and my hand smells like the things you do in the dark when no one is watching. Plus, my sheets are stiff, and my spunk is dried on my skin.

"Great, I'm fucking thirteen again," I mutter as I go for another shower.

Lena hasn't texted me like she does in the mornings after

she leaves breakfast downstairs, and I can't bring myself to be the first one to shatter this uneasy silence. I slap my face at the memory of the things I said to her. Fuckity fuck fuck.

"Hello?" I call out, but as I suspected, it's just me.

The house smells like bacon and pancakes, and though my stomach growls, I don't chow down. Something is missing. It takes me a moment to realize what it is. The usual Post-it with her name and her smile is nowhere in sight.

Is she embarrassed?

I'm not.

Well, if I'm honest with myself, I am a *tad* embarrassed. She heard me moaning her name into my fucking fist. God, I forgot what that fucking felt like, the rush of it, the want and need of another person. Not just a person, but her.

I only want my name in your mouth.

I shove the food down my gullet, each bite tasting like more and more of the things I can't have. Last night was a mistake. I wonder if she's going to tell Scarlett? When I look outside, her car is gone, and I am in a full-blown panic that she isn't coming back.

For a moment, I want to go to the pool house to make sure her things are still in there, but my hands tremble at the thought. Plus, that is her home, her space. Until the end of this month.

I call the number Kayli gave me the last time she was here. I've been talking to this counselor for a little over a week. He's okay. Far better to talk to than the other shrinks everyone tried to match me up with at first. Chris called me back after that freak-out of a voicemail. I don't know what it is, but he doesn't talk *at* me like the others. Perhaps it's also easier because he knows nothing about me, except for the specific background Kayli and I gave him. I trust Chris. Well, I trust him enough to feel a fraction of safety when I unload my feelings over the phone. Feelings I can't tell Scarlett or Jack or my boys, not that I'm brave enough to even call them.

I start telling him about Lena and Mari and the pool and how we ended up on the phone.

"I don't understand," Chris says in his deep, clear tone. He reminds me of Fallon in the way he's levelheaded. "What happened?"

"We got a little too close last night."

"You allowed her to see you?"

I run my palm over my eyes. I feel like a goddamn child whispering secrets at a slumber party. "Over the, uh, phone. I think she's gone. I think I scared her."

"What did she say?"

She said she wanted me. She cried out my name when she came and I cried out hers. Even without touching her, I felt how good it could be, how good it should be if I wasn't in this fucking box of a house I never should have built in the first place.

"What did she say when?"

"When you called her this morning. You called her this morning, right, Patrick?"

I grunt a denial. "I didn't think."

"Look, Kayli said you didn't want a psychologist. I am no longer a practicing psychologist, but I do want to help. I can't help if you don't want the same."

"Of course, I want help," I say. "Do you know how hard it was for me to pick up this phone to talk to *you*?"

"I do. I also know how—difficult—last night must have been for you. But do you think you're taking the right steps in the wrong order?"

"What do you mean?" I nearly shout.

"I mean, you wanted to call someone because you want to get better. Do you want to get better for yourself or for Lena?"

"Both." My brother is waiting for me on the other side of the country, and in thirty days, Lena will be out of here and I don't think I want her out of my life forever.

"I think you should consider whether or not you're moving too quickly. What about Lena's needs? Have you thought of how sustainable this will be?"

"You're not helping me with those questions, Doc."

"I'm not here to be your friend. I'm here to try to parse out the thoughts you're giving me. I promised Kayli that if I thought you needed further help, that I would recommend people."

"No. This is fine," I say. "What should I do?"

Chris is quiet for a little while. "Talk to her. Talk about what last night meant to both of you. What are some smaller steps you can take? Go from there."

That sounds like bullshit advice, but I know that he's right.

When I hang up the phone, I stay in my gym all day, alternating between running and lifting weights with the volume dialed up to the max. What am I doing? What does Lena need? What can I offer her from a distance I can't close? I can't seem to find an answer that satisfies me, so I keep sweating.

When I get out of the gym, my house smells like dinner. I almost can't believe I've been in my gym that long. But every part of me relaxes because she's back. She's home. I dive into the beef Bolognese left for me on the counter. The first time she cooked for me was the same night I puked when I stepped out of the house. I'm not going to tempt fate by repeating the same mistake, but the boxing bag is still in the garage . . .

The first time I spoke to Chris he asked what I wanted. What was stopping me from moving forward all these months? I stared at my reflection in my bedroom mirror while I listened to him. I saw the thick scars on my chest, the hundreds of scars on the left side of my face, the one cutting across my left eyebrow and disappearing into my hairline. I said I didn't know what I wanted and I didn't know what was stopping me, but those were lies.

I clean up the kitchen so Lena has less to do in the morning, then I go wash my sweaty skin off. I walk past my reflection, but then return to it.

This.

This right here is stopping me.

Lena deserves better.

Jack deserves better.

Everyone who makes the mistake of being in my life deserves better.

Lena makes me happy and I don't deserve to be happy. What if I ruin her the way I ruin everything that I touch?

But then, when the night is dark, and I'm in bed, I feel possessed as I call her. The phone rings a single time before she picks up, her voice heady and sweet. Like she was waiting for me.

"What are you wearing?" she asks.

And I say, "Absolutely fucking nothing."

9
Don't Turn Around

LENA

August

This thing between Patrick and me is the first secret I've ever *truly* kept to myself. I was always the worst secret-keeper to my friends, accidentally revealing my friends' crushes in the middle of Earth Science class and on the school bus home. I don't like secrets and I definitely don't like keeping things from my sister. But this is for the best. When I think of slipping into my bed at night to wait for Pat's phone call, my heart gives an extra fast pump as I push the shopping cart down a row of lampshades past a young guy in a forest-green cap.

Thankfully, Ari decides to give me a call because I need a sober distraction.

The moment our FaceTime clears up, and I plug in my earbuds, she asks, "Did you get a tan?"

"I *am* tan."

"I mean you look glowing." She gasps. "Is something happening? Something is happening with the Soccer God, isn't it?"

"Don't be ridiculous." I don't think I sound convincing enough, so I throw in an eye roll.

"It sucks you have to move out of the nice house and back to a crappy shed with seventeen people."

"It's a house and I have five roommates this time."

Ari sets her phone down and begins fixing her hair into a ponytail.

"Where is your phone? And I thought you were getting a haircut?"

"I have a tripod for my desk, obvs."

"*Obviously*," I say, moving on to the rug area of Western Home Decor. On the way, there's a giant section of taxidermy which I consider pranking Patrick with. "What about the hair? I put money in your account last week."

I see the moment Ari decides to lie to me. She shrugs and says she decided to go to the movies with her friends instead. She rests her chin on her hands. "I like the fuzzy pink rug. It's very retro."

"I don't think that Patrick is going to want a dead unicorn in his living room."

"Then get it for me." She grins into the camera with her whole face.

I sigh. "How's your mom?"

"*Your mom.*" Ari turns her face to the side and pouts a little. "I wish you two would get along."

I've tried to get along with her since I was eleven and it never took. "We do."

Ari can *never* know that the reason I'm working for Patrick is because her mother stole my identity. That I could have sent her to jail but I'd never do that to the memory of my dad or the future of my little sister.

I swallow the anger that boils to the surface of my skin and keep going down the aisle.

"Don't look now," Ari says, eyes wide, "but there's a guy checking you out."

I wait to turn the corner and casually tuck my hair behind my ear. There is in fact, a guy who looks vaguely familiar. He was also just in the lampshade aisle. It could be that we're both browsing the same things. He seems incredibly interested in a white fuzzy rug now that I look at him, though.

"Hey, don't I know you?" I ask him, loud enough that the old lady cruising by in her chair glares at me. "We go to school together, right?"

"What are you doing?" Ari hisses into my earbuds, but I can tell she's thrilled at my behavior.

"When you call out a creeper, he has no choice but to scatter. Like when you turn on the lights and the vermin hide."

"He could just be into you. And we don't *have* vermin," she says, "but point taken. I'll remember that."

"Me?" the guy asks, leaving the white throw rug back where he found it. "Yeah, I'm in the same art program. Just browsing."

"Okay. Have a nice day." I exaggerate a smile and start to push my cart away. I need a rug, but I also need an end table.

"You, uh, ready for the new semester?" he asks, stepping into my path.

I shrug. "As I'll ever be."

"You still living at the Donatello Ranch?"

I shake my head. I should ask how he knows where I live, but I've come to expect that around here. "Back to campus housing. Sorry, what was your name again?"

He scratches the back of his head and adjusts the bill of his hat. There's something overconfident in his wide pink lips. "I'm Keillor. We had Surrealism and the Modern Artist together. And I'm one of your new roommates."

"Oh," I say flatly. Why wouldn't he just start with that? The only person I spoke to in that class was Mari because our professor spoke so fast, if you didn't listen you got lost. "You could have *led* with that. I'm Lena."

For a moment, I forget Ari is on the phone until she snorts and says in my ear, "What kind of name is Keillor?"

"Nice to meet you," I say, but busy my hands with the grip of my cart.

He looks around with bright blue eyes. "So, the Donatellos, huh?"

"What about them?" I ask, and I feel like a cat that's just been spooked. The hair on the back of my neck stands.

"Just what they say around town. I grew up here." He crosses his arms over his chest.

I get a strange hot flash of protectiveness. Whatever gossip he wants to share with me about Patrick and his family, I don't think I want to listen to.

"Listen, Keillor, I don't feel comfortable talking about my boss, so just drop it, okay?"

He looks stricken, but nods. I forget about the rug and head for the antiques section, knowing well enough that he's not going to follow me.

"I thought he wasn't your boss," Ari says smartly.

"*Ariana.*"

"Fine. That was still weird. Come hooooooooome."

"I only have a year and a half left," I say. "And I'll be home for Christmas."

"You'd better."

"I will," I say, and this time, I'm glad I can keep that promise.

"Looks like it's just you and me," Kayli says, taking off her doctor smock as she steps onto the patio.

This is our third monthly food and wine night and the first time without Scarlett, who is busy revising her book. Kayli's just finished with Patrick and it takes all of me not to ask how he is because she can't tell me.

"I hope you're okay with pizza," I say, holding the delivery box. "My head is all over the place lately. I forgot to thaw out the burgers when I left for town this morning."

"I have never said no to pizza," she says with a wink of her blue eye.

She picks out a wine since I know nothing about them except "red" and "white." I build the fire easily now that I know where (and what) the kindling is.

"What's got you all over the place?" Kayli watches me with a new sort of intensity. I wonder if she's trying to make some sort of diagnosis on my mental state. I don't think she'd do that, but I have an aunt who swore she could tell you your illness by reading your palm. I know, that's not possible.

I take the glass of cold white wine she offers and sit in the Adirondack chair farthest from the fire. You would think we wouldn't need a fire for the middle of August, but the nice summer weather seems to have come and gone.

"I've been very conflicted about things."

"This about school?" Kayli asks, sipping slowly.

"Kind of. I feel rusty. Like a bike left in the cold for too many winters."

"You're not a bicycle."

"Motorcycle?" I offer.

"Have you tried to paint at all this summer?"

I shake my head. I wish I could tell her that it has nothing to do with school and everything to do with Patrick. My vagina is the rusty bike in the cold. But I'd started down this path of half-truths, so I continue. "I've done some sketches, but they all end up in the fire. Plus moving stress."

"I'm sure Pat's going to miss having you around."

"Why do you say that?" I ask.

Kayli gives me a secret smile. "I don't know what's in the food you're feeding him but he's smiling. That's as much as I'll say as his doctor."

I am thankful for the setting sun that casts a pink glow over both of us because it hides my hot blush. "Happy to help?"

Kayli nods methodically. "You're different, too, you know."

"How?"

"When I first met you, you had this tension in your shoulders. It's like you're holding the weight of the world."

"No one can do that."

"Well, you have your family back in New York and your life here. School. Patrick's house. Yourself. Each one of those things makes up your world. In that sense, you *are* holding that up. I just hope you're taking care of yourself as well."

I want to tell her that I am. Every night for the last two weeks, Patrick and I get under the covers and whisper filthy things until we come and then fall asleep. We never talk about it during the day, and yet, if he doesn't call me the minute the sun goes down, I call him. I turn to the horizon, the bleeding reds and oranges behind the outcrop of tall trees in the distance.

That presents a problem today when Kayli usually stays until way past dinner.

I'm not going to make her leave just so Pat and I can rub ourselves down. She's one of the few friends I have here. Patrick will wait, even if my heart gives a little tug at the thought of him. I can't keep this feeling pent up and I finally break. A little.

"Kayli, have you ever had a long-distance relationship?"

She smiles, folding a slice in her hand to get ready to eat it. "Once. It didn't work out. It never really does."

That's what I keep hearing. "Yeah, you're right."

"You rekindled something back home?" she asks.

The first time we met I told her that there was no one. And that was true. I give her a noncommittal nod. Half lies and half-truths have become my specialty. "I haven't seen him in, well, forever."

"Are things the same between you?"

"Things are *way* better than before. Perfect really. Well, it's all over the phone, if you know what I mean."

She stares at me like I've grown another head, but then widens her eyes with realization. Her eyes get small and her smirk playful. "Oh. Scandalous! Is it . . . good?"

"It's amazing how much you can do with your own fingers and the sound of their voice, but I'm a little frustrated. More than a little. It's tough wanting to just break down that wall and see him."

"And it's not exactly economical to fly there and back."

"Right."

I begin to sink into that desperation that comes with being a few yards away from Patrick and not being able to touch. To know what he really feels like. Every night, he says all of these things, but even though it feels good, and even though I love the sound of his voice, is this what I'll have for the rest of our time together?

"It's not like we're dating anyway," I say. "It's just sort of physically. Or one-way physical."

"Oh, I don't like this. You were so happy ten minutes ago!

Go back to the good part. I'm sorry I said what I said. You can try. It's different for everyone."

As if he's sensing that we're talking about him, Patrick chooses this precise moment to call me.

The moon and stars are barely out and he must not have seen that Kayli's truck is still there. I pick up the phone before she can see who is calling.

"Hey," he says, his voice low. I shut my eyes and push down *the rippling sensation* that spreads across my belly just listening to his voice gives me.

"Hey! Can I call you in a few?" I don't wait for an answer when I hang up.

"Do you need me to go?" Kayli busts out laughing.

I set my phone upside down and finish my wine. "Of course not. As Leslie Knope says, 'Ovaries before brovaries.' I hope we can keep having our dates when I'm back in school. We'll meet at Scarlett's, though, because my house won't be good for visits."

"Are you all set for the new semester?" Kayli asks, nibbling on her crust.

"Actually, that reminds me. I had this weird encounter today at the store." I tell her about Keillor, my new roommate.

"Hard pass. The Keillor brothers always were in a rivalry with the Donatello boys ever since they were kids. Girls, football, cars. Tommy is the youngest and the only one still in school. Not surprised he'd be nosy. But listen, if you need a place to stay, you can rent a room from me for what you're paying now. It's a little out of the way toward Big Sky, but it's better than five roommates."

"I can't pay you five hundred a month to live in your home."

"Of course, you can. I'm even sure Patrick would rent the pool house to you for even less."

"That *would* be great, but I can't ask him to do that. Besides, I have to work at the studio for extra credits to finish my degree sooner."

"Want to leave us so quickly, huh?"

"It's something I just thought about today. I need to get back to my sister. I realized that when I was on the phone with her. It would be great if I can finish up by next summer."

"It's great that she has you, I hope you know that, Lena."

I take a deep breath and admit something I haven't to anyone else. "I wanted to adopt her two years ago. Filled out the paperwork and all."

"What? That's huge."

I nod and refill my glass. "She was a wee thirteen-year-old. But no judge was going to hand her over to a college dropout. At least, that's what my stepmother threatened me with."

"I know lawyers, Lena. Just say the word."

"I will," I say, emboldened by her friendship. She didn't even try to talk me out of it, like I don't know what I'm doing the way Sonia spoke to me. "Ari still has three years of being a teenager and I'm not letting my stepmom mess them up."

"I've only known you for a short amount of time, but I know if anyone can do it, you can."

"Thanks, Kayli," I say. We watch the fire reduce to ash and embers, and then I walk her to her car.

I start to head back into the pool house when I realize my phone is ringing. Patrick. A tight coil digs into my stomach as I answer.

"Why didn't you tell me about what happened at the store?" he asks, more worried than anything else. But there's a tense, angry chord to his voice that makes my heart sputter.

I look at my phone. "How do you know that?"

"You didn't hang up. I heard everything."

"You were spying on me?" I ask sharply.

He sighs hard, a sound I've come to love in the middle of the night. "I'm sorry. I wanted to hear your voice and then—I shouldn't have done that."

I stand in the blue pool light, fighting the anger and frustration and *want*. There's still the want. I listen to him take a deep breath and release it slowly.

"Lena?"

"Pat?"

"Come inside."

"Really?"

"I think—I think so."

With a thundering heart, I open the kitchen entrance door. I haven't been here in this time of night ever. The house is completely dark. Every single light is turned off. The only source of light is the moon shining through the glass walls, swollen and full, as spotlight on me as I step into the living room.

"Patrick?" My heart is a bass drum in my ears.

"Lena," he says, softly behind me. I begin to turn around, but he grips my hips. "Don't turn around. Please."

I hold my breath and fight the urge to spin on my heels and face him. I want to look into his eyes. I want to run my hands across his chest. I want to do all of the things he's been promising every night in the shadows.

But I stay put because I know that this is what he needs.

When the pressure of his hands leaves me, I ache for it. I whisper, "Don't let go of me yet, *please*."

I feel his hands wrap around my torso, trembling fingers flat on my stomach. I sink against the solid weight of him, the firmness of his chest. His chin rests on the back of my head, and I can feel him breathe me in. It isn't fair that he gets to do that and I don't.

"Can I kiss you here?"

I nod, brushing my hair away.

When Patrick lowers his lips to the crook of my neck, it is everything I imagined and more. They are soft, pressing a reverent kiss on my bare skin. That kiss hollows out my insides and leaves me craving for more when it's gone.

"Why?" I ask.

"Why what?"

"Why would you tell me to come in here and still keep me at arm's length?"

"I'm trying, Lena."

The fact that his arms are wrapped around me, that I can feel how solid he is, is proof that he's trying. Something hitches in my chest and I hold it in, like a wish I'm too afraid to speak out loud.

"What changed?" I ask.

"I heard what you said about your sister. Because I am trying to be better for you and I'm afraid of your reaction when you finally look at me."

"Don't you trust me?"

"I want to."

"That's a no."

"Do you trust me?" he counters.

"I think I could. I trust you right now. But you can't eavesdrop on me. Maybe you can start by trusting that I'll tell you when something is wrong. Can you do the same, Pat?"

"When I came back to this house—" He holds me tighter and I brush my fingers across his arms. I can feel thick scars. I can feel the shudder of his breath as he speaks. "I came back here to die. I wanted to die. After the accident. I was going to do it. But I couldn't."

"Oh, Pat."

"I don't want that, Lena. I was in a bad place. I thought the people in my life would be better without me. But something else happened. I suddenly couldn't leave. I couldn't let anyone see me. I found a way to live and for a while, I thought I was doing the best I could and then you walked in here. You make me want to try to get better again. To be a better man. But I need a little bit more time."

I let tears run down my face and brush them away with my palms.

You take in too many strays.

That's what Mari would say. But I know part of what Patrick is saying is a part of me, too. I did not come here to die. I came to Montana to run away. To hide. To forget about myself and leave a part of me behind.

I don't want to do that anymore.

"Stay here," he whispers in my ear.

I rest my hands over his and feel the rough skin of scar tissue.

I don't let go. I want him to know that I'm not going to let him chase me away.

"It's a little difficult to stay here without turning around."

I feel his chuckle against my back. "I mean, here, in the pool house. Kayli is right. I'll rent it to you. You can have it. Whatever you want."

"I want you." I take his hand and guide it down my belly, and to the waistband of my shorts.

I can feel him harden against me. He shudders. "Lena."

His hand is firm against my stomach, like he's afraid to touch me, afraid to keep exploring. I don't want to push him.

"Okay," I say. "I'll stay. We'll figure it out in the morning."

I lean my head to the other side, brushing my hair away. I close my eyes and feel the sensation his lips bring to my skin, like I have been reduced to the fizz of champagne.

It doesn't make sense how someone whose face I haven't seen makes me feel this way. But in this moment, I decide to not let that bother me. To memorize his mouth instead. To long for it.

"Good night, Lena," he whispers.

And I'm not ready for how badly I want to follow him into the shadows.

10
Colder Weather

PAT

September

The cold snap settles in a week into September. After months in California and Vegas, I'm not ready for it after just having gotten used to summer again.

But there are benefits, too.

Lena is staying at the pool house and she started school. She doesn't feel right living here for free, so I told her that she could pay the same rent as she would have at the house off campus. We find a new routine from the one we had this summer. She has to wake up too early to eat a proper breakfast, but I leave the coffee percolating and I ordered her a travel mug. The only day she has completely off is Sundays, and then I leave her to catch up on sleep.

Part of me has already started moving too fast. In the mornings when the air is so cold I can see my own breath and the sun has only just starting rising, I take ten steps outside of my house. Chris told me to take small steps, didn't he? In a way, with Lena at school, I have more time to focus on doing this one thing for her. Hanging the damn boxing bag in the garage.

"What then, Pat?" Chris asked me. "What does that have to do with allowing her to see you?"

I need to be able to do this one thing for her. It meant something to her. She hasn't asked for anything, but she had asked for this. Her dad taught her how to box. I asked her for a little more time and now I have to have something to show for it.

Yeah, that night in the living room was a big step. It has been fueling me ever since. The feel of her skin on my lips. She smelled like fire and grass and something sweet like vanilla. Every part of me was trembling. I thought I'd combust against her. I still don't know how I found the balls to tell her to come inside the house.

Chris said that I shouldn't do things that I'm not ready for, but he doesn't know the real situation between us. He doesn't know how I feel about Lena, how I would do anything she asked of me.

Except look at her. Except touch her. Except leave the house.

Those thoughts rebound in my head with the passing days. That is a truth I can't escape.

First, I get to the garage. I hang the bag. Then, what? I could stand there and surprise her. Is that really how I want her to see me? No, that isn't right. I am not one for romantic gestures. That was more of Ricky's thing. I would ask Scarlett but Lena and I agreed we wouldn't say anything about what's going on between us.

Scarlett would probably say some sappy shit like prepare a nice dinner. Ricky would probably tell me to hire a small jet and fill it with strawberries and champagne. Do I just take a fucking picture of myself and send it to her? Wait for her reaction? Would she want me the same way if she looked at me now? She says she would, but what if she recoils from me? What if she's like those nurses on that day? It would undo me in a way I wouldn't know how to fix again. And I know that's an unfair thing to ask of her.

For now, we have the nights on the phone. I haven't touched her since, and it is like a ghost limb now that I have held her once. Now that I know I won't want to let her go again.

But it's for the best.

That's what I tell myself at least.

Two weeks into September and I get halfway between the house and the garage.

LENA

"Better, Lena," Professor Meneses says. Her light-brown hair is brushed back into a neat ponytail and her round glasses always look like they're about to fall off the tip of her long, crooked nose.

I wouldn't call my sketch better, but it's a start. My fingers feel stiff and not because I spent last telling Patrick in excruciating detail what I was doing with the vibrator I bought at the local Feminist Club fund-raiser. It's been almost four weeks into the semester and I feel behind the others. We're studying the human body, and as much as I love staring at a naked stranger with a flacid penis for hours, I'd rather be naked. In bed. Talking to Patrick.

"Your movements are beautifully frustrated, Lena," Professor Meneses tells me on her second lap. On the other end of the room Mari's cat-green eyes find me and she snorts.

I pinch the piece of charcoal between my fingers and smile. "Thank you?"

Meneses quickly moves on, and like all the other sketches this week, they're unfinished. They don't even look like people, just smudges of ash. I snap pictures of them and send them to Patrick.

Pat: *Not exactly the nudes I'd expect.*

Me: *The only ones you're going to get.*   ;)

Pat: *You coming home? I can order.*

Me: *I'm sorry, I picked up studio hours. Ari is already mad that I didn't call her at midnight on her birthday yesterday because I fell asleep.*

Pat: *Jack's birthday was the day before on the twenty-eighth.*

Me: *Surrounded by Libras. Kind of love that.*

Pat types and stops.

Me: *Wait up for me?*

Pat: *I don't know. I have a really packed schedule of reading Scarlett's latest book.*

Me: *How do you get to read it?*

Pat: *I believe she calls me her beta reader. I asked her if I could call it alpha reader, but she didn't like that.*

Me: *I kind of love this aspect of your life.*
Pat: *It only took thirty-five years, but I finally read books.*
Me: *Maybe you can read the really dirty bits to me tonight.*
Pat: *Tonight, Lena.*

I pocket my phone. I'm the last one to put my things away. Mari is at the doorway flirting with one of the girls from class. Keillor and his girlfriend are leaving the room, hand in hand. He hasn't said a word to me since the day at the store, and I'm glad that's all sorted out as just an awkward moment.

"Lena," Professor Meneses says in that smoky voice of hers. "Will I be seeing you at my exhibit tonight?"

Shit. That's tonight?

Tonight, Lena. It felt like a different kind of promise. But this is too important. She's my teacher, and I'm sure everyone else in the department is going to be there.

"Of course," I say. "I have studio hours, but what time is it at again?"

"My darling, you work yourself to death. Take the night off. There won't be anyone here because everyone will be at the exhibit. At least, I hope. Mustn't jinx myself." She knocks on the nearest easel. "Six o'clock!"

I wave as she leaves the room. "See you tonight."

Tonight, then. On the bright side, this means I'll be able to be home in time for my naughty storytime with Patrick.

PAT

Lena is coming home early, which is both good and bad for me.

She has to change for a party, but she promises to come back for tonight. The plan is to have dinner ready for when she gets here. In the imaginary advice between Scarlett and Ricky, Scarlett wins. I find a nice bottle of wine, one of the many gifts my agency had shipped to me after the accident.

"I can do this," I say out loud.

I go to one of the boxes I keep downstairs full of only family things. I rummage through one until I find my mom's box of index card recipes. She used to painstakingly write her favorites down from magazines and friends. Brigid Halloran learned to make Italian dishes to impress my dad when they first met, and he, in turn, serenaded her with her favorite Irish ballads he learned from his grandparents.

Mom's best dish was a rabbit tagliatelle. I don't have rabbit, but I have beef and I hope it works out. My parents weren't perfect in many ways. They fought and yelled and were just trying to get by with three loud, reckless boys. But they showed their love in other ways. If I could be a fraction of my parents, then maybe I could be on the way to becoming the person that can deserve Lena. Jack. The kind of person that can ask for forgiveness. Right now, I'm the guy that managed to burn pasta.

I fucking *burned* pasta. How did I even do that?

I grab the pot handle before the smoke detectors can go off and yank open the kitchen door. The wind bites my skin, and I march around the garage where the garbage cans are. I throw out the entire pot.

It isn't until I'm inside the house that I realize I walked out there and back again.

I grab the sides of the counter.

Holy shit.

Did I really just do that?

Before I can celebrate, I get a text from Lena: *Heading to the party.*

I part the blinds in the kitchen. She's at her door, clueless of the fact that I was just out there. She's stuffing her arms into a flimsy leather jacket. Her dress is my favorite shade of red, a crimson that matches her lips. When she walks, it reveals a slit at the side of her thigh. Her tall ankle boots make those legs appear so much longer. I have never wanted to go to her so badly.

I grab the doorknob. I just did this. I can do it again. I twist the handle but I freeze up again.

No, no, no.

That vertigo sensation crashes over me again as I shut my eyes and I see the flash of headlights. The splatter of blood on glass. I haven't seen these images in so long. My heartbeat races, and this time it isn't because of Lena.

I take several steps back.

This can't happen. I can't take one step forward and fifteen back. I can't do that to her. She can't see me like this.

I grab my phone: *Have fun.*

Lena: *Tonight then.*

Me: *Tonight.*

That's all I can manage before I go to my gym. I crank up my music as loud as it can go, not caring that I'll probably shatter my eardrums one of these days. I have to get it together before she comes back.

For a moment I want to call someone. Scarlett. Jack. Chris. I have people that I want to talk to but none of them will tell me the thing that I want.

I want to be better. I want to stop feeling this way.

I scratch at my chest, my scars hot under my skin. I breathe through it. I lie back on my bench press and try different numbers, but no one is picking up today. It's Friday night. My little brother, even in a physical rehab clinic, is probably doing something other than hiding in a gym.

I feel desperate. A dark, ugly feeling crawls from the depths where I thought I'd buried all of my fears. An anger I thought was gone rips through as I get up and ram my fists into the nearest wall. This time, I hit hard enough to break through the Sheetrock. I've hit this spot enough that sooner or later I was going to break through. Isn't that what is supposed to happen? You do something enough to make progress and here I am not making progress. Here I am ambling through my shit without her. No matter how hard I try, I'm still a fragment of myself. Blood runs down my fist from the open gash of my knuckles. I take off my shirt and use it to staunch the wound.

I race upstairs and grab the first aid kit from under the kitchen sink and do my best to clean it up. I wrap my hand with a bandage and some tape.

"I can do this," I tell myself.

I just need to work out this frustration, this fear. I'm so close, I can taste it. I put my music on the highest volume and push my body until I'm weak and trembling. Between reps, I feel the cold wind on my cheeks from when I stepped outside. I try to hold on to that until the anger evaporates. I lift two free weights and do arm raises, my hand stiff and stinging with sweat.

Then, there's a pounding on my door. When I look at my watch, three hours have passed.

It's Lena.

"Patrick!" She shouts and shouts my name. "What happened?"

"I'm fine," I shout, defensive. On edge. She can't see me. Not this way. She deserves better.

"Pat." Her voice is trembling. "There's blood. What did you do?"

"Just leave, I can't do this right now—"

But she doesn't leave.

"I—I know who you are. I know everything that happened."

The minute she says that, I feel my body give out. I drop the weights with a loud crash, and the memory I've tried the hardest to push away comes surfacing, paralyzing me, until I relive the entire wretched thing.

LENA

Professor Meneses has carved out a market for herself painting her dachshund as different presidents of the United States. The studio space is an old court building now used by the art department. It has beautiful columns and polished hardwood floors. The paintings are hung in gold frames worthy of the Met. I don't really understand the dog, though, and it's things like this that make me question why I went into art, but after one glass of champagne, the dog begins to look kind of charming as George Washington. Still, events like this make me feel out of place.

I tell Mari as much. She's a vision in a sparkly black cocktail dress that makes everyone in a hundred-mile radius feel overdressed. It's fantastic.

"You, Magdalena Martel, are exactly where you belong. With me. You'll see. I'm going to curate exhibits at the Louvre. I'll be a tastemaker, not an artist. You're the artist."

"Not lately."

"I have faith in you. When you start painting again, it will be exactly the right thing at the right moment."

I look into our glasses of champagne. "I don't think I got the same drink as you."

She throws up her hands in an exasperated way, and, in turn, splashes me with what's left in her glass.

"Oh shit. Sorry!"

"That's fine," I say. "Pretty much in line with what this day is shaping up to be."

After the most stressful week of my life, between my stepmom hitting me up for more money, the hospital bills that are still somehow multiplying, and my general coursework, I still haven't started the assignment. I was hoping to get in some hours at the studio tonight, but instead, I'm here. Professor Meneses has given us the theme of "home" because she wants to torture all of us.

I haven't painted a single thing since school started. I thought that all the orgasms Patrick has coaxed out of me through our phone sex marathons would have helped, but they have just added to my stress levels. When I get home, all I want to do is crash. I've missed his calls the last four nights, and as much as I want to hear him, I also grow increasingly frustrated with the distance between us. I tell myself that tonight will be different. He was making so much noise in the house. I really hope he isn't trying to cook for himself. I'd be in more of a rush to get home if I could crawl into bed with him, feel him against me as I fell asleep.

A girl can dream.

I leave Mari for the bathroom where I blot the excess liquid. I should've gotten a better picture of me in the dress earlier to send to Pat. This is, after all, my lucky one. Everyone has something like this in their closet. Some magical object that possesses a divine power to help them get laid. At least, that's what every romantic comedy ever taught me. Good thing the red fabric is dark enough that you can't really tell I got a champagne shower unless you look real close.

When I exit, I nearly collide into my professor. She's wearing her large round glasses.

"Magdalena," she says, "thank you for coming. I can't wait to see what you're going to have in store this semester. You know, I was on the admissions board when you submitted your portfolio."

She has told me this several times, but at least it's a compliment.

"I can't thank you enough."

"No need. You have more than talent. You have a vision."

That sends my nerves on alarm because the only vision I've had lately is of me getting an F and a blank canvas that will haunt me forever and ever.

"Excuse me, I see a reporter friend of mine. I can't wait until you're on this side of things, darling girl."

I let out a sigh and grab another glass. These things usually run long, but I might cut out soon and surprise Patrick with an early call.

There's a full-length mirror and I take a couple of snaps for Ari. She responds in ten seconds with a cheesy smile and thumbs-up. "I hope Señor Soccer likes it."

"She's definitely wrong on that one," I mutter to myself.

"Who's wrong?" Keillor asks, walking around the column with a bemused smile on his face. He's wearing a blazer over a punk band T-shirt, and his dark-blond hair is roughly combed back.

"No one," I say curtly.

"So, Lena. I thought you weren't working at the Donatello place anymore."

"I'm not working there anymore. I live there."

This has Keillor intrigued for some reason I can't understand. It's not a sexual vibe he gives me. It's different, like a vulture circling around a promising nearly dead animal.

"Why are you so interested in the place?"

He looks over his shoulder to make sure we're alone. "Listen, I have a friend who would pay good money for a picture of Halloran, that's why. Between you and me, if you're tired of working for shitty minimum wage at the studio, these pictures can set you up for a while. I don't know about you, but my tuition isn't cheap. Maybe we can split the payday."

I stare at him like he's grown scales on his face. What in the world? I drain my glass because if I were anywhere else, I would have poured it over his head. Besides, I need to wet my mouth because it is dry as the desert. "Why would anyone want to pay for pictures of a soccer player?"

Keillor stares at me with cool blue eyes. He shoves his hands in his pockets. "You're serious?"

Mari comes up beside me and wraps her arm around my waist. "What's up, bro?"

"Nothing, just filling Lena here in on her boss."

"He's not her boss," Mari says. "*Goodbye.*"

She holds up her hand and it's like she mentally removes him from the room. He starts to leave, but not before slowing down beside me, like a drive-by.

"Look it up. Patrick Halloran," Keillor says. "You know where to find me."

And then he's gone.

"Ignore him. He un-ironically owns pictures of dogs playing poker, that's why Meneses tolerates him. And before you say anything, yes, I will be the snob in this room full of dogs dressed up as the founding fathers. At least the colors are complimentary." Mari pauses. "Lena, you don't look so good."

I know that name. That time I Googled Patrick Donatello MLS, our Google overlords tried to correct me. *Did you mean Patrick Halloran?*

I didn't think anything of it because the first article that came up was about his injury and how he'd never play again.

"I think this champagne is making me sick."

"Oh no, traitorous drink! Want me to drive you?"

I shake my head. "It's not far. I didn't finish it."

But really, I can't wait to get out of here and get on my phone.

I leave without saying goodbye and jump in my freezing-cold car. I type in the name. The service is spotty, but after a little while everything downloads at once.

Pictures after pictures. Headlines that make me gasp out loud. Brutal visions of a car accident. *The* car accident. For at least an hour, I don't even drive, I just sit in the parking lot and stare at a man I've been living with for four months. A man who is a stranger. I scroll through the hashtag of his name. Each image a barrage of information he's tried to keep from the world. From me.

Patrick, older now than the photo I found from his soccer team. Broad shoulders and beautiful. So beautiful it almost aches to look at him in magazine stills. He stares into the camera like he's doing the world a favor by being wrapped in furs, covered in oils, spread across a bed with faceless women draped around him. Everything about him is perfect. His cropped golden hair. His emerald-green eyes. His full pink lips framing blindingly white teeth. His muscles smooth and defined. This Patrick doesn't even look real—like someone carved the ideal man and Patrick walked out from the clay.

Then, in videos he's a different person. Streaking through the Met, threatening to trash a priceless vase. Stumbling out of clubs with models wrapped around his arms. Shaking a bottle of champagne to shower a line of people who scream in adoration. Tripping on a red carpet at some sort of premiere. Stepping on his co-star's dress.

I've heard of him.

I grimaced when I heard of the overnight success. Not because it wasn't deserved but because I think I pitied him? A star fallen from grace so quickly, it was inevitable to be a scandal all over the place.

Almost at the exact moment that I was driving across the country to Bozeman, Patrick was drunk, racing his car down a California boulevard and getting into a three-car collision.

"Holy shit," I sigh.

The least surprising of it all is seeing his likeness on a book cover. Scarlett West. I feel like I've been punked even though it isn't any of my business. This guy is not the one that I've come to know. Isn't it?

How much do people really change?

Is a near death experience enough to make someone different? *Yes, it is,* I think. *Of course it is.*

That doesn't mean that a person is better, it means they're changed. They can choose to become better. Patrick told me that he was trying to be a better man. How much of his past matters to me?

I think of that answer the entire way home.

I instinctively think of it as home because that is where Patrick is waiting. I mentally replay the images that people took around the accident, vultures like Keillor. Patrick's face was covered in so much blood it was like he was wearing a red mask. They took pictures of that. How could they do that to him?

People were hurt, but no one died, did they? Is this why he hasn't let anyone but two people into his life, his home?

He let me in, briefly, slowly.

Why me?

I turn onto the long road that leads back to the house.

I have the choice to go into my pool house and confront him about it over the phone, or wait for him to tell me himself. But I already know that I'm going to go with a third option.

I can't unsee this. No matter what, I have to talk to him.

I park in front and head straight into the house. The lights are off in the foyer and living room but the kitchen light is on. It smells like something burned.

"Pat?" My pulse races as my feet carry me into the kitchen.

I freeze. There's a bloody shirt on the counter and an open first aid kit. More blood splatter in the sink.

Music is blaring from his gym.

"Patrick!" The panic in my voice sends adrenaline rushing through me. I pound the door until I hear him. He tells me to leave, but I want to make sure he's okay.

"I know who you are," I say.

He doesn't respond. I wait and wait and the music keeps playing. I press my forehead against the door. I know I am not supposed to enter here, even if I don't work here anymore. It is something he has asked of me. There's a loud bang, like the clatter of metal slamming into metal.

"Are you okay?"

My heart races in a way that clouds my mind. What if he tried to hurt himself? What if the blood on the counter means something else? What if he can't answer and needs help?

"Pat? Please—"

When he doesn't respond, I know I have to make sure he's safe, even if he gets angry with me.

I turn the doorknob. It is like wading through freezing water. My limbs move in slow motion, my breath trapped in my chest as I brace for the mangled bloody sight of him.

Patrick is in the fetal position on the floor. His hand is a fist against his chest. When he notices I'm in here, he covers the left side of his face. My eyes dart where blood is smeared in a divot in the wall.

"Patrick?" I say his name again as he pushes into a stand. He faces me.

I want to go to him, but I don't think he's going to accept my touch, so I hang back. I have the vague sensation that this is what it might be like to stand in the middle of a ring with a lion, beautiful and dangerous all at once.

His face is not the one in the soccer photo and it is not the one that I've spent the last hour scrolling through. But he is *my* Patrick.

His torso is covered in zigzags of thick scars, each one a river of pearl. The left side of his face is a concentration of more scars than I can count. They form a pattern, like the shower of a sparkler, the tail of a comet. Part of his left ear is missing, his shoulder-length blond hair tucked behind it. His nose is broken in the middle, which makes him look severe, but his mouth. His mouth, with a fine scar that runs over the left corner and to the tip of his chin, is perfect.

I'm trying to smile. I want to say, "*There you are.* I've been waiting for you," but he moves so suddenly that I jump. I can't help but jump back.

"Get out!"

I stay put. "You don't mean that."

"Yes, I fucking mean that. I told you to stay out of here." He turns sideways, giving me the right, unblemished part of his face. "Don't. Don't look at me, Lena. I don't want that pitying fucking look in your eyes. Not from you."

"I *don't* pity you. How can you say that?"

"Then why are you looking at me like that?"

Because I've finally seen your face. Because I love this face. I could love you.

He doesn't let me say any of it, and I realize, in this moment, that he might be so broken, nothing I say will help him.

"You can't pull me close and kick me away when you feel like it! That's not how relationships work."

He scoffs, a bitter smile as he crosses his arms over his shoulder. I have never seen Patrick so bare and so boxed away at the same time. "Tell me, Lena? Did you go searching for something on me? What happened to giving me time?"

"*No,*" I say, my voice hard, my fists shaking at my side. "You don't get to make me into your bad guy. I've given you time. I've done everything I could to make this thing between us work even if it leaves me empty. Part of me always knew you would *never* truly let me in. I didn't even know who you were, Patrick. But I stayed because I wanted to." My vocal chords feel raw and pinched. "You asked me to stay."

"Now I'm asking you to leave. You have your answers. This is who I am. Is this what you wanted to see?"

"Yes," I say, and that is the only thing I can be sure of in this moment. "I wanted to see you. Thank you for showing me who you *really* are."

His chest rises and falls rapidly, and then he turns face forward. He advances two steps and I stay put. He leans into the light, beautiful and broken. "Don't act like this is a face you want to wake to every morning, Lena. Don't lie to yourself!"

I can feel the moment my heart breaks. I think it broke a long time ago, but I'm not sure I can place it. Perhaps it was that night under the full moon in the living room when I begged him to let me see him and he didn't. Perhaps I knew then that it wasn't ever really going to work out, but I hoped.

I turn around and he doesn't follow me.

He slams the door and I slam the one at the front of the house.

With unsteady fingers, I text Scarlett: *Can't explain. On my way. This is over.*

I turn the key in the ignition but it won't start. My mind is as numb as my fingers. Whatever tears I had are gone. I swallow the pain slicing down to my core. Maybe there was never anything there to carve out. Maybe that's why I've never been able to make a relationship work, even one like this.

"Come on, baby," I cry to my car, but no matter how many times I turn the keys, or hit the gas, or bash my fists on the steering wheel, it doesn't turn on. "Come on!"

I hold the wheel, trying to steel myself, to calm down. I can't stay here and a Lyft isn't going to come out this far. I try to call Scarlett, but it goes to voicemail a couple of times. What if she isn't home? I can walk there along the road, but I remember what she said once.

Just take the trail on the left for two miles and you'll be at my house.

Two miles, I think. I used to walk from Union Square to the Met all the time. I can walk that far. Every motion, from turning on the flashlight on my phone, to putting on my jacket is automatic. Possessed, even. I pass the firepit where Scarlett and Kayli and I had some of my favorite nights out here. I've never even been out this far into the property, but I see the forked path and I take the one on the left.

I walk and walk until my feet start to hurt from rubbing against the sides of the ankle boots. My breath comes out in clouds and the cold is seeping into my bones. My hands are too numb to accept the thumbprint on my phone and it takes me four tries to type in the code. I don't know what time I left. I don't know how far I've walked. All I know is that every tree looks exactly the same in the dark. The hot anger that felt like lava when I was in the house is cooling, leaving hard chunks of regret. I drop my phone so many times, that on the last one, the screen cracks.

Slowly, the horrible realization of what I have done dawns on me.

I walked into a patch of woods in the dark in a dress and heels. It is probably forty degrees, getting colder by the minute, and my jacket is a flimsy pleather. It is pitch black and my phone light flickers at best. The trail is no longer clear, and I know that I'm going the wrong way because I'm winded from climbing up instead of going flat and straight.

I hug my body tight because sometimes you have to be your own best comfort. And then, I let out a long, frustrated scream. The kind of scream I've been holding inside for so long it leaves me feeling tired. My joints hurt, my throat aches, and I finally sit down on a log.

I did not come to Montana to die in the woods. It doesn't really occur to me that there might be animals in these woods until an owl hoots from somewhere. Shitshitshitshitshit.

I try my phone again, my fingers too numb to feel the splinters that come from swiping across the screen. Scarlett is calling me back!

The second I answer my phone utterly and completely dies.

11

Love Is a Wild Thing

PAT

"What have I done?"

The swell of anger ebbs too late because Lena is gone. My heart hammers in my chest as I wade through the house in the dark. Her car is still parked out front and the lights of the pool house are still on. I sit at the kitchen counter and relive that awful moment when she walked in and I told her to get out. Maybe I can fix this in the morning.

I've already given up all my chances at forgiveness from her. How many times have I told her I was sorry? That look on her face, the sadness in her eyes. The anger that pinched her lips together to stop from crying—or yelling, "There is no fixing this anymore."

Get out. Why did I say that to her? That is the opposite of what I want. *Stay. Hold me. Be with me. Love me. Don't run away.* I could have said any of those things, but I panicked. I saw the fear in her eyes.

But who wouldn't have been afraid? She came home to blood on the counter. She came home to the smell of something burning. Something wrong. *I know who you are.*

"Fuck," I sigh into my palms.

I have no right to call her, but I tell myself to do it. Even if it's to say goodbye. There are already ten missed calls from Scarlett.

Now, an eleventh. Lena must've told her about what happened. I don't feel like having her yell at me, even if it's what I deserve, so I hang up.

She instantly calls back.

"What?" I answer.

"Don't *what* me, Patrick. Where is she? What happened?"

"She's in the pool house. Everything she told you is true."

"She hasn't told me *anything*. I can't reach her."

There is real panic in Scarlett's voice. Dread seeps into my heart. I remember Jack's face on impact. I remember the moment of stillness just before the headlight collided into us.

"She sent me a text saying she was coming here. What is over?"

I can't even focus on Scarlett's words as I walk to the front of the house. Lena's car is still there, but when I step out barefoot and the sensors come on, I realize that the door on the driver seat is open, the lights still on. I didn't notice. How could I not have noticed? I was so relieved to see that red piece of junk there that I didn't *see* something was wrong.

"When did she say that?" I don't know how long she's been gone. How long was I sitting at the counter reliving the sight of her face? "Her car is here but the keys are still in the ignition."

"An *hour* ago, Pat."

I know what we're both thinking. It takes five minutes to drive to Scarlett's property if you cut across the rocky path on the outskirts of the woods, and fifteen, twenty tops, if you take the long way down the driveway and onto the main road.

I run around the pool. Into the house that has been hers since she got here, Scarlett shouting my name on the other line.

"Lena?" I shout but I know she isn't here. She must have left the lights on before she went to her party. I think of her walking out in that dress, those boots. Goddammit, Lena.

"Pat, what happened?"

"We had a fight," I say, breathlessly. "We've been—I don't know how to explain."

"Don't explain. Go get her. Lord knows she probably decided to walk here! I'll meet you halfway on the four-by-four."

I hang up and run back inside the house. My blood is rushing, my heart beating so fast I have to close my eyes for a moment. I see my brother waking up in the ambulance.

"Pat, Pat, we're alive," he said, crying for the first time since he was ten when he broke his leg falling off a dirt bike. "We're alive," he kept saying all the way to the hospital and the entire time I kept thinking, *No, I'm not,* until I said it out loud and he didn't respond again until the next day.

I didn't feel alive. I haven't felt alive until Lena walked into my house and breathed life into me. She shook me awake with her fierceness, her words, and I hate myself for giving her nothing but ruin.

I take a deep breath. This is how I can be a better man. I have no other choice. There is no time for doubt or fear. I have to go. I grab a heavy-duty yellow flashlight from the garage and stalk into the woods out back.

I know these grounds like the back of my hand, even with the new scars that decorate the left one. When my brother Ronan was still alive, we used to take the trail to the right and see who could get to the top of the hill first. Ronan used to say that the trails felt wild sometimes, that it was why he could never get lost because he knew the woods better than the rest of us. He was right, he did. There's something about this patch that makes you feel lost the second you walk in. Even when you start taking the clear path that leads to Scarlett's house, the trees are thinner to the right, they feel like there's more space to breathe and walk. You get turned around, lost.

Lena would have gone this way. I know it the way I know that she sings to herself no matter what task she's doing, the way I know the little sigh she makes after our clandestine phone calls, the way I know she is just as lost as I am. If she is crazy enough to forgive me, I want to kiss every part of her. If she doesn't, it won't matter as long as she is safe and whole.

I climb up the hill and keep shouting her name.

LENA

I am officially *that* city slicker Scarlett and Kayli have complained about all summer.

It is cold as fuck. I'm wearing boots, but they're heeled and the inner zippers have rubbed the skin on my ankle bone raw and bloody. The edges of my dress are ripped from getting caught on branches I didn't even know were there. I lick the lipstick on my dried lips, and listen to the hoots and hollers of nighttime creatures. They sound pretty judgmental the longer I sit here.

I read somewhere that music keeps away bears. "Are bears nocturnal?"

It might be the dumbest thing I've ever wondered while out here, including the time I thought jackalopes were real that first time I let Mari take me to a bar. Mari. Why didn't I call her? *You don't let people take care of you.* Even so, I know my best shot right now is to start singing. I rub my hands together for friction but that's going to get tiring real quick.

Does Patrick even know that I'm gone? Maybe Scarlett will come and find me when she realizes that I've made a stupid choice. I'm *sure* of it. Or maybe, just maybe, what she'll find in the morning is my frozen carcass being pecked at by feral squirrels. Squirrels if I'm lucky.

My breath is warm and my throat itches from singing. When I exhale, I sink into the bark of the tree behind me. Why don't I ever think things through? I wonder if Patrick and I would have gotten off to such a bad start if I had listened to my mom's advice. Be nicer. Pliable. Amicable. That was her, and I love my mother. I love her so much that each and every day I'm not painting, I tell myself that I can't give up because she is waiting for me to succeed.

The good thing about freezing to death in a pitch-black wood is that I'm too cold to cry. My tears freeze halfway down my face.

I look up at the moon and stars peeking out from the canopy. There is no way I'm capable of pulling a Moana and finding my way out of here using the freaking stars as my guide. Trying to keep walking would be dangerous. I can wait for daylight, and if hypothermia hasn't set in, I'll get to Scarlett's. She should be here by now, shouldn't she?

And then what? Not see Patrick again? Have her or River or Kayli go retrieve my stuff like that one time I had such a bad breakup the guy wouldn't let me in his place again and I had to send my neighbor Howey to go get my Fleetwood Mac record and my favorite shampoo?

It *was* expensive shampoo.

Now, after literally cooling off, I know I shouldn't have run. Patrick shouldn't have yelled at me. The hurt in his voice cut me deeper than anything else. I take in too many strays and this is the one that was rabid, the one that bit me back harder than I ever thought possible. How could he think that I would react to him that way? Then I think, what must it have been like to have me barge into his space? He was trying.

He wasn't trying hard enough, another voice tells me. I think it sounds like my dad.

Then, I hear a hard crunch, the echoing snap of a branch breaking in half, and my scream as night birds take flight.

PAT

Jack's voice echoes in my head as I race deeper into the wood. *We're alive.*

Why did I tell him that? Why did I respond to my baby brother with, "No, I'm not."

I could have said anything. I should have said I was sorry for getting us into that mess. For picking a fight with that guy that led to that race in the first place. When we came to during the accident, the first thing out of my mouth should have been begging for his forgiveness. Maybe I've been trying to heal something that has always been rotten. I am not a good man. But I can't let that stop me from finding her.

"Lena!" I shout.

It doesn't take an hour to get to Scarlett's, but it's pitch dark and freezing outside, though cold sweat runs down my spine. I know that if something happens to Lena I could never forgive myself. This time, I wouldn't be able to do it.

"Lena!" My voice is answered by the caterwaul of an owl, or some sort of night bird.

Then I realize. No, not a night bird. Lena.

It's her. She's singing.

My heart swells with relief at the sound of her awful, truly terrible voice, leading me all the way to her. I stumble into a brush covered in leaves and fallen branches. There, nestled between the roots of a tree is Lena.

Her cheeks are tearstained, and her hair has leaves caught in the dark strands. Her dress is ripped and she's hugging herself tightly for warmth. She screams when she sees me and this time, I know I deserve it. I will take all of her scorn, her rage, her anger. I accept all of it because I've found her.

I sink to my knees in front of her, holding my hands up so she knows I'm trying to help her.

"Oh, Lena," I say.

She lets go of a strangled sob, but she reaches for me and I scoop her into my arms.

"I *hate* you," she tells me, half a sob, half a laugh. But wholly, completely Lena.

I carry her back the way I came from, and as she rests her hand against my chest, I say, "I know."

LENA

"I know," he says.

Patrick is in the middle of the woods holding me. Patrick left the house. The same guy who couldn't bear to walk down the hallway when we first met, or the idea of me seeing him, is carrying me into the open.

"You didn't bring a jacket," I say, holding tight around his neck. He's hot to the touch, but he shivers.

"I wasn't thinking," he says, and grips me tighter.

I take the flashlight and hold it forward so he has one less thing to worry about. We continue the rest of the way without speaking, which is best for me since I can't stop shaking.

I know when we've arrived on the other side of the trees when I hear Scarlett's high-pitched scream of relief. My eyelids are heavy and I lift my head from Patrick's shoulder and find her waiting for us at the clearing with a small open-frame Jeep.

"What in the world?" Scarlett asks. She's fluttering like a butterfly, flapping her arms around me to make sure I'm okay. Then she looks at Patrick, her eyes wide and furious. "You haven't stepped outside in nine months and you can't put on a shirt? Are you crazy? Do you want to freeze to death, too?"

Patrick makes a frustrated, growling sound and maybe I'm delirious because I laugh. I let go of Patrick. Even walking on grass hurts, but I manage to get into the passenger seat. With the Jeep's headlights, I focus on little tasks, like putting on my seat belt and turning off the flashlight on my lap.

"Lena," Scarlett says, and when I look up at them, they're waiting for an answer I didn't hear the question to.

"Huh?" I ask.

"Scarlett said she'll take you to her house," he says. Somehow, he still looks as unreal as those old photos I found of him today. A beauty that is raw and brutal and makes my heart give a painful squeeze. I could stare at him forever.

I shake my head and reach for his hand. "Take me home. We have to talk."

Pat and Scarlett exchange a nod, and she gets in the driver seat, still shaking her head and muttering like a mother hen. Patrick grabs on to the Jeep's frame around back and then we're bounding over a gravel path around the trees. If I'd taken this road, I would have surely broken an ankle.

"Do you have any idea what I thought?" Scarlett shouts over the breeze. "I thought you were dead! Frozen to death in a ditch."

"I'm fine," I say, but my teeth are chattering and if I could crawl into the fetal position, I would.

"Fine, my ass. I'm going to call Kayli to come check on you."

"Really, Scarlett. I just need a hot shower."

"I already messaged her," Patrick says. "She's on her way."

I turn around. I can't take my eyes off of him like this out in the open. He holds on to my stare with his own.

There you are, I think and grin.

When we get to the house, Scarlett takes off my shoes, then leads me to Patrick's room.

I am *inside* Patrick's room. He looks displaced, like he isn't sure if he's helping or hindering. Like he's afraid to be near me and touch me, even after all that.

"Get me some tea," Scarlett barks at him. "You know where the tea is, right, hon?"

"Fuckin' hell, Scarlett," Patrick mutters, but does as he's told.

I stand at the center of the room and take in the smell of varnish. How can a house still smell *so new,* I wonder? His bed is neatly made. Does he do this every day? Mine looks like a tiny hurricane rolled across it day in and day out, my pillows somehow on the floor when I wake up. The bathroom is to the left, and the tall glass window to the right gives me a bird's-eye view of the pool house. Scarlett rummages through a tall dark wood armoire and brings out a white comforter and extra pillows. By the time she's done, I have a literal pillow fort around the fireplace. My skin is warm but I'm still shivering inside. I don't dare sit on Patrick's bed. Mostly, because I don't want to get it dirty but also because I feel like he should invite me to do so first.

"Sit," she orders me gently, then picks up a remote control that ignites the fireplace with a loud pop.

"This really isn't necessary," I say, but Scarlett throws a blanket around my shoulders and I can feel myself relax in front of the crackle of fire. My skin is warm but I'm still shivering inside.

Patrick returns with a mug of tea. I can smell the chamomile and his sweet, nervous sweat. He found a shirt to put on, the long sleeves taper to his muscles like second skin. I take the mug he offers, and I can't help but notice that he keeps giving me the right side of his face.

"I'll be back," he says, his bright green eyes dart from me to Scarlett to the door. I want him to stay, but I know he needs space as much as I do.

Scarlett gives me a long look. "Lena, what in the hell happened?"

I sigh and tug the fleece blanket tighter around my shoulders. "I don't even know anymore."

"Start small."

I tell her about the party and what Keillor told me. About driving here and how in about five minutes, the delicate balance Patrick and I had found together broke.

"Oh, honey. You didn't do anything wrong, you know that, right? I love that boy, but he's not in a good place."

"I know." I know and I still pursued him because I thought that I could handle it.

You take in too many strays.

There's a knock at the door and Scarlett and I both snap to attention. Kayli is there dressed in tight jeans and a first-date blouse.

"Uhm, Patrick is outside," Kayli says, tugging off a red scarf. "Like outside of the house."

"What is that boy doing?"

"He's moving boxes in the garage. Do I even want to ask?"

"No," Scarlett and I say at the same time.

"Well, you're going to have to tell me something because I got this emergency message from Patrick during my second course," Kayli says, sitting in front of me. "It's a good thing I was in town."

"Oh no! I don't want to take you away from a date."

"It was *not* a good date. Though I always feel like Superman a little. 'Be right back, mister man. Duty calls.'"

For the first time, I notice the briefcase she carries. She sets it on the bed and brings out her stethoscope, a blood pressure band, and a thermometer.

Because I won't budge, Scarlett gives her version of the story. "They got into a fight and she took the shortcut to my house."

Kayli raises her eyes in surprise and she puts on the earbuds of the stethoscope. "Lena, Lena, Lena. Inhale." I wince at the cold of the metal and she listens to my breathing until she's satisfied with what she hears.

"Bite down on this."

I take the thermometer in my mouth like a child, then let her take my blood pressure and shine a light in my eyes. She even has me walk in a straight line.

"I had one glass of champagne at a party," I complain.

"Just checking," she says, looking at the thermometer. "Your temperature is a little lower than I would want it, but you'll be fine in a few hours. We can bring your temperature back gradually. Blankets, fire, tea, check. Shower is fine but *no* baths."

As the two of them make sure that I'm not horribly hypothermic, I feel cared for in a way I haven't in a long time. Scarlett goes back through Patrick's closet. I'm a little jealous of her ability to go through his things, to touch his shirts and socks. She hands me a T-shirt and long johns.

"I want to shower," I say. "I also got dirt everywhere."

"I'll clean it up," Patrick says, appearing at the door. His hair falls over his face and he brushes it back. He wipes a hand on the front of his shirt, and leaves smudges of dirt.

Kayli and Scarlett exchange a look that says what I feel—we are in a bizarro world.

"Pat," Kayli says, almost relieved.

He frowns, crossing his arms over his chest. "Can we—I need to talk to Lena."

"Lena?" Scarlett asks me.

"Go, I'll call you later," I promise them. I hug Kayli for an extra second. I have real, true friends.

I watch from the pillow fort on the floor and he stands at the threshold of his own room.

We wait until we hear the sound of engines starting and wheels crunching gravel and dirt. We wait until the automatic lights outside shut off.

"I'm really fine," I tell him.

"I'm sorry, Lena."

"I know you are." I pull a pillow across my lap. "At a certain point, you have to stop being sorry and stop doing things to be sorry for."

He takes a deep breath and nods. "You can stay here, if you'd like. I'll take the guest room."

I chuckle. "It's a good thing I did such a good job of making them homey."

He smiles, but I notice the way he keeps his body turned to the side that is unblemished, unscarred.

My stupid, wretched heart gives a tug because I want to reach out to him. He might have left the house for me, but I don't think it's caught up to him. He looks more shocked than I feel.

"I need to shower," I say.

I stand, bits of dirt and the leaves we tracked in litter the floor. I take slow, even steps. Every single one is like stretching time between my fingers, weaving it like a cat's cradle. I can't get trapped here.

Without touching him, I face him. All of him. I don't know how to ask this. Me, the girl who blurts out whatever she wants, *can't* ask this of him.

"You can join me if you want," I say, and start walking away. I get all the way inside the bathroom before he follows me. It takes me a minute to get over how amazing this bathroom is, with warm brown stones, and white glistening tiles that look like pearl. I leave the lights on the lowest setting, a faint golden glow that makes this all feel like a dream.

I can feel Patrick's presence behind me. I move my hair to the side and point to my zipper. I remember the last time he put his lips on my shoulder. I remember the way my skin reacted to him. Now, as he unzips the back of my dress down to my spine, it is the same heat. I push the sleeves down and turn to face him.

"Why are you afraid to hold me?" I ask.

"I'm afraid," he says, his chest rising and falling, his hands framing my bare shoulders, "of everything when it comes to you, Lena."

I drop my dress down to my waist, then over my hips. "Why?"

"I don't want to hurt you again. Everything and everyone I've ever touched, I've broken."

How can I convince him that it doesn't have to go that way?

"We can start again. Slowly," I say, reaching for a strand of gold hair over his left eye. "Do you trust me now?"

"Yes," he says, his voice a deep caress against the bottom of my palm.

He pulls off his shirt and tugs off his sweat pants, leaving a messy pile of clothes. He steps into the glass shower. Like the outside of the house, it's also completely glass. Two white-tiled benches built into the walls. I follow him in, watching the ripple of his back muscles as he works the handles. Two waterfalls come in with perfectly warm water. In seconds, steam rises.

I close my eyes and step under one of the waterfalls above us. My hair is a tangled mess but that doesn't matter. What matters is that Patrick is smirking at me.

"What?" I ask.

"Just you." He keeps his body turned at that angle, grabbing hold of a sponge. "You go from scaring the crap out of me to getting me naked."

"First of all, I scared myself in those woods. Second of all, you're wearing boxers and I'm still in my underwear. This is like we're in the pool instead of your orgy bathroom."

I try to joke but it's a front. I can't deny how strange it is being like this with each other, like we're still watching each other between a glass wall. He lathers his chest and stops around his abs. I've never been self-conscious about my body, and maybe that's because I had a dad who taught me how to fight and a mother who taught me how to love myself. It must have been difficult for him to have so much about him change when he was literally being consumed by the public. Even now, I'm drinking him in like cold, delicious water.

"Technically, this is a his and hers shower," he says. "My contractor talked me into it."

I narrow my eyes. "Are you sure he didn't mean his and seven hers? This shower is the size of most Manhattan apartments."

That draws a laugh from him. He steps out of the waterfall, brushing his hair back. "I don't need anyone else in here but you, Lena. I mean that."

"I know you do." I push down my underwear, kicking it off with a nudge of my toes. I give him my back and the breath he exhales gives me goose bumps. He unclasps my bra. Brushes the straps down. When he caresses the skin of my shoulder, I feel settled. The fear I felt in the dark slips away. In the amber light of the bathroom, I turn to face him. He looks like a figure carved from stone, broken and filled in with gold to be made more beautiful than before. But I also see the sadness in his eyes is so deep, I wonder if we'll both drown in it in the end, because it matches my own.

"I don't hate you," I say. "I didn't mean it when I said that."

His mouth quirks and all I want to do is leap on him and bite his lips. "It's okay if you do."

He tugs off his boxers, and I bite my lip at the sight of his thick erection. A soft moan escapes me, and I want so desperately to touch him. He looks down at my neck, my breasts, my waist. I take a step closer to him.

"I can hear you thinking," I say. "It's like when you're texting."

"You noticed that, huh?"

"Can I touch you?"

He nods, and I let my fingers reach for the side of his temple that's covered in scars. He closes his eyes and exhales. He closes the distance between us, my chest against him, his dick against the flat plane of my belly.

His eyes flutter open, wet lashes blink at me. "You almost screamed when you saw me."

I swallow, try to replay that moment. "No. I almost screamed because I didn't know what was happening. You were bleeding. I was scared, too."

I think of what Hutch said in the car that time. He said that it was easier to talk to someone when you weren't looking at them. Isn't that what we've been doing? We've been talking to each other through messages because we can find boldness under the cover of night. Is that why we only learned fragments of each other? I've held back in other ways.

"And now?" he asks.

"Now I want to look at you. Just you."

He takes my free hand and guides it to his face. I kiss the scar along his jaw. He holds his breath as I stand on my toes to reach his cheekbone.

"The moment I saw you," I say, "really saw you, I knew this was you."

"What do you mean?"

His hands slip down my forearms and then up to my shoulders.

"I saw a soccer photo," I say.

I watch his reaction. It isn't what he was expecting I'd say. "That's a throwback. That feels like a lifetime ago."

I want to kiss him on the lips, but it doesn't feel right yet. I kiss the underside of his chin, the bare skin of his throat.

"Are you disappointed?" he asks, his Adam's apple bobs once.

"No," I say. "Because what's in here, what I feel when you whisper to me, when you tell me the things you want to do to me, I still feel that, Patrick."

There's a scar that runs clean down his left eyebrow, so deep the hair hasn't grown back. I can't imagine the pain he must have gone through, that he might be still going through.

"I wasn't a good person," he says. "The accident didn't turn me into a good person, Lena. You deserve more. Better than this."

Steam rises around us, and though we're more or less squeaky clean, we don't make a move to get out.

"You told me that you were trying. Are you still going to keep trying?"

"I want to."

"What else do you want?"

His voice is tender, eager. "To feel you. Can I feel you, Lena?"

"Yes," I sigh.

He nods, takes my chin in his fingers, then traces the skin of my throat. My breasts feel full, and aching. My nipples pucker from the sensitive touch of his chest against me.

I inhale sharply as we almost slip. He catches me around my waist with one hand and plants a hand against the wall to hold us up.

"What's funny?" he whispers in my ear.

"It's good you had seats built here," I say, wrapping an arm around his neck to hold on. He grips me tight and we walk backward through the waterfall and sit. I shift to straddle him, his back against the white tiles. His hands grip my hips as I settle my weight on the top of his thighs. He hisses and he takes his dick in his hand.

"Fuck, Lena, look at what you do to me." He runs his fist up and down his length.

"Can I?" I whisper.

He nods once, keeping one hand on my lower back so I don't slip off. I wrap my fingers around the head of his dick, tracing my thumb against the sensitive skin of his frenulum. He exhales sharply with every slide of my hand.

"Lena," he whispers, and I catch the tail end of my name with my mouth.

I want to be everywhere at once. I want to keep stroking him. Kissing him. I want to feel the pressure of him inside me. He grips the back of my neck and presses me to his chest. I let go of his hard cock to rake my fingers through his hair.

"Touch me," I tell him and he does, frantic and hard and reverent.

"God, Lena, you're going to break me."

One of his fingers slips between my folds, stroking like he's beckoning me to come for him.

"I want you," I say, and it feels like we're echoing everything we said over the phone, and now we can say them to each other in person.

"Be specific. What do you want me to do?"

"Fuck me, please," I whisper. I move my hips, my wetness sliding against his cock.

He grumbles as he licks kisses on my neck. "Not here."

I scream with pleasure as he lifts me in the air, water spraying everywhere. He slams a fist to turn the water off, and then he's carrying me out of the bathroom and into the bedroom. I'm slippery all over, and when I slide back down against his chest, I feel the ache of his dick against my opening. I stare deep into his eyes and moan.

"I'm not going to make it," he grunts.

"Really?" I ask, disoriented as we haven't even started yet.

But as he kneels on the pile of blankets and pillows in front of the fireplace, I realize he means the bed.

"Lena?" he whispers between kisses on my neck.

"Pat?"

He moves up to my ear. "I need you to know. There hasn't been anyone but you."

I take the kiss he hovers over my lips. I take his face in my hands, so vulnerable. "Same."

His tip stretches my opening as he shudders against me, enveloping my breasts with his reverent tongue.

"More," I say, moving my hips in small circles. "I want to feel all of you."

"I've dreamed of you," he tells me, his face lit by the shadows of the flames. He pushes my leg aside with his knee and pumps once, reaching deeper inside me. I grab hold of his shoulders and sigh. "Every night."

"Show me, show me what we do in your dreams."

He slides farther and farther, slipping into my wet pussy. I can feel the pressure building in anticipation of this. He kisses me, driving into me harder and faster. I want to be crushed by the pressure of his body, I want to feel that breathless moment over and over, until I unravel so much, I don't think I'll be able to be put back together the same way.

I come hard and fast. I hear him the moment he's close. That sexy grunt at the back of his throat. He pulls out and runs his hand up and down his slick, wet dick.

"Right here," I say, tapping my lower abdomen. He stares at me with that intensity again, only this time, neither of us are afraid. His warm seed spills on the plane of my skin and I run my finger through it, like I'm finger painting on canvas.

"Lena," he moans, a smile I've never seen etched on his beautiful face. A face that tells me this night isn't over yet.

PAT

I watch her play with my come on her skin. When she brings it to the tip of her tongue and licks it, I'm hard again.

I don't think my heart can take this. She is the sexiest woman I've ever had under me. For a moment, I'm dizzy with the feeling she brings out in me. It is strange and overwhelming. Unlike all the other times, I don't try to push it away. I let it fall over me like the water from moments ago. It passes, and I feel better than I have in weeks. In months. And I know that I am not healed but I am closer than I thought possible and it is, in part, because of Lena.

She lets her leg fall to the side, unveiling her sweet, beautiful cunt for me. Neat lines of hair guide me to the sweet spot of her clit. I take her into my mouth and she gasps, saying my name with a shocked sigh.

I want to keep surprising her. I want to let her know that I will get through this. That if she will wait for me, I can come out the man who deserves her. With the stroke of my tongue around the swollen, sensitive bud, I fuck her with my fingers. Her slick wetness all over my face and nose. I want to breathe her in until I smell like her.

She calls out God's name and mine, and I can feel the walls inside her contract around my lucky fucking fingers, because I get to make her feel this way.

When she's finished trembling, I drag my tongue from the bottom to the top and look up at her. She's biting her lower lip.

She reaches for me, and for a moment, I desperately want to feel the sensation of her skin on mine. But I turn my face so she's got the smooth, unblemished side. There's a frown on her face, and I don't want her to frown. I want to see her bite that cute fucking lip again. I want her to keep screaming my name.

"Get up," she says, and my legs are already moving before I've had a chance to process her words.

She gives me a little shove onto the bed. I am not used to women who push and pull this way. She's dominant in a way I've never experienced and my body does everything she asks me to. Lie back. Look at her.

She traces her fingers on my skin, but doesn't scratch me and I wonder if it's because she's afraid of hurting the scars on my legs. With Lena touching them, a part of me shudders. I want this. I want to feel her mouth on every part of me. Why is there still a trace of fear there? Fear that I'm dreaming again.

I was dreaming that first night that changed everything. When she moaned so loud, I could hear her all the way from the pool house.

As she takes the swollen head of my cock in her mouth, I exhale a long-held breath. My dick was made to be sucked by her, my whole body changed to give her whatever pleasure she asks of me. I don't hold back how good it feels to be touched this way. I grab hold of her hair so I can see the way I disappear into her mouth, along her throat. All those nights on the phone were an experience I'll never be able to re-create, but this? I could dissolve around her, melt into her. Lena can have all of me if she just asks.

"I'm going to come, baby," I whisper.

The wet smack of her lips sends a sharp tug of desire. She puts pressure on my sack and grins, bites the bottom of her fucking sinful mouth as she tugs my dick with her hands.

"Then come," she says, and kisses my cock along the length, working her way to the head. I grab hold of it, and stroke while she licks circles that have my head spinning. Glistening, pearly come pools against her lips, trickling down my shaft and her chin.

"Stay with me," I say.

"I am with you."

She massages my thighs with her hands, and, despite being naked and covered in my fluids, she looks sweet, innocent. That fear returns, the one where I repeat everything that just happened. Fuck, was it really just two hours ago when I thought I'd lost her?

I know who you are, she said. And with those words, I dove back into the hole I've been trying to crawl out of.

She climbs up on me and I clutch her full, round ass. My dick is spent, but when she touches my chest with her palms and her small round tits get hard, my dick is at attention.

"I mean, stay with me, tonight." *Stay with me for always.*

"Okay, Patrick." She brushes her hair aside and closes her eyes as she sinks around my cock. "I'll stay."

12
Body Like a Back Road

LENA

October

When I wake up, I'm in Patrick's bed. The fire is off.

In fact, the floor is clean of the dirt and leaves we left behind. I sink back into the pillows, let myself feel everything we did last night. There's a pleasant ache in my upper thighs, and a soreness between them. My mouth is swollen and when I trace my lips, I remember every single thing I used it for.

"Patrick?" I say his name and rub my eyes.

The window shades are still drawn and the bathroom door is wide open. I don't have class today, thank goodness because I don't know how I would be able to get my life together after the ups and downs of the last twenty-four hours. I don't even remember falling asleep.

I get out of bed and open the door. I can't believe my ears. There's music coming from downstairs. I realize that I'm naked and covered in sex, so I return to the shower where everything started. There's something about this quiet, this stillness of the shower that I appreciate. It's like he knew that I would need to be by myself for a little while. Or maybe he just wants to avoid the awkwardness of the morning after.

After rummaging through one of Patrick's drawers for clothes, I go downstairs. Patrick is making breakfast. I can't believe my eyes. He's in a long-sleeve white undershirt that hugs his muscles. In the morning light, his rumpled beauty steals my breath. His hair is long enough that he can tie a length of it at the nape. Strands of it escape as he turns to grab a packet of bacon. He blows the hair out of his face in a gesture that is somehow incredibly sexy in its sweetness.

He's listening to a song I can't name, but the only word I catch is "Cadillac" and that's when I let my presence be known with a laugh.

Patrick turns to me, and I see the moment he thinks about retreating. One moment he's confidently moving back and forth between the kitchen island and then when he sees me, he stops. He stares. He lowers his eyes. But only for a moment.

Oh fuck. It's awkward. Neither of us really close the space but stay right where we are.

"I thought you might sleep a little longer," he says, settling bright green eyes on me. "I could get used to this look on you."

In one of his soft white T-shirts and shamrock boxers, I twirl in place. His eyes lock on the chocolate circles of my nipples where his shirt is see-through. "Don't think I didn't notice the shamrock tattoo on your ass."

He barks a laugh. I don't think I've ever heard him laugh this way. "My parting gift from when I lived in Vegas."

"I'm going to need that story," I say, still keeping my distance.

His smile turns rueful. "Come here," he says, and those two little words seem to break the spell between us. I go to him, his arms extended and waiting.

I reach for his lips with mine and taste the sweetness of orange juice on his tongue. He kisses me slowly, holds me hard, pulls me closer. His kiss has a different effect than it did last night. Now, we are in the light and we can't blame our actions on a spur of the moment, on adrenaline, on the tornado of hormones and emotions we felt in such a short span of time.

This kiss is his promise to try harder. It is the kind of kiss that sends arrows of pleasure through my limbs, it makes me want more. I know he feels the same when I feel his erection strain through his sweat pants.

"We should probably talk about some things we did that were reckless," I say, between kisses.

"We really should." He grips my middle and lifts me up on the countertop so we're face-to-face. How can two people line up so perfectly? He gives a tiny thrust of his pelvis, putting pressure against the wet fabric of my borrowed boxers. Lucky indeed.

"Last night was—" I search for the right word but it's hard to put just one to it. Amazing feels trite. Perfect feels too romantic. "Everything."

He threads his fingers between mine and kisses my forehead. God, I love his little touches. "But?"

"I have never had sex without a condom before," I say. "And it's sort of scary that I want to do things like that with you."

When he lowers his face to mine, he looks deep into my eyes. "You're right. Before you, the last time I slept with anyone was the morning of the premiere. I was reckless, but the good thing about almost dying is that they run every test."

I know that he's trying to joke but I see the twinge on his forehead. "Pat . . ."

"Kayli gave me a clean bill of health. But we should have used a condom. Are you on the pill?"

"I have copper in my uterus," I tell him.

"What?"

"An IUD."

"A . . . bomb?"

"Not an *IED*. Intrauterine device. It's birth control." I laugh, falling back on the counter and he follows, kissing my throat. It is so easy for me to forget myself and sink into his touch. I've never wanted someone like this before—so much I want to forget reason and logic and responsibility.

"Do you feel okay from last night?" he whispers, nipping my earlobe and sucking it into his mouth.

That sends an unexpected sensation down my collarbone and into my center. "I'm a little sore, but I want you."

He tugs my boxers off, and I squeal at how cold the marble top is on my skin. He cups my ass with his hands, squeezing and rubbing warmth into my skin.

I push down his sweats by the waistband in a frantic rush, then use the sides of my feet to get them completely down. I seize his cock with both hands and watch the pleasure move across his face as his eyelids flutter when I begin to stroke up and down.

"*Now.*"

He breathes hard. "Then spread your fucking legs."

My breath hitches at the command in his voice, and my knees inexplicably drop to either side. He rests his glorious cock on my slit, a crooked grin on his mouth as I squirm with expectation.

"Patrick," I sigh, toying with my hard nipples. "I want you now."

"How badly do you want me?"

"More than I want to breathe."

At my words, he makes a wordless groan and catches my mouth in his. He pulls back his hips and enters me with a hard grunt. He pumps inside me faster than last night, and I match his pace with a frenzied pulse thrumming through me because I want this feeling, need this feeling to never stop.

And then it does.

Patrick jerks off me. "Oh fuck."

The fire alarm goes off, the kitchen filling with smoke. The bacon and the entire pan are burned beyond recognition.

He grabs the pan handle and hisses because it must be hot. Then he turns off the burner.

"You okay?" I ask, pulling my shirt down.

He looks at his hand, the red line across it. I wonder what he thinks when he sees it. But when he turns to me, he isn't thinking about his nonthreatening burn.

"Who said you could get dressed?" he asks, a deep frown between his brows.

"I thought that's all you had for me today," I tease, leaning back on my elbows, extending my leg out to him. He catches it, kisses the inside of my knee and keeps moving up. His tongue draws out a moan when he licks up my sex.

"I'll show you what I have for you," he says, and the vibration of his laugh hums on my skin.

I brush his hair away from his face, trace the smooth outline of his right jaw. "So, *not* bacon."

"Well, if you don't want it."

"Please, Patrick," I sigh. I run two fingers between my wet folds and close my eyes at the shocks of sensation that come with it. He wrenches my hand and takes my fingers into his mouth. His tongue smothers and licks.

"I want to be the only one to taste you," he says, and nuzzles into my neck. "I want to be the only one to fuck you."

With the alarm blaring, I feel disoriented, dizzy. If there were a real fire, I have to pause and consider if I'd finish fucking Patrick or run out. That thought is a little more destructive than I'd like, but I feel the thrill of it as he sinks into me so deep, I arch my back to take it.

He scoops me into his arms and carries me. I wrap my legs around him tighter, the pressure of our pelvises together feels so fucking good as I bounce against him down the hall and into one of the guest rooms. It's the first room that I finished.

We fall into bed with him on top of me, the weight of him squeezing sounds of pleasure from my throat until I come around him and he follows moments later. When he rolls off me, we lay on the bed, staring at the ceiling. The day is gray outside but at least there is color in here.

He turns to me, and I know that I could stare at him like this for days. "You know, Lena, you were right."

"About what?"

"It is salmon pink."

PAT

So, both of my attempts at cooking have turned into shitastic messes. At least I'm wealthy in cookware because after break-fast sex, Lena finds a pan from I-don't-know-where and makes pancakes and bacon.

"I need to pick up eggs and more things for dinner," she says, munching on an extra crispy piece. She's relaxed, rumpled, sweet, looking like we've done this a million times, which I would like to. Only 999,996 times to go.

Her ink-black hair falls over bronze shoulders covered in freckles. I wonder if I can count how many beauty marks are on her body. If I lose count, I'd just start over as long as I got to keep her naked and with me.

"Pat," she says.

"Sorry, what?"

"I said, can I take your car later? Selena is still out of commission."

I frown. I don't want her to leave, but I realize that she's going to have to go back to classes on Monday. She's going to have more school functions and places to be. It's one thing leaving the house and staying on my property, it's another having to stand in front of others with their judgments and their staring.

That's a problem for later. For the next two days, I have her to myself.

"Keys are in the car," I say, and take her hand into mine. I lick the maple syrup from her fingers and watch a blush creek up her neck.

"I can't fucking believe you keep keys in your car! What if someone took it?"

I cut the pancake with the side of my fork. These are almost as good as the ones my mom used to make us in the morning. "Even if someone were stupid enough to trespass on my property, I have cameras in the garage and around the house. We're not in *New Yawk*."

I mostly say it to light her up because she gets instantly flustered and cute.

"How *dare*," she says, unable to finish her sentence. For the next five minutes she launches into listing every single good quality about New York City. While they include my favorites like pizza and bagels, I realize that the only one I care about is sitting right in front of me.

"You forgot one thing, the only thing that matters about that hell city," I say.

Her brows are knit so tight, they're almost touching, and her pout is irresistible. I get up from my stool and go to her, nestle myself between her legs.

"What?" she asks.

I cup her face in my hands, tilt her chin up to look into her big brown eyes. "It gave me you."

She tries to suppress her smile, but she can't, and a sense of pride fills the hollow parts of my chest because she is smiling for me. I did that. But then I think of all the other times I've done the opposite. How could I do that to someone I care about?

"Okay, Groucharella," she says, giving me the tiniest eye roll. I hate Scarlett for teaching her that. "I'll be right back."

But I don't want to let go of her hand. I kiss her all the way to the door, pressing my body against her. I sink my hands into the sides of the boxers to start to pull them down. I am so hard I can't see straight and the way she toys with the outline of my dick against my sweats isn't helping.

"Unless you're going to come with me to the store, I have to go and get dressed," she says playfully. There's an underlying challenge.

I lick my lips and look over her shoulder at the frosted glass of the kitchen door. Yesterday feels like days ago. My heart races at the thought of going out there, but it doesn't make me want to throw up like before. I did it yesterday, I can do it today.

"Okay," I say.

Her eyes widen. "Are you sure?"

"You just asked me and I'm saying yes." I put bravado behind my voice because if I have to put on a brave face for Lena, then maybe I'll trick myself into believing I can do anything.

"Pat, you don't have to. I shouldn't tease you that way."

"I'll keep you company. You can drive." I hold her stare. All those times I've looked at her at a distance and I never got to see the beauty marks on her face. It was like looking at the night sky when it was cloudy and now that I can see her, hold her, I want to do everything in my power to be able to keep this going.

She bites her bottom lip, and for that moment, I forget about everything. All I want is to put my mouth on that mouth. My body on her body. I kiss her, and she melts against me, so slowly that I feel like time is coming to a crawl.

"I'll meet you outside in five," she says, and I see the struggle in her eyes as she pulls away and walks out that door.

And I'm left standing there repeating in my head, *I can do this I can do this I can do this.*

"You're a terrible driver," I say, sitting in the passenger seat of my truck. I grip the handle above the window, which I've only ever used to hang things from.

The truck took time to start because it's been a few seasons since I've turned the ignition. When Fallon and the boys drove me out here, we were in a rental.

Lena glances at me, narrowing her eyes, but when she catches sight of my knee bouncing in place, she places her hand on top of mine. "I drive well enough to have gotten myself out here."

"You drove from New York? In that thing?"

"What did you think?" She laughs. "Did you think I could afford to have *my* car, that relic from days gone by, shipped here?"

I flush hot, a little embarrassed. I sit back and lower my baseball cap over my eyes. It's ridiculous because the windows are tinted and they're rolled up, so, even if anyone drove past us, they wouldn't be able to see me. "I'm sorry. We didn't grow up with money, but the second I came into it, I went a little wild."

She smirks at me. "Sex, drugs, rock and roll also applies to actors?"

"Actually," I say, realizing there is so much about me that Lena doesn't know. I don't exactly want her finding out from a YouTube video or anything. "Before I was an actor, I was a dancer."

That has her attention, but she needs both hands to steer as she tries, and fails, to merge onto a highway. Someone beeps behind her. She curses up a storm fit for a sailor and in that instant, I want her dirty little mouth even more.

She turns her head to me for a second. "Like a stripper?"

"I'm actually a little affronted you didn't guess ballet first."

We both laugh, and she hits the gas, pulling onto the highway. My heart is racing about a thousand miles per minute every time I see another car. Thankfully, we're blessed with Montana traffic, which is about fifty cars instead of hundreds. I take deep breaths, as instructed. While she was getting dressed, I called Chris. He told me that I'd made a huge step and shouldn't push myself. I have to treat my mind like a physical injury and I've had plenty of those. He also said it might be good for me and Lena to take a drive because people are more honest when they're driving or some such. So, this is me being honest.

"How many careers have you had, exactly?" she asks.

"Let's see, I was a paper delivery boy when I was ten. In high school, I worked on cars out of the garage my brothers and I built. You now call it the pool house. I was a major league soccer player for about six months and then I got the compound fracture to end my career. Ronan passed away shortly after, then my folks, and I was in a shitty place. I did nothing, except for worked on cars back home. Oh, I figured out what was wrong with your car, by the way."

"Oh yeah?" she asks brightly.

"It's an old piece of shit."

"*You're* an old piece of shit."

I take her hand in mine and kiss the inside of her wrist. "I *am* ten years older than you and I'm not sure if I should be bothered by it or not."

"I'll go with not. We have enough things to deal with."

"Like?"

"Like don't change the subject. Tell me about your dancing days. Did you wear thongs? Do male strip clubs have poles? Wait—what was your act? Do you still talk to any of them?" I feel her eyes on me with that last one.

Right. Honesty and driving. Fuck me.

I think of my days with Mayhem City and the brothers I made there. Can I still call them brothers if I treated them like shit and abandoned them? Isn't that what I did to Jack? "I haven't talked to any of them in a while. I was closest with Ricky—stage name Rick Rocket."

"I am not even touching that one with a ten-foot pole." She giggles.

"Believe me, he's untouchable. He's fucking tiny compared to the rest of us, but he's dapper as fuck, with an Australian accent, and about a thousand custom-made suits in his closet. He's the reason I didn't wind up at a dead-end job I hated. I mean, I love cars, but I never wanted to be a mechanic as a job. I wanted it to be my hobby. Something I did for fun on my days off."

"What did you want to be?"

I stare at the open road, the trees with russet and yellow leaves against a pale-gray sky, mountains in the distance. What did I want to be other than Indiana Jones and RoboCop? "I don't remember. I feel like I tried everything I thought I wanted to do and the world was just dead set against it. I miss dancing, though. I was good at it."

"I believe that," she says.

"Why?"

She flashes me a sexy, sleepy stare. "Because you know how to work your hips for a white boy."

I laugh so hard, I can feel it in my abs.

"Would you do it again?" she asks.

"No," I say without hesitating. "Not like this anyway. I don't know. Dancing now wouldn't be the same."

She squeezes her hands around the wheel. "You're beautiful, Patrick. All of you. Every part of you."

"Half of me is, maybe," I say, and I don't like where this conversation is going. That hot feeling returns and I rest my head back. "Please, Lena, don't make me go through this."

"Okay," she says, taking my hand and guiding it to her thigh. "Okay. Where are they now?"

"Who?"

"Your boys. You called them your boys. Where are they?"

I clear my throat and shrug. "You know firsthand what I've been like. In January? I was worse, Lena. I pushed everyone away and they stayed away. There's only so much someone can take before they give up on you. I'm not so sure I'm better, but I think I'm trying."

"How do you know they gave up on you?"

"Well, they aren't here. Are they?"

"When was the last time you reached out?" she asks.

I lick my lips. Thankfully, she's turning into the parking lot of the supermarket. "Four months."

"You don't know that they've given up. Maybe they're waiting for you to be ready." The lot is packed, and there's only one spot, but the one thing she can do is slide into that parking spot like a knife in butter.

She flashes a pleased smile at me. "See? I can do one thing you mountain dwellers can't, and that's parallel park."

It's just before lunch, but it's a Saturday. There are people pushing carts and bringing groceries out. Neighbors and friends stop and talk to each other. I sit back and take off my seat belt, not because I want to get out, but because it is suffocating me. An older woman with sandy-blond hair and a pinched face stares at my truck, parked right next to hers.

"Do you know her?" Lena asks, patiently waiting for me.

I squeeze her thigh. "She was my brother's high school math teacher. After our parents died, I was basically the one to go to PTA meetings." I've had the same version of this car for about ten years. The only thing that changes is how tall it keeps getting, but the license plate is the same. The locals, the real locals, know this is my car, or at least, guess at it from the double takes people keep making.

"Do you want to wait for me in here and keep the car warm?" she asks.

I do, but I don't want to admit it. Why is this so hard? It's been months . . . "Can you get cherry pie?"

She leans over and kisses me hard, biting my lip in a way that's got me sprung in the next second. "I'll be right back."

The minute Lena's gone, I feel the absence of her. A sick part of me wonders if I can get away with jerking off in my own car. Of course, that's when my cell phone rings. It's Jack. He never calls on the weekend.

"Hey, are you okay?" I ask.

"Easy, tiger," he mutters. There's a loud commotion behind him, cheering and music and laughter. Did I send my brother to a *party* rehab center? "I was going to ask you the same thing. Just got off the phone with Scarlett."

"Dammit, Scarlett." I tap my fist on the window.

"Don't damn her, bro. Especially since how she tells it, she did you a solid." Someone honks their horn next to me because some guy is on his phone instead of backing up, blocking traffic. "What is that, where are you?"

I sigh. "I'm at the Fresh Market parking lot inside my car while Lena buys groceries."

"Holy fucking shit." I hear the gasp and awe in his pause. "Pat! This is great, this is huge—"

"Easy, *tiger*," I mutter back. "I don't know what this is yet."

"How do you feel?"

That's the part that's harder to answer. "A little freaked, if I'm honest. I couldn't get out of the car."

"But you got out of the house," he says, with more enthusiasm than I've heard from him in a while. "More than once."

"What about you? Where are you?"

"Oh, this guy in the hospital has made a great recovery, so his dad decided to buy us all Yankees tickets. It's hot as balls here and my wheelchair keeps getting sticky from the floor, but we're sneaking some beer. Look at that. We're both having good days."

"We are, aren't we?"

"So, *Lena*," he says, suggestively.

"Nope."

"What do you mean, nope? I'm your brother."

"You're my *little* brother. I'm not going to tell you about my sex life."

He cackles. "Who was your errand boy for *years* because you were too embarrassed to buy your own fucking condoms?"

"Safety first," I say, and then we're laughing like we've scrubbed our sins clean. There's music in the background, signaling a lineup change, and a roar from the crowd. "I fucked up yesterday."

I tell him about everything that happened and he listens. "I didn't think, I just went. I had to find her and make sure she was safe."

"Hey, do you remember when I got lost in that same way when I tried to run away?"

I didn't remember, not at first. Then I think of the day he describes. Mom had just died and Dad wasn't handling it well. Ronan was still in Washington and I was busy having girls sneak me into their bedrooms and barns while their parents were away. Jack packed a bag and took off. "She took that exact trail, too."

"And you found us both." He chuckles, and I wish I could be there with him. I wish that I could shake off this weight from my shoulders and walk down supermarket aisles picking out fucking cereal with Lena and drinking beer at a baseball game with my brother.

You can do this.

"There's Lena," I say.

"I want to meet her."

"You will. I promise."

"Don't be a stranger, Pat."

I hang up as Lena opens the door and unloads the cart with bags. People stare at her, this beautiful woman with ropes of dark hair and bright brown eyes. I don't like the way some of the men leer at her as she returns the cart to the little shed, so I punch the horn, and they scatter like pigeons.

"What was that?" she asks, pressing a cold kiss on my face.

"My hand slipped," I say.

She doesn't quite buy it, but we drive and I tell her about the call with Jack. "He wants to meet you."

"Good because Ari wants to FaceTime with us. I told her we might have to work our way up to that, but that you'd at least talk to her."

I like this. I like making plans with Lena. I don't even feel the same anxiety I had moments ago. Between talking to Jack and having her back with me, I'm settled. I'm good.

We're almost home when she says, "Wait, you didn't tell me your skit."

"My *set,*" I correct her. "And I will tell you if you don't laugh."

"I make no promises."

"Then I won't tell you."

She gives me that sexy little pout and pulls into the garage. "What *if* you show me instead?"

"Okay," I say, opening the door. "But I want to show you something else first."

She arches a brow, but I simply tug her to the third closed garage door. She stands there with a smile that makes me dizzy by how beautiful it is. I almost forget why we're standing there.

I push the garage door open.

"When did you do this?" she asks, her mouth open.

The punching bag is hung at the center of the garage. "The space was built for a gym, and it looks empty. But I think with time, I can get everything moved out here. Maybe the basement can be a bar or an arcade or something or an actual den."

I'm rambling. She presses her hands on either side of the bag and looks at me. Tests out the balance and weight.

"This is what you were doing when Kayli was checking on me?" she asks.

I rake my fingers through my hair and nod.

She angles her head to the side, watching me. "Can I ask you something that might be uncomfortable?"

"Yes."

"I know you've always worked on your body. But did it get more intense while you were here?"

I hold the punching bag on the other side of her. I think about every meal I stopped myself from enjoying, every day I toiled away on a carefully curated workout routine. I told myself that deprivation was discipline, but I know that's what's added to this.

"I guess, it's the only thing I could control. It was like being in my own personal jail. I'm not just vain, though Scarlett might say otherwise. After I got injured, the first time, I saw the way people reacted to me when I looked a certain way. Like I was broken and fragile. The second accident? I couldn't—I don't know. It's the only way I could release my anger. It started as an obsession. It still is. Even if I don't want anyone to see me."

"But you've let me see you," she says.

"I trust you, Lena. I was afraid of your reaction to me more than anything."

She walks around the punching back and rests her hands on my torso. "I've had this reaction even before I saw you, Patrick."

I know that she means it. I know that it matters. But a part of me that is still locked away, still lost, doesn't want to hear it. I kiss her forehead.

"Come, I'll bring the groceries in."

"Can I try out our new toy later?" she asks. *Our* toy. I like the sound of that. "I have my own gloves."

With that promise, I carry all the bags inside. It is maybe ten minutes before I resume kissing her, her high-pitched moans twisting my feeling into so many knots I will never come undone.

"Come," I say. But instead of taking her to the bedroom, I take her to the living room where there's a box of books stashed in a corner.

"More presents?" she asks playfully.

"I said I would show you what my set was." I pry the box open and hand her the small rectangular book.

Her eyes dart from the cover to me and then back. A wide, purely sinful smile tugs at the corners of her mouth as she reads the title out loud. "*Save a Horse, Ride a Cowboy.*"

13

Save a Horse, Ride a Cowboy

LENA

Patrick won't do his dance set for me, but he does finally make me a meal that isn't burned to a crisp. He grills steaks outside, barefoot, smelling of the sex we had on top of the boxes in the living room. Plus, the house still smells burned. I boil some star anise, and make sure my timer is on while we're out here.

I'm already halfway through the book, lounging on an Adirondack chair with a view of the mountains on one side and Patrick's buns on the other. I lift the edge of his hoodie over my nose. It's about four sizes too big for me, but it's soft and comfortable. It smells like a man. Sweat and a fragrance that reminds me of leather and pine. I never thought wearing the clothes of a man you've slept with would be so satisfying? It's like a little part of me is claiming this. It's a *tad* possessive and a little sexy. Even enveloped in his clothes, I know that I've never wanted this of another man before.

"I can't believe you haven't heard of Scarlett's books before you met her. They were everywhere last year."

I take a long stalk of grass and use it as a bookmark. I pick up my beer and drink. The bitter hops make me grimace at first, but then I actually like it. "Excuse me, I've been busy reading books for school."

"Still."

"I am not caught up on popular things unless it's something a fifteen-year-old girl likes, and I trust her opinions more than I do other critics."

He takes the tongs and flips the steaks. From this angle, he is all scars. When he sees me watching him, he pulls up his hoodie and walks over to me. Pat kneels on the grass, giving me the right side of his face.

"I agree with you, but, still. That was my act. The cowboy act."

"You've never been a cowboy a day in your life."

He smiles widely and I drink it up because a part of me fears it won't last. "True, but I'm from Montana and Ricky is nothing if not a showman first."

"Was he like your ringleader in a naked circus?"

He takes my beer, eyes searching the darkening sky. I catch him soaking up the feeling of being outside in small increments all day. I wonder how weird it must be for him to have been locked inside that house one minute and out here the next. Because of me. I wonder if I've done him more harm than good.

We have one more day of being together before I have a week from hell at school. I've ignored every phone call, except for Ariana's today, and I know I'm going to owe Mari an explanation for leaving her at the gallery.

"Lena," he says, bringing my attention back to him. "Where did you go?"

"I have to tell you something," I say.

He makes that rumbling sound in the back of his throat that makes me shiver. "Don't tell me you're pregnant, I'm not that good."

I roll my eyes, but I see the nervousness in his face. He scratches his short beard and places both hands on his knees waiting for me.

"Do you remember that guy I told you about from the gallery? Keillor."

He frowns. "What about him?"

"He was the one who told me who you were. He said that there were people who would pay money for a picture of you."

To my surprise, Patrick skips the part where he's angry and nods methodically. He breathes evenly, almost resigned. "Yeah, that's not new. When I first got here, I almost shot a paparazzo who got all the way to my front door."

"Patrick!"

"It was a *blank* and he was trespassing," he says, by way of excuse.

I shake my head. "And people tell me that New York is dangerous."

"I wasn't aiming *at* him, just trying to scare him. It was the only way to get them off me, fucking leeches."

"It's been months since the accident. Why the interest again?"

He shrugs, but I can tell it's going to bother him. "After the crash, papers were pouring offers our way. I've never turned down so much money in my life, but I couldn't bear the thought of more cameras. Pictures comparing me to the way I looked before, the man I'll never be again. I'll give my agent a call, not that she'll return it. But I'll leave her a message."

"Patrick?"

"Lena?"

"If you burn those steaks, I swear—"

"Oh shit," he darts to the grill, and I go inside to shut off the boiling star anise. The smell has cleared up enough, but we build a fire and eat outside on tin plates. The sky is bright with so many stars, I want to cry just looking at them.

"Why the long sigh?" he asks. His plate is nothing but bloody runoff from his steak, and potato skins. He chucks the scraps into the fire and sets the plate in the grass.

"It's going to be a long week."

He traces a finger over the top of my hand. "We still have tomorrow, Lena."

I take the kiss he offers. I let my plate fall as he tugs me onto his lap. I sit against him, the warmth of him and the fire leave me nice and toasty. His nose is against my neck, soft lips cupping the ticklish parts of me.

"We have tonight, too," I say, and press my ass against his erect dick. I giggle, and twist my torso to kiss him. Thank goodness for these wide chairs that fit the both of us. "Are you tired?"

"Not even a little bit," he says, kissing my neck. I can see his breath in little puffs and the contrasts of hot and cold make me shiver. "It's been . . . difficult the last few months. I couldn't—you know."

"Get it up?"

"Yes, I believe that's the technical term." He growls against my skin, and I feel the flutter of his lashes on my face as he moves toward my lips. He pulls at the waistband of the too-big sweat pants I'm wearing, snaking his fingers toward my waiting, wet pussy. Now, he knows just how to press me to get me wriggling.

"When did it change?"

"It didn't happen right away," he confesses, brushing my hair to the other side to get the part of my neck he hasn't kissed yet. "There was something about you that lit me up from the second you got here. You started turning things upside down. You've turned me upside down. And then I saw you by the pool."

"That day we—" I gasp as a shock of pleasure rips through me, his expert fingers filling me.

"That day I heard you and you heard me. You make me so fucking hard. Your body, your mouth." With his free hand, he traces the outline of my lips. "Your angry, filthy fucking little mouth."

I suddenly feel so hot, I take the hoodie off and glance back at him.

"Fuck, you're so beautiful. You are impossibly stunning, Lena."

I want to tell him that I feel the same way about him, but I wonder if he'll reject it the way he did in the car. I only shut my eyes and breathe short breaths as he drags his fingers around my clit.

"Patrick," I whimper. "I want to ask you to do something."

He kisses my shoulder. "Tell me."

"I want to feel you come inside me."

I feel him groan, breath hot on my skin. "I want to, baby. God, Lena. I fucking hate the idea of someone else touching you this way."

I twist in place to face him. Under the firelight, his scars have a pearly sheen. They look like a shower of sparks. They are beautiful in a way I wish he would understand. I kiss his scarred cheekbone and feel his dick harden beneath me. I bite my lip and smile. I love the way he looks at me. It sets something loose inside of my chest.

"Are you telling me you want to claim my pussy?" I ask.

He grunts against my neck, biting a little harder than he has before. "When you talk like that, it kills me."

I jump with the slap of his palm on the side of my ass. He's yanking his pants down, freeing his erection, lining up the head against my wetness. I arch my head back, resting it against his shoulder. He grips my hips hard, and I sink down his length, slow and steady, feeling every inch of him.

He pulses into me, drawing waves of pleasure from me as he kisses my spine and fucks me at the same time. He moves faster. I feel his teeth. His nails. His tongue down my back. I squeeze my thighs together.

"Come inside me, Patrick," I turn back and whisper in his ear.

He comes with a shudder, a wet warmth spreads through me. When he stops moving, I turn around, his essence dripping between us. I sink back on his dick and he takes my breasts into his hands as I writhe myself into an orgasm that, I swear, makes a dog bark from miles away.

"That's a wolf, Lena," he says, chuckling and kissing my clavicles.

"What?" I gasp.

"God, you're so fun to tease."

I pout and he sucks my bottom lip. "I'm cold now."

"Let's go to bed." I like the sound of that.

He smothers the fire in the pit, and we dart back inside as the sun sets and temperature drops. We shower, and fall asleep so tangled that I'm not sure where my limbs start and his end.

I wonder if maybe, I've claimed him tonight, too.

14
La Cura

PAT

I hate it when Lena isn't here. For two weeks, I only see her for dinner, which I make. Now, I'm not complaining. She did the cooking all summer. It's just that when I get in the kitchen, it doesn't taste the same. Thankfully, no more pans have been sacrificed since the last one that ended up in the trash.

After she leaves in the morning, I busy myself in the garage giving the punching bag a few rounds. It's a nice change of pace sweating out in the garage when it's cold. When she isn't too tired from school, Lena joins me. Though, that first attempt, she walked out in a red sports bra and shorts and we ended up fucking on a mat instead.

It gets easier to take walks around my property. To walk by myself. When I close my eyes, I can still see the crash. I see it and hear the screams. It isn't going away. Chris says that it won't and that I should be prepared for that.

"Does Lena know you're speaking to me?" he asks.

"No one does. I don't want them to get their hopes up in case I can't get better."

"But you are getting better. You're opening up to her. You're processing your grief."

"No one died in the accident," I say, staring at the woods. Clouds gather in preparation of a storm. I hope Lena gets home before then.

"But you lost part of your life. You lost your brother, your parents—did you ever seek help for that?"

I think about it. "What if I deserve everything that's happened to me?"

Chris is quiet for a bit. It's weird talking to a guy I've never seen before, but isn't that how it was with me and Lena for a while? Not that I'm going to start calling him at midnight to have phone sex, but still. He knows so much about me and I know little of him. "I want you to start doing something once a day."

"Please don't say vitamins. Or praying. Or meditating."

He laughs. "I want you to ask yourself the same 'what-if' questions but flip them around. See the other side of things. What if you deserve a girl like Lena? What if you keep making progress? Even if it's just once a day and one question. The more you spiral into the darkest, grimmest possibilities, the worse your anxiety can become. It isn't a remedy, but it's a way to cope."

After we're done talking, I start with one. The biggest what-if I could possibly ask myself.

What if I'm in love with Lena?

I can't sit on that one for too long because at that moment I get a call back from my agent. Miriam is the kind of New Yorker who moved to Los Angeles with the expectation of hating it, and then stayed for fifteen years.

"Hey, baby, how you doing?" she asks when I pick up.

Talking to other people, to people who aren't Scarlett and Kayli is weird. I've known Miriam since she "discovered me" after the book cover went viral, but I've known Ricky far longer, and it's been just as hard trying to reach out to my former mentor. What if I try one more time?

"Better," I say, thinking on the right word. "Better" *isn't* it. I still haven't seen enough doctors to pronounce me *better*. My body is healed, my heart is healing, but my mind? I don't know. I can leave the house, but I haven't tried leaving the property since that day we drove to the supermarket. "I think."

"Hey, I'll take that over the miserable lump who's hung up on me ten times in six months." She laughs, a throaty sound consistent with the three cigarettes she smokes a day. One to get her going with her coffee, another before she enters her office, and one just after dinner. She might be the kind of Angelino that drinks green juices and sucks up hydration bags before an award show, but she's still the same woman who grew up in "the Village" scouting bands and partying until sunrise. "I figured if you were calling me, then it was serious. You didn't happen to change your mind about the exclusive with *People* magazine, did you?"

"No. But I got wind of someone snooping around. Can you figure out where it's coming from?"

I hear her exhale. I realize it's lunchtime in California. "Nothing's come through me, kid. But I'll check it out, okay? Anything else?"

"How are you?"

"Business's good. Signed a new kid looking to be the next Chris Evans."

"Everyone wants to be a Chris," I say.

"You wouldn't have been. You're just Patrick Halloran, the one and only."

I sigh, combing my fingers through my hair. I should think about a haircut soon. "Miriam, I wanted to say I'm sorry. For not calling you back, for hanging up, for—"

"You went through hell and back, kid," she says, taking a drag. "I get it. Hurt my little heart, but I get it. I'm here when you need me."

She was never one for small talk, but the minute we hang up, I can breathe a little deeper. That shortness of breath that happens when I talk to someone from my old life alleviates. Just a little, but it's a start.

What if I call Ricky and the boys next?

LENA

I throw another painting away because it doesn't feel quite right. Meanwhile Mari is lost in her own head, bopping away to an EDM mix that gives me heart palpitations when she blasts it through the studio speakers. Every now and then, she calls out things that are on her mind—people she thinks are cute, toiletries she needs to buy on Amazon. It's become her work process and that's fine with me since my work process has been repainting my canvas white.

"Do *not* bail on me for the Halloween party this weekend," she shouts because she has her headphones on. When I speak and she can't hear me, she takes them off. "Sorry. What?"

"I said, I don't have a costume."

"That excuse is weak, Martel, and you know it. Bring your boy toy."

"He's not my boy toy," I say, but he's definitely my *something*. "Besides. He is a *man*."

"You can't fool me. You haven't smiled this much in the year I've known you. He built you a boxing gym."

"He hung a bag in the garage. He has more time to use it than I do."

"Don't diminish the gesture!"

I don't know why I want to hide my happiness. I don't know why I want to act like it isn't a big deal when it is. Patrick and I are fucking like rabbits in heat, and the days we don't get to see each other, we're practically doing it half asleep. I crave him even when he's wrapped around me in our bed. I feel like if the world intrudes, it might break our spell.

"Whatever he is," Mari continues, "I'm happy for you. If only he could double as your muse, you'd be set for the rest of the semester."

"Muses are not real," I say, but she's already got her giant headphones back on. We're always the last ones to leave the studio, and the first ones to arrive. Tonight, I leave first.

"Halloween!" she shouts as the door swings behind me.

When I get back home, Patrick is waiting for me with dinner. He's practically perfected the beef Bolognese. I've essentially moved all of my things into the main house, into his bedroom. I don't want to think of it as our bedroom because that feels like jinxing it. The house isn't finished, after all. Slowly, but most surely, we're breaking down the remaining boxes in the living room together. I have an idea for a color-coordinated bookshelf, but despite the boxes of Scarlett's books, we need many, many more.

"You've been busy," I say, wrapping my arms around him.

He kisses me like he hasn't seen me in days, tugging my hair back to expose my neck. Each and every time, I react the same way, my toes springing up to better reach his mouth. "I guess with everything out in the open, I realize how much stuff I keep that I don't need. It feels good. But now, I'm left with needing new furniture. There's a whole empty room that needs something, though."

"Is there a secret room?" I ask. I trace the outline of his jagged ear and he lets me, shivering lightly at my touch.

"It's not a secret, but it is in on the second floor which—"

"Which you *forbade* me from going to. I guess, other than your bedroom, I was just sort of accustomed to it."

He rests his forehead on mine. "Will you please come look at it?"

"But I'm hungry," I whine.

"There will be plenty of time to eat. Just one look."

I take the hand he offers and follow upstairs and into the room that has always been off limits. I don't know what I pictured the first time I was here. He already has the guest rooms and the torture room in the basement. The upstairs space is the in-progress library, and the downstairs is a living room. I think of what my mother would have said about this big house, this man all alone up on a hill surrounded by nothing but trees and mountains. She would have said he needed a family. I picture Ari taking ownership of one of the guest rooms and another one, painted all sorts of colors—maybe an underwater blue . . .

Whatever he is, Mari referred to Pat. He's not whatever. He's mine. My stomach flutters with something I never let myself want. A family with Patrick. I know I'm being stupid and getting way ahead of myself, but when I look at him, I can't imagine not waking up beside him.

"Close your eyes," he says.

"Pat—"

"Please, Lena. My Magdalena."

"You've been listening to my playlist." I smirk and do as he's asked.

The instant he turns around, I peek. The door opens and I rush past him because I recognize what's in the corner. My easel. There's a long wooden table that still smells of varnish, and new paints and brushes arranged in a neat row. Each wall is an ice white, the only decorations are a series of photos on the wall. Printed-out photos framed in elegant black.

"Your sister emailed me the photos," he tells me.

"How did you know what to buy?" I say, looking at the table.

He smiles, pleased with himself. "Your syllabus and supplies are on the website."

"Pat," I say, and turn to him a little breathless. "This is amazing. I've never had a studio before. You didn't have to do this."

He takes my hands in his, kissing each and every one of my knuckles. "It's not entirely selfless."

"How come?"

"When you're gone, I feel it right in here." He presses his palm against his chest. "When you leave the room, I still smell you. When I sleep, I dream of you."

"Every night?"

He shrugs. "Sometimes I dream of an all-you-can-eat buffet at Red Lobster."

"Gross."

"Don't knock it 'til you try it."

"I don't know how much work I would get done with you down the hall," I say, half serious and half playful. I bite my bottom lip. "You're distracting."

"We can set up boundaries. When the door's closed, I'll stay out." He kisses my cheekbone reverently. "Unless you invite me to come inside."

I moan as I kiss him because he knows just what to say to get me to melt at his fingertips. The only thing that stops me from ripping his clothes off is my rumbling stomach.

"What do you say?" he asks me.

"I accept your studio, Patrick Donatello. On one condition."

He arches a brow. "Which is?"

"Will you be my date to the Halloween party?"

He inhales, bright green eyes searching my face for something I don't know how to answer. He licks his lips, a frown coming and going from his features. I'm pushing too far. Too much. I'm messing this up.

"Never mind, it's silly. I love—I love that you did this for me. No conditions."

"Lena?"

"Pat?"

"I would love to be your date for the Halloween party."

15

The Monster Mash

PAT

"Aren't you a little tall for a stormtrooper?" Lena asks from behind me.

The stormtrooper costume is one I've had for a few years. I was blond enough and slimmer then, so I was Luke as a stormtrooper. Now, the black material stretches a bit over my biceps and thighs, warping the plastic white armor in some places, but it still works.

With my helmet in hand, I turn to where she leans against the bedroom door.

"Oh sweet Christ," I swear under my breath because I'm straining through the cheap black nylon and white plastic. "Do we really have to go to this party?"

She does a little twirl in the white Princess Leia costume. It's a Rated R version of the one I grew up with as a kid. A lot less Wholesome Princess and more Alderaan Girls Gone Wild. I especially love the addition of the hip-length slip that displays her thighs.

"I considered going as a slutty cupcake," she says, "but it was this or slutty Wookie and I wasn't sure if I wanted to traumatize you or not."

"As long as you're not slutty Darth Vader, otherwise this role play is going to be real weird. Come to think of it, I'm just a plain stormtrooper now." I set the helmet on the bed and grip her around the waist. Her hair is pinned in two buns at the sides, and with every step she takes, I get a flash of her light-brown skin.

She's got boots on, so she doesn't have to push up on her toes too much to kiss me. I wonder if I can convince her to stay in for the night. To let me get my head under that skirt.

"Come, we're already an hour late."

"Can anyone really be late to a college party?" I ask.

"I promised Mari."

I succumb to her will and follow her downstairs with my helmet under my arm. Before we get in the car, she kisses me, flicking her tongue against mine.

"You good?"

"I'm fine, Lena."

What if I really am fine? I think.

She drives, and I hold my helmet in my lap. It's like all of my adrenaline is in my legs, because I'm more jittery than I've ever been before.

I can do this. I can do this for Lena.

"We don't have to stay long," she says.

At that, I frown. "You don't have to make excuses for me."

"I'm not." Her words are tight. "I want to make sure you're comfortable. Usually when people say they're fine, they aren't."

"Look at me, baby," I say. "Do I look fine?"

I try to put everything I've learned with Chris over the last couple of weeks into practice. This morning, while Lena was in the shower, I got in a call to him, and he encouraged me to wear something that made me feel comfortable. The helmet will help with that.

"You're fine in so many ways, Pat," she says, a suggestiveness in her sexy voice. "It means a lot that you're here with me."

When we get to the house and she parks at an angle on the lawn, which is probably illegal, she holds my hand. I grip it tight.

The house is decorated from porch to roof with cobwebs and an entire elaborate graveyard complete with skeletons in various stages of resurrection. I already forgot whose place this is, but their neighbors must be pissed at all the cars surrounding their property.

I put on my helmet, then step out of the car. For a few steps, it feels like wading into mud. I focus on each and every single movement of my body. Shut the door. Adjust the helmet on the face. Take a step. Then another.

Thankfully, people littering the front lawn are too young and too drunk to really pay attention to me. This isn't the small neighborhood that I grew up in. These aren't the families that knew mine. This is the college town with enough people that I am just a guy in a costume trying to impress the woman he's falling in love with.

"Pat?" Lena asks, and her voice, clear as a bell, rings through my thoughts. Her voice is the thing that brings me back. Her touch anchors me. I am out of the mud, crunching on leaves, on solid ground.

I tug on Lena's hand and bring her ear close. Damn this helmet. "Thank you for bringing me out, Lena. I'd completely forgotten what it was like to see college kids puking before midnight."

At that, she barks a laugh and we waltz in through the door, crowned with bright orange lights. Everything is filtered through the pane of my helmet, making the hanging lights that much brighter. I can hear my breath, feel it get hot in here, which, I can already tell, is going to be a mistake.

Lena finds her friend Mari right away, sitting on a tall armchair dressed in a flowing robe and a garland propped on her long, dark curls.

"Who are you supposed to be?" Lena asks.

"A Greek goddess," I say, my voice too deep, too muffled under this thing.

But Mari isn't scared. She makes a scandalized face, completely pleased. "See?! I am Aphrodite, goddess of sex."

"She's the goddess of love," Lena corrects.

"I'm about to *well, actually* you on this one," Mari says, "But she was literally born of the sea when Zeus spilled his god jizz into the waters. That's about sex. Not love."

"On that note, I'm going to get us some drinks," Lena says. "Pat, can you keep Mari company so she doesn't get into trouble?"

"How dare?" Mari asks.

I think of how Lena also said the same thing to me. Have I really been hiding for that long that everyone under thirty has come up with a different way of speaking?

Lena gives me a small look, one that asks, "Will you be okay without me?"

I don't know. I don't want to let go of her hand. I don't want to find out the answer.

But it's like the time my brother Ronan shoved me into the lake and said *swim*. I swam all the way to the other end of the lake because the only other option was drowning. I nod, and she's gone in the throng of bodies covered in glitter, lamé, and superhero costumes. While I don't care for their lack of rhythm or inability to keep a beat, I miss music. I miss dancing.

"So, you're the mysterious recluse," Mari says, her voice climbing over the music.

"Guilty. But you can just call me Pat." I take the empty seat beside her.

"Just so you know, whatever way you hurt Lena, I will return the favor seven times worse."

I want to laugh at this girl, over a decade younger than me, swathed in gossamer fabric, and glittering powder on her skin. But there is nothing humorous in the way she juts her chin out and gives me a stare that defies her size. She is all heart.

"I won't. If I do, I promise you can use me for target practice."

She seems pleased with this answer.

"I'm used to getting this little speech from dads," I tell her.

Mari sniffs her long Roman nose, pushing her hair aside. "Everyone is allowed to fight for the people they love, within reason. That role isn't for just dads or whatever idea your generation has about patriarchy."

I laugh, the sound robotic against the plastic of my helmet. I consider taking it off. Who would look at me and stare? Who would take a photo and plaster it all over the internet? Though, in this crowd, I might be safe since celebrities get rinsed and recycled so quickly. Plus, I never got to be famous, just infamous.

"How old exactly do you think I am?" I ask.

For the first time during our conversation, I think she might actually look abashed. Thankfully, Lena returns and sits on my lap. I realize the problem with this scenario. How am I going to drink this beer without resorting to a straw?

Mari and Lena get into a conversation about the holidays. This is going to be my first year without Jack. I try not to think about that, and the fact that Scarlett has invited us to her house for Thanksgiving. I would know everyone who is coming, and it would be a safe place since I can't exactly wear my stormtrooper helmet everywhere I go.

You can beat this, I remind myself.

I keep my hand on Lena's thigh, and she absentmindedly brushes her fingers on the inside of my wrist. I have never been with someone who touches me this way. I grew up skinny, but my brothers and I were breaking six feet in height before we reached high school. I have never been a small man. She doesn't exactly make me feel small, but when Lena touches me, she makes me feel breakable. Like she's handling me in a way that's *careful.* I don't want her to be afraid to touch me. I want her to know that she can be rough around those sexy fucking edges. She's like that in the bedroom, but in public, she pulls back. It's not that I want her to do to me the same things here that we do in the dark. That's not it at all.

What do I fucking want? I want this girl, this woman to love me hard and unconditionally. I want her to know that I will be strong enough to hold her up the way she has done for me.

I take off my helmet.

Mari does a double take, and I think I might have done the impossible. I have rendered her speechless.

The room is dark, and the air humid from the costumes and bodies dancing beneath a strobe light. Why do college kids want strobe lights and smoke machines at their parties? I can feel Lena stiffen against me, a sharp little intake of breath as she turns her torso to settle wide brown eyes at my face.

I'm scar-side to Mari, who only smirks and says something I'm not quite sure I understand. I drink from my beer and keep drinking because I feel like my mouth has become a desert and nothing will quench it except for this thing in my hand and maybe Lena's mouth.

Her mouth. She leans up to press a kiss on my jaw.

I feel my dick twitch, and I decided to stop picturing the things I want to do with her because this costume is old, and I'm afraid my full erection will rip the seams.

"Well, *hello*," Mari says, and without the helmet, I can see her dress is the color of Caribbean seas, her eyes a sharp green, and the glitter on her skin a gold that brings out the warm brown.

"Hello yourself, princess," I say, and I soak up the way the two of them fall into giggles.

I sit here, like this is a perfectly normal thing. Like I am the kind of guy who is better. Like I'm a regular guy on a regular date with his incredible girl.

"Oh, this is my song!" Mari shouts. "Dance with me, please."

She's taking both of our hands. A familiar panic starts to build between my ribs. Sitting in a dark corner with Lena and her best friend is one thing, but it's another to stand in the center of a throng.

But I pop my helmet back on and follow the girls. The song has a hard and fast beat that even I can't follow, but it doesn't matter because Mari and Lena seem to sandwich me playfully.

This look on Lena's face, sheer happiness without the worry of our families or her school or anything—I would do anything to maintain it. Mari "whoos" behind us, but then the song changes to one I actually know. Slow with a heavy bass. I grab Lena and pull her tight against me, her skirt riding up high, so the top of those slits reveals the black lace panties she's wearing. Somehow, we dance into a dark hallway all alone.

Lena's eyes spark with lust, because she can feel my dick pressing against her thigh. She rubs her hand across it and I lift my helmet to taste her waiting mouth. Her nipples are perked up and showing through that flimsy little dress.

"Take me home," she whispers in my ear.

I don't know what makes me harder—the feel of her body against me or when she calls my house *home*.

We push through the crowd. For a moment, I catch that smirking Keillor kid in the corner, drinking from his red plastic cup. He tries to catch Lena's eyes as she's leaving, but she doesn't look his way, and when he sees me, he says, "Sup, Donatello."

I say nothing, despite the unreasonable slap of rage against my chest. This is the guy who wants to sell my photos to the highest bidder. He doesn't know it's me, can only make his best fucking guess, but for the briefest moment, I make a fist.

What if he caught a photo of that kiss just now? What if he saw us in that corner before?

I think of what Chris said earlier this month. What if I do another thing I'll regret? What if I just keep following Lena outside? What if this night continues to be great once we get home and naked?

I walk and walk. Lena's round ass is my North fucking Star.

She drives us home, singing in her god-awful, beautiful voice.

"You are truly terrible," I tell her, removing my helmet for the last time tonight.

She glances at me. "That's not going to get you any cookies tonight."

"Please," I scoff. "You always say that and you can't resist me, Lena."

"In that case, I'll just keep singing."

I take her hand and kiss the tops of her knuckles. "It still sounds—perfect. In Spanish and all."

She only purses her lips, but when we're home and kissing up the stairs, that purse melts away into a perfect circle gasping as I spread her legs and nestle myself between her thighs like I've wanted to all night. I push the black lace to the side and slurp up her sweet, wet pussy.

The white plastic of my suit has started to rip when I sit on my knees to have a better position of her. I yank off the gloves and fuck her with my fingers until she's utterly demanding my cock.

Amazingly, the buns of her hair have stayed in place and she makes no motion to remove that dress. She crawls on her knees and gets on all fours. The way she moves the fabric to reveal her ass is an art form.

"Get inside me, trooper," she says.

I can't reach the ridiculous fucking zipper, so I rip the flimsy seams and whip out my dick. She sits back as I guide myself inside her, parting her ass so I can watch myself disappear in Lena. She cries out, sinking her hands and face on the mattress like she's praying. Then, she reaches back and slaps her ass cheek, leaving a red print that fades when she moves her hand.

"Do you want to slap my fucking ass?" she asks.

I do. More than anything I do. I pound harder, my heart seizing in my chest. I slap her full, delicious cheeks and when she makes high-pitched sounds, pushing hard against her, I can't hold it back anymore and come.

"Don't move," she tells me.

I push myself into her and she fucks my dick, riding herself into a climax.

When we're finally finished, we are a mess of tattered clothes and panting breaths. Her hair has finally come undone, falling over her. She's unreal. She's the kind of perfect I don't deserve.

"Thank you for tonight," she says, and when she kisses my neck, something in my chest hurts.

"Thank you for wearing that." I slap her thigh and pull her leg across my stomach. "One thing, though. Mari called me something and I'm not sure whether or not to be offended."

"What did she say?" she asks, biting her bottom lip.

"What the hell is a zaddy?"

16
Save Me

LENA

November

I paint for hours, listening to a mix of songs that Patrick made me. I recognize the songs that I've played over and over again since I moved in, but there are others that he said he loves from Dolly Parton and Willie Nelson and Johnny Cash. Ari says you get to know someone by the kind of music they listen to. The chords that make them melancholic and hopeful. The lyrics that stick to your head far longer than any pop-quiz answers that vanish after you take the test. Every time Pat shows me a different part of himself, I feel like I'm falling in love with him a little bit more. I'm sure it's love that I'm feeling.

Sometimes, when I wake up before him, I watch how peaceful he is while he sleeps. His beauty startles me every time, and I want to whisper to him that I love him. But then he wakes up, and we sink into each other's warmth and I lose the nerve.

A cold November breeze fans through the open studio window. I'm wrapped in one of Patrick's hoodies, which has become my preferred way to dress inside. The strong scent of linseed oil and paint makes my nose itch from hours of inhaling the chemicals, but I've finally finished my first piece of the semester. The assignment was "home." I painted a portrait of my mother surrounded by flowers. I wasn't even meaning to, but I've found myself missing my parents more and more. I have plans for a matching one with my dad next since I have tons to catch up on. But the final assignment is the trickiest. It's a free for all. Anything we want. I guess it's Professor Meneses's way of throwing a wrench in her course since she's always so regimented.

"Babe?" Patrick calls for me from down the hall.

In the last two weeks, he's kept his word and never disrupts me during my studio hours, but he will do it to make sure that I eat.

I hang up my apron, move my painting to a stand to dry. Only five more to go. Thankfully, the next one is watercolor. I pack the oils away and lay out the pots of acrylic I'll need. I unfurl a roll of canvas so I can keep working after dinner.

"Lena?" Patrick says, and this time I hear the anxiety in his voice.

I drop everything and slide to the library in my socks. The shelves are built and the fireplace is crackling. Patrick is sitting and staring at a photo album. I don't think I'll ever get tired of seeing him like this—rivers of scars across his naked torso, a mess of golden hair getting longer every day. He is so big in every way, and so vulnerable in others. He scratches at his beard and looks up at me with glassy green eyes.

"What's wrong?"

He shakes his head, and I see the struggle there. "I haven't seen these in ages. I didn't even pack them up, I think."

I sit beside him, pressing my shoulder to his. I take the photo, one of those standard Kodaks where the colors fade easily. In the picture, two little blond boys sit on a green hill. It's the same view Patrick and I have from the deck. Between them is a brunette baby in diapers. Patrick and his brothers. It is like walking through a mirror and stepping into a past that doesn't belong to me, but he's taking me with him.

"I always thought Jack had taken them with him to Seattle."

He pulls out another one. They're a little older, the older brothers holding Jack by his tiny hands to help him walk. One with their mouths covered in red and orange dye from eating popsicles. Ronan and Patrick look so much alike as kids, I wouldn't be surprised if Patrick revealed that they were twins. But I can tell my boy apart from the bright green of his eyes, like rough-cut crystals.

"You look happy," I say.

"We were. In the ways it mattered, at least." Patrick turns to me, and I offer him a kiss.

"Also, you make the exact same faces still," I say. "Playful, sweet."

He laughs, and shows me his parents. I see him in his mother's face, his dad's cheekbones and jaw.

"What in the world are you doing in this one?" I ask, picking one up where Ronan is holding his arms open and Patrick has a toddler Jack around the waist.

His eyes crinkle at the corners, a booming laugh that nearly tips him back. "This is the time Ronan and I tried to use Jack as a football."

"Patrick!" I say, shocked.

"Ma was not happy." As he breathes, trying to steady his breath, I know how hard he's trying not to cry. He swallows hard and stares at the photo again. He touches the side of his hand to his left eye and then closes the box.

My stepmother said she hated when men cried because it made them weak, and what was the point of weak men? I hated her for saying that because she was talking about my dad. There was a time during his illness when we both knew he wasn't going to get better and that we would have to live without him sooner than we thought. My dad cried and Ariana and I cried with him. But Sonia couldn't—wouldn't—handle his tears. Crying is for anyone who feels pain. Maybe if we stopped caring about who does the tear shedding, everyone would be able to communicate a little bit better.

"When Ariana was born, I put a 'for sale' sign on her and left her in the living room," I confess. It's something I've never told anyone.

Patrick flashes his white teeth, and his green eyes brighten. The sadness dispels, and then it is just the two of us and our memories. He tugs me over his thighs until I'm sitting between his legs. I rest my head on his chest and I feel complete in a way that startles me.

"Magdalena Martel. There is a dark side to you."

I lean up and kiss his jaw. "You know my dark side better than most."

He goes for my lips, and then we're kissing on the floor. He's on top of me, parting my legs with his knees. My body surrenders to him so easily, so willingly. He props himself on his elbows and I trace my hands over his chest. He kisses the tip of my nose.

"Don't kiss my eyes," I say, turning my face.

He chuckles. "Why?"

"My mom used to say that if someone kissed your eyelids they were telling you lies behind your back."

He nods and kisses my temple instead. "And I thought my family had people beat on the Catholic superstition stuff."

"Superstition and guilt."

"Do you have any pictures of you as a kid?"

I shrug. "They're at home."

"Good thing your sister loves me and will probably send them to me if I ask."

"Ovaries before brovaries," I say. "But I was definitely the cutest baby you've ever seen."

He nuzzles my neck, finding a spot that makes me squeal from how ticklish I am there. His fingers cup my waist and move down my thigh. I wrap my leg around him, pressing the heel of my foot into his firm ass cheek. He answers with a hip thrust.

"We'd have a cute kid," he says.

We lock eyes, and I can see the moment he realizes he's spoken out loud. His eyelashes flutter and whatever he wanted to say next gets stuck in his throat. I laugh to let him know that I'm not reading too much into it.

"Hypothetically," I say, tracing a finger over his left pectoral. "We would have very beautiful kids."

Heat fills my chest and I lick my bottom lip. There's a 0.3 percent chance that I could get pregnant on an IUD. One of my friends had a copper one, and it shifted. Now, they're about to welcome their third kid. I used to think I didn't want kids. The world is too ugly, too mean. There are too many people already and it feels like no matter what we do, there's no way that we'll get ourselves together as a species to make it better. But after looking at baby Patrick and his brothers, and after the sincerity with which he said that, my ovaries give a painful squeeze. Or, it's just my period cramps. Probably my period cramps.

"Lena," he says, tentatively.

For the last couple of weeks, he's hesitant when he says my name, like he's setting up the stage for something bigger. A silly, girly, ridiculous part of me is waiting for him to tell me that, maybe, he loves me. Is that what I want? Is that what he needs? I read somewhere that the first three months of any relationship feel like some sort of paradise made individually for us. What happens come December when we get past the blissful stage? What happens when June rolls around and I've finished school early? Am I really going to stay here after working so hard? Am I going to move Ariana across the country, too?

"Where did you go, baby?" he whispers against my ear, a warm finger dragging the outline of my jaw.

"Just thinking about the future."

"Because of what I just said?"

When I touch his chest, I feel how fast his heart is beating. "Yeah. But not in a bad way."

I decide that the only way to really understand each other is to be honest. As honest as I can be with these feelings. We aren't sitting in a car, but we can't waste gas just to have real conversations. I take a steadying breath and tell him my fears, condensing my thoughts about our bliss stage.

"I don't know much about relationships," he says, flipping over and lying beside me. "But I know that when I'm with you, I'm a better version of myself. I know you have to decide after the end of the school year. But I'm not going anywhere, Lena. I don't think I can go anywhere. That's not fair to you. You should do what's best for your career and Ari and you."

He lets go of my hand and taps a nervous beat on his abdomen.

"You're as much a part of my life as Ariana and my art," I say. "Whatever decisions I do make, you're included in it. As long as you want to be."

He locks eyes with me. "I want to be, Lena."

We lay side by side, listening to the fire eat away the logs, until our fingers search for one another at the same time and we become a tangle of limbs once again.

"I can't," I whisper, biting his earlobe as he tugs at the front of my leggings. "I have my period."

"I heard somewhere," he says, grinning devilishly, "that your orgasms are stronger during your period."

I roll my eyes. "Please don't tell me you read it on some dude blog."

"*Cosmo,* actually. It might be wishful thinking," he says. "But I can certainly try to deliver."

He kisses the crook of my neck, nipping hard enough to draw a high-pitched sound. I can't deny how much I want him, every minute, every day. It only gets stronger the more we're together, and that's scary. That kind of building pressure isn't always good, I think. But I still find myself following him into our bedroom. I undress and get in the shower first to clean up a bit before I let him back inside. My breath is in knots at the sight of him, so fucking tall and muscular. His hair a tangle of golds, curling at the ends in the steam. He picks me up like I'm weightless and pins me up against the wall with his arms hooked under my knees. He presses himself inside me and stays there without moving as he kisses every part of me he can reach. My skin is raw from his beard against me, but I don't want him to stop. I beg him to move, to fuck me harder and faster until he's wrenching an orgasm from me. When he pulls out, I kiss his open, panting mouth. I could look at him forever.

"Patrick?"

"Lena?"

"Would you let me paint you?"

He presses his forehead against mine, the rainfall washing us clean. I see the doubt and fear, still fresh on his face. "I want to do anything you ask of me, Lena. Anything. But I can't do that just yet."

PAT

Thanksgiving Day brings gray skies and crisp, cold air that smells like it's going to snow soon.

Lena and I walk through the trail that leads to Scarlett's property. I carry a bottle of whiskey in one hand and Lena has the cherry pie she made last night. I definitely got my hand slapped trying to sneak a taste. Scarlett gave us very specific instructions of what we were allowed to bring because she's been planning this all week.

From the moment I woke up, my nerves feel ripped open and frayed. Perhaps it's left over from the conversation Lena and I had last week. She's already thinking about her exit plan. She says that I'll be a part of it, but what if she goes where I can't follow? I made it to the grocery store, but I didn't get out of the car. I went to a party and I took off my helmet for two minutes, but I haven't tried again since then, especially after the call from my agent.

Miriam said that the paparazzi site XYZ had put out a call for recent photos involving the stars of *American Speed* for the upcoming one-year anniversary of the movie and accident. Will it really be in a little over a month? Daisy, my co-star, is happily starring in an independent film with a big-deal director. Everyone from the director to producers to the other actors have moved on with their lives.

"Remind me who's going to be there?" I ask.

Lena makes her cute thinking face. "The guy she's dating, I think. I forgot his name, but he works at a school."

"Scarlett and the jock," I say, chuckling.

"There's Kayli, Mari, and you remember my friend River and her fiancé."

"Is Montana a haven for wayward New Yorkers now?"

She nudges my side with her elbow, and I sling my arm around her. I hate that the encroaching winter means jackets covering her beautiful body. That's more layers for me to take off, but I don't mind the work. I kiss the apple of her cheek. What would I do this time next year if she isn't in my life? My chest feels a painful tug.

I can't think about what it would be like to lose her. I have to remind myself that she's here, that while I have her, I need to do everything I can to make her happy, to show her what our life can be like.

What if I do all of that and she still leaves?

What if she doesn't?

I stop to kiss her better, to kiss her hard. She balances the pie on one palm to better wrap her arm around my neck. Our puffy jackets make a swishing sound as we get closer and closer. I walk her into the sturdy bark of a tree.

"I find myself between a rock and a very hard place," she says.

I laugh as I explore the spot under her ear, my brain calculating the best way to take her in the middle of this trail while not dropping our Thanksgiving offerings.

"Patrick Donatello, if you make me drop this pie, I swear—"

We break apart, sighing away the pent-up frustration. You would think with all the sex we've had the last couple of months I'd be tired, bored even. The old me would have left her in the middle of the night. Would I even have remembered her face? That version of me wouldn't deserve to be in the same room as a woman like Lena. Thinking of it makes me cringe inwardly.

When she threads her fingers around mine, she becomes a lifeline, pulling me out of the storm of my thoughts. We reach the end of the path and I can't help but remember standing in the same place holding a shivering Lena in my arms with her dirty, ripped dress. I don't deserve her.

"You good, baby?" she asks, as our boots crunch on the gravel path leading to Scarlett's house.

I don't want to worry her with everything that's going through my head. I'll sort it out with Chris after Thanksgiving. For now, I assure her it's nothing to worry about. Just nerves. This is the first time I'm in someone else's house surrounded by people. The only ones I haven't really met are River and her fiancé.

I can do this.

I wipe my feet on the mat in front of Scarlett's house. She moved back here after the divorce and the place hasn't changed since I was a kid. The same rose garden is out front, the same creaky wooden steps. The Christmas wreath and decorations are a new addition, though, which is surprising since she said she barely had time to get dinner together.

I ring the bell, and Lena steals one last kiss from me, which is a terrible idea because I'm already wound up, and I'm pretty sure a raging hard-on was not on the list of pre-approved things Scarlett said we could bring to dinner.

Scarlett opens the door. At least, I think it's her. I haven't seen her dress up since Vegas. She's in a cream-colored sweater that shows off her boobs—believe me, I feel so wrong noticing that—and her auburn hair falls in shiny waves.

Her light-brown eyes take in the sight of me and they get glossier by the minute.

"Oh, Pat," she says.

"Don't get weepy on me now, West," I mutter, and scoop her into a hug. "Did you brush your hair?"

She swats my back, and I set her back on the floor. The lights in the house feel too bright. White twinkling ones line the entryway to the living room and the kitchen. Everyone seems to be congregated around the small kitchen table.

We're the last ones to arrive and it's only two in the afternoon. Even Mari is here, dressed in a tight black velvet dress. She's chatting with Kayli while drinking wine and arranging a cheese plate.

"Pat!" Kayli says, offering a wide smile and her open arms.

This feels awkward. Too many eyes on me. Too many sorry

expressions. What if they aren't sorry? What if they're showing support instead?

I embrace her, and she rubs my back. "I hope you brought the good stuff."

"Nothing but," I say, and hand over a bottle of Blanton's.

"Come in, you two," Scarlett says. "I got a late start but it's all hands on deck." Scarlett takes the pie and sets it on a dessert corner. There's something shifty in her eyes, and I wonder if my jeans don't conceal my erection like I thought.

"Okay, I'm in charge of the playlist for the next hour," Mari says, swiping through her phone.

"That doesn't seem like such a good idea," I say, and wink at her. She calls me an old man, and I keep following Lena around the kitchen table.

I meet River, a gorgeous blonde with blue eyes as sharp as knives. There's a steady quiet to her, and when she looks at my face, her eyes don't linger on my scars. When she introduces us to her fiancé, Hutch, I pause at the memory I have of him. He's the guy that dropped Lena home in July. Months later, I feel a twinge of embarrassment at how I reacted. He's a couple of inches taller than me, with a short crop of dark-brown hair and brown eyes.

"Hey, Patrick," he says in a voice so familiar I nearly jerk back. "Chris Hutcherson."

I force myself to grip his hand tighter and take a deep breath. It's incredibly fucking weird being face-to-face this way with my therapist. "Hey, man, nice to meet you."

He gives me a nod that tells me he is, in fact, who I think he is. He slaps my shoulder good-naturedly, and moves on to Lena.

"What do you need us to do, Scarlett?" Lena asks. There are various pans in stages of prep. The oven is blazing, and though the kitchen is small, it feels like being home. The kind of home that welcomes you back even after you've been gone for too long.

I glance around the room and realize there's someone missing. Scarlett's coach boyfriend. I'm about to ask when she turns a nervous stare to me.

"Pat," Scarlett says, twisting the bottom of her sweater. "I have something to tell you."

I rub my hands over my face, a knot forming in my chest instantly. "Why do people think that's ever a good way to start a sentence?"

"I have a surprise for you. At least, I thought it would be a good surprise to invite him because you've been doing so well. But he's been here for so long I might kill him myself if things don't work out."

"Scarlett, what are you talking about?"

"Don't get mad at me for bringing him here, okay?"

I snap my attention to the door leading to the living room. I walk around her, taking long steps, ready to see my brother's face. Of course, she's talking about Jack. Who else would it be? But why would I be mad at her for bringing him here?

Unless—

Standing in front of the roaring fireplace isn't Jack.

Dressed in a deep-green velvet blazer and black jeans is Rick Rocket.

"Heya, kid," he says, a smile ticking up his bearded face and glass of amber liquor in his hand.

"Hey," I say, a tremble in my voice.

I don't know what to do because I can *feel* everyone behind me staring at us.

The last time I saw him, that I can remember, was after that long-ass drive. Fallon and Aiden and Rick. The brothers that chose me, that tried to put me back together and I wouldn't let them.

"I'm sorry."

He sets down his glass on the fireplace mantel and opens his arms. "Come here, mate."

"I'm sorry, Ricky," I say again. I hug him, and he's solid as ever. My fucking eyes are burning and I know everyone is watching us and Lena's probably crying, but she was also crying while we watched *How the Grinch Stole Christmas* last night because she felt bad for the Grinch and of course she does, since she's got a heart three times bigger than anyone I know, definitely more than me.

Ricky slaps my back a few times and clears his throat, like the big fucking man he is. "We'll be all right, kid. 'S good to see you. You're copying my look and everything."

He tugs on the bottom of my beard and punches my shoulder lightly.

"What the fuck are you wearing?" I ask, now that I have a good chance to look at him. There's more silver in his blond hair than I remember, deeper laugh lines at the corners of his eyes.

The most shocking addition is a solid platinum ring around his wedding finger.

"Did you get fucking *married?*"

Ricky's eyes widen with sheer white fear. "Fuck no. This is the latest tech to keep track of my sleep habits. My doc wants to keep me fucking monitored twenty-four-seven, can you imagine that?"

"Why? Is something wrong?"

He shakes his head, but I see the lie forming on his lips. "No, not at all. High blood pressure, lack of sleep, but at least business is good. Show's good. Boys are good."

I want to ask about them. Do I have the right to after the way I treated them?

"I want you to meet someone," I say, and hold my hand out for her.

Lena breaks apart from the throng jamming up the hallway. Chris ushers the others back to the kitchen to give us privacy. I was right. Lena's dabbing at the corners of her eyes when she stands in front of Ricky.

"Hello, gorgeous," he says, and hugs her. "So, you're the one that's brought this sorry lump back to life."

She reaches for my hand, and when she sets those deep-brown eyes on me, I know that I am the luckiest man alive. "It's been pretty mutual. How are you liking Montana?"

His pale-blue eyes dart to where Scarlett comes in with a little red bell and I don't think I'm imagining the smirk there. "Okay, people. Dinner isn't ready yet, but there's still work to be done. Let these two catch up. Mari and Kayli, you make the mac and cheese, Lena—stuffing. Chris—remind me not to burn the bird. River—you keep making cocktails."

We take the two upholstered armchairs in front of the fireplace. There's a pile of clothes tucked in the corner, which I won't point out in case Scarlett freaks out some more. Lena had offered to help her clean yesterday since we knew how tight Scarlett's deadlines have been, but she declined.

"Has she been like this all day?" I ask Ricky.

Scarlett only reappears once to pop a drink my hand. She doesn't even look in Ricky's direction before she stomps away.

He raises his brows, scratching the back of his neck. "Try days."

"I can't believe you're here," I say. "How did Scarlett get a hold of you?"

Ricky rubs the sides of his beard. "She's persistent, I'll give her that. I thought she was just another groupie trying to get a hold of you. But then on the twentieth nonstop call, I had to pick up. Gave me the lowdown. I got here three nights ago."

I try the drink River made. It's like a Manhattan but sweeter, and delicious. "Huh. No wonder she didn't want Lena coming over yesterday."

"About that," Ricky says, ice-blue eyes darting to the living room entryway. "Scarlett's, uh, kind of mad at me."

I look at him, confusion making my eyes strain. "Why would she be mad at you?"

He tries for a look of innocence. "It's a long story."

"Turkey isn't done yet, and I could use stories that aren't about me."

Ricky settles in with his drink in hand, very much the king of the castle. "Well, once she told me how well you were doing, I said I'd come out. The hiccup was that my assistant booked me on the wrong date and to the wrong airport. I'm a big boy, you know, so I rented my own damn car and drove from Missoula. I got to her place and she was fighting with some bloke. I grabbed him by the neck and we got into a blue."

"Wait, what?"

"Her ex. The coach."

Understanding hits me. *That's* why the boyfriend—ex-boyfriend—isn't here and she's so flustered. "Let me understand this. You got here, punched her boyfriend, and she's mad at you? That doesn't add up."

Ricky waves his hand in the air, like he's trying to clear the board. "She said she had it under control, which she might have. But I was tired and he had a punchable face, Pat. You should've seen him. Anyway, she's been irritated with me ever since. I also watched her kill a turkey and make eye contact with me the entire time. Women out here are—"

"Easy now," I say, laughing my warning. "These are my people."

"I'm just trying to be a *good* houseguest," he says, slapping his knee.

"Uh-huh," I say. Trying to picture high-maintenance Ricky, who gets a weekly pedicure, spa treatments, and goes to the gym six days a week living with Scarlett. The woman who mows her own lawn and chops wood to *think* and lives off chips and diet coke while she's on deadline. "Bro, you must be driving her bat-shit crazy."

"That's one way of putting it," Ricky says, his eyes darting to the hall again.

There's something he's holding back, and I wonder what's happened in these past two days that has him uncharacteristically frazzled. Maybe it's been so long, I'm reading him wrong. He slaps my arm, and his eyes settle on my scarred face. I think of the first time we ever met. We were both at some party in the Hamptons and I was a shitty waiter surrounded by women. He looked me up and down and nodded his approval. He said, "Hey, kid, I've been waiting for my drink for an hour."

"It's good to see you, Pat."

I look down at my drink, and play with the rim of the glass. Then, I find the courage to ask something I've been dying to know since I saw him. "Tell me about the boys."

LENA

While the rest of us are making sure everything is being cut, cooked, salted, and mixed, Scarlett is going through her checklist.

"Where's your coach?" I ask Scarlett.

She crinkles her nose, and I see the moment Hutch looks out of his element and concentrates on chopping apples for the sangria.

"As of yesterday, he's no longer my coach," Scarlett says.

"Damn, Scarlett. I'm sorry."

Scarlett shrugs, but she doesn't seem terribly bothered over it. "It wasn't going to work out. I'm fine. Really. He didn't understand my schedule and that I wasn't going to have time to go to Texas to meet his family."

"He wanted you to meet his family?" I ask. "That's huge."

"Yeah, but I wasn't going to say yes even if my schedule allowed. It was just supposed to be fun and stress free while I finish this series." She moves hair away from her forehead, and I wonder if it's a good time to tell her she smudged flour on her nose. I decide to walk to her and clean it up myself, which gives us all a laugh.

"At least that's good?" I ask, tentatively.

Hutch clears his throat and we all turn to look at him at the same time.

"Are you analyzing me?" Scarlett asks.

"Me? I wouldn't dream of it," he says, smiling all the way to the fridge to get a can of Moose Drool.

"Lay it on me," Scarlett says, pursing her lips and making a beckoning sign with her hands.

Hutch shakes his head, and I kind of agree with him. But Scarlett insists and so he sets his drink down and meets Scarlett's eyes.

"You say you're fine, but are you trying to convince us or yourself? You've been forgetful all morning, but it isn't because you're careless. It's okay to let the people who care about you take care of you and be there to listen. Something else is bothering you."

I feel his words in my bones.

Scarlett nods slowly, like she's listening to a faraway song the rest of us can't pick up. "Jake and I had a really big fight three days ago when I said I couldn't go to Texas next week, and I said things that I didn't mean. I even called him by my ex-husband's name at one point. And the thing is, I don't miss my ex. Part of me just wanted something physical, and I know I was wrong because I didn't tell Jake that I wasn't looking for anything serious. Then Ricky shows up and punches him, and—"

"Hold up," I say, surprise rippling through the room. "Ricky punched him?"

"You definitely left out all the good stuff," Mari says, popping a cheese cube into her mouth.

"I suppose it's a good thing *Ricky* showed up when he did," Scarlett says, "because I was ready to get my shotgun from the porch."

I scoff and throw my arms in the air. "What is it with you guys and your shotguns?"

"You'll never get used to it," River says, while filling a bucket with ice.

Scarlett rolls her eyes and continues. "Anyway, Ricky's been here since then, moving around all of my things and criticizing me because I don't have a hair dryer. I air dry my hair, okay? I made this beautiful loaf of sourdough and he wouldn't eat it because he's on some fucking Whole30. Why did he even come for Thanksgiving if he wasn't going to eat?"

Hutch bites his lips and we share a knowing look. I wonder if Scarlett would kick me out of her house if I suggest that maybe she likes having Ricky around, but just then Ricky comes marching out of the living room with a very amused Patrick at his heels.

"Excuse me, Duchess," Ricky says, "I have a gluten sensitivity."

Scarlett's cheeks are red as she brushes a stubborn bit of hair away from her eyes. I realize—wait, is she wearing lip gloss?

"You didn't have a gluten sensitivity in the middle of the night when you ate my Pop-Tarts. And you're drinking whiskey. Do you know what that's made out of?"

Ricky unbuttons his velvet blazer, the fitted shirt beneath tapered to his solid body. "You told me to make myself at home. Maybe you shouldn't say things you don't mean, Duchess."

"I told you not to call me that," she says, this time holding her chopping knife in his direction.

"How about some music?" Hutch asks me. "Mari?"

"On it!"

"As long as it's something Patrick and Ricky can dance to," I say, smirking at the beautiful men.

The two of them suck in a breath so sharp, it draws everyone's attention to me. The others dissolve into laughter, while Ricky comes over to me to pick me up into a strangling hug and says, "Oh, I *know* I'm going to like you."

We spend the next few hours eating the appetizers and drinking sangria and whiskey punch on the deck. Ricky says today is the exception to his *gluten sensitivity* so that the liquor will keep him warm. While the turkey is on the last half hour of being done, River and Mari set up a giant Jenga game in the backyard. Hutch and Patrick chop up firewood for the pit. Kayli told them that they were out, but I highly suspect it was to get them grunting and doing manual labor in their tight T-shirts. Scarlett brings out a bow and arrow from her garage for the target practice that hangs on an old tree.

"Americans," Ricky mutters, but I notice how he lingers, like he's waiting to see if she'll look at him.

"Hey, don't look at me," I say and bring my sangria to where he's sitting. "Though maybe that target practice would have come in handy when I had to live with my stepmom."

Scarlett aims. She glances at Ricky, a tiny smile creeps on her face before she fires and hits the white outside of the bull's-eye. Ricky and I high-five.

"That doesn't sound like you, Lena," Scarlet says. "I know you had problems but . . ."

She lets the question go unasked. What did she do? Was she really that bad? In this yard, I feel safe in a way that I haven't in so long. There are people who love me, and despite the forty-degree weather, I feel *warm* and it has nothing to do with the drink. I look at Patrick standing a few yards away laughing with Hutch. He's not the only one who should open himself up,

I exhale tiny frosted clouds. "She stole my identity."

Scarlett lowers the bow and turns to me. "What?"

I laugh at her reaction and the surprise on Ricky's face. I tell them all about how I was a week from quitting college, how that's why I went to work for her and Patrick and answered the ad. How I have more debt on my shoulders than I ever thought I'd be responsible for and I know this isn't what my parents would have wanted for me. And yet, I wouldn't have it any other way right now.

"Oh, come here, baby girl," Scarlett says. There is no judgment. No pity. She hands me the arrow and helps me aim. I let go. Something unsprings, breaks, and I feel that freedom of the arrow.

Ricky starts to walk away toward the Jenga game, but I clear my throat. I give Scarlett a meaningful look.

"Where do you think you're going?" Scarlett asks him. "You're next."

Ricky smirks. "For lessons or target practice, luv?"

I go over to Kayli, River, and Mari. The Jenga tower wobbles on the deck table precariously.

River lifts her chin in the direction of the bull's-eye. "How much do you want to bet they're going to screw tonight?"

"I don't need to take that bet," Kayli laughs, her cheeks pink. "I *know*."

"No one fights that way unless they're into each other," Mari says, poking my side. "You should *knoooow*."

I touch the center of their Jenga tower and it comes crashing down. They threaten to kill me, but I run inside to check on the turkey.

When the turkey's finally ready, we gather in the warm living room to eat and go around saying the things we're thankful for.

"I'm thankful I've allowed myself to take time off when I need it," Kayli says.

Mari follows, raising her glass. "I'm thankful for you all welcoming me into your home. It's rough being away from my family around the holidays."

River holds Hutch's hand and whispers something to him. "I'm thankful Hutch is letting me elope and not be a bridezilla. You're all invited to our Caribbean wedding, by the way. And also, to having Lena around."

I feel the tears bubbling to my eyes, but Patrick grabs my hand and squeezes. I mouth a thank-you to her and reach over the table to bump fists.

"For found family," Hutch says, raising a glass.

"I'm thankful for deadline extensions and last-minute party preparations," Scarlett says, and we all laugh. I notice how she licks her bottom lip and seems to chance a glance at Ricky. "But honestly, I'm thankful for all of you. It's my second holiday since the divorce but the first one that I'm not alone. It means so much to me."

"Glad to be here, Duchess," Ricky says to her, his voice husky and playful. Even *my* toes curl when he speaks like that.

Ricky stands, stuffing one hand in his pocket. "I'm thankful for Scarlett." We all turn to her, feeling the same gratitude for this woman. "For not giving up on trying to reach me. For opening up her home so I can be here. For taking care of Patrick. I've had a great couple of years professionally, and a shitty one personally, what with losing one of my balls and all."

"Ricky," Patrick says, half standing.

"I'm well, Pat," Ricky assures, and Pat settles back. "Clean bill of health now. I'll show you the scans. This isn't about me. Like I was saying. The ups and downs—they'll always be there, but as long as you have family, nothing else matters."

We cheer, and I can feel the tension in Patrick by the way he squeezes my hand.

Everyone looks at me. "I'm thankful that I finally decided to continue my dream because I got to meet all of you. To Scarlett for giving me a job. To Patrick for—" I look up at him, and I lose the words I want to say because none of them are enough. "For being everything. When I'm with you, I don't feel homesick because—I guess—I'm already home."

My cheeks feel hot as Patrick tugs me to him and presses a kiss on my lips.

Patrick's next. He looks around the room, smooths out the front of his shirt nervously but when he speaks, he's sure.

"I'm thankful for the patience of everyone in this room. I gave up on myself a long time ago and the only reason I'm still here is because you didn't. Scarlett, Kayli." He looks at me. "And you, Lena. You brought me back to life."

I look into his eyes and I want to tell him how much I love him. But when I do, I want it to just be the two of us.

"Cheers," Scarlett says, and we toast one final time.

We eat until we're too stuffed to move. We move the party into the backyard, where Hutch and I build a giant fire from the wood they chopped. Kayli and Mari dance with River, and Ricky whispers something to Scarlett that makes her blush.

Pat and I FaceTime our siblings. Ari is adorable when she's with him, and Jack is so charming, Mari comes over and tries to steal Patrick's phone to check him out.

When we're ready to leave, Hutch and River give us a ride back. Kayli and Mari are spending the night.

At home, Pat and I shower and fall into a Thanksgiving coma. I doze off, sleeping in the crook of Patrick's arm, my leg across his body, his hand on my rump.

"Good night, Pat."

"Lena?"

"Mm-hmm?"

"You can paint me for your project."

I half think I'm already dreaming that he's telling me this, and still, I find his mouth in the dark. His tongue. His throat. I slide on top of him, feeling the delicious throb of his cock. I decide I am not as full as I thought because I will always make room for the way Patrick feels inside of me.

17
Patience

PAT

December

The first time I was on a set for *American Speed,* I was cocky. I walked in there knowing that I had the lead role. I fucked up over and over, forgot my lines, and I never apologized to the hundreds of people I delayed with my bullshit. I never thanked the crew, the director, my co-stars for how many times I was wrong. I don't know why everything went so quickly to my head. When I was with the boys of Mayhem City, I worked harder than I'd ever had. I wanted to be good. I wanted to be seen. But after the movie, I felt like I was being given my dues and then no one could tell me anything.

Standing naked in Lena's studio, I feel the heat of anxiety I didn't have when I was filming. I'm aware of the sunlight refracting from the snow outside. It's been snowing for a week since Thanksgiving, and we haven't left the house. I've been mentally preparing myself for this moment, but now that I'm in here, I don't know what to do with my body.

"Where do you want me to stand?" I ask, tugging off my shirt and boxers. I hold them in my fists, and she takes them from me.

"What do you do before your workouts?"

"Stretch."

"Then do that a little while I finish setting up."

She's in my long johns and a Wonder Woman tank top that's covered in paint, despite the apron wrapped around her neck and waist. Her hair is tied neatly into a bun and three skinny brushes are pierced through the center. My little artist. I would do anything to keep that smile on her face, because as she looks at me, I don't feel bare or exposed. I feel like I am exactly where I need to be.

She moves me like a mannequin, adjusting my arms so that I don't look as stiff as I feel. It almost reminds me of the way Ricky used to adjust my stance when I was dancing, only when Ricky did it, I wasn't sporting a semi.

"Don't even think about it," she says, warningly, but still biting that sexy bottom lip.

I have no idea what she's doing on the other side of that canvas as she paints, but for the next week, we rinse and repeat. Being naked for Lena this way makes me feel aware of my body in different ways. I'm not hiding. I'm letting her put me on display. The promise I make to her is that I can't see the painting until it's done. When she isn't painting me, she's painting other things. I lose her to this studio, but it's where she belongs. She works day and night and all I can do is help with what she needs.

One night, after a long session of me standing on my feet, I complain that I need a treat. She gets on her knees and takes my dick into her mouth, licking me until I come on the strip of canvas that covers the floor. I return the favor by laying her flat and drinking my fill of her. When she comes, she kicks out with her leg, accidentally knocking over the watercolor bins behind us. The water is cold and she squeals.

"Turn around," I tell her, and she barks, "*You* turn around."

But she does it anyway, rolling onto her belly. I spread her legs with my knees and guide my dick into her folds. Her hands spread on the canvas leaving smudges of her handprints in blues and pinks and greens, each and every color mixing in together. Even my knees drag the splashes on the blank canvas as I pound into her. There's paint all over our skin, and just before I feel ready to come, she slips off me. She pushes me to the ground and climbs onto my dick. We tussle that way, fucking every way we possibly can, making a mess of color and sweat.

When we're finished, my hair is stiff with paint and probably more.

"You'd make a good redhead." She laughs when she sits on my abs.

"How dare?" I ask and that makes her fold in half with giggles.

"I honestly don't think we'll ever be clean," I tell her.

"I like you a little dirty." She bites at my ear.

She decides to keep that canvas and stretches it on a frame when she's satisfied with the colors.

LENA

I finish my painting of Patrick in mid-December, which gives me just enough days to make sure it dries properly before I have to show my work to Professor Meneses.

I am proud of the work I put into making sure he looks like the man I love. Just thinking that—love—keeps surprising me. That feeling has been there for so many months, but I never let myself say it. I want to believe that he's having the same emotions on his end, but a part of me is scared. I've never said it to someone and meant it. When I tell Patrick that I love him, I don't want to take it back.

The night before I have to bring my painting in for show, I make dinner. I can't remember the last time I cooked, except for the help I put into Thanksgiving dinner. Patrick has taken care of our meals, including doing the things around the house.

Cooking relaxes me and helps me focus and is an excuse to sing around the kitchen. While the pernil roasts and the rice cooks, we sort the books in the living room.

"Isn't this going to make it harder to find a book I *want* to read?" Patrick asks, putting the last blue book into the blue section.

"Don't ruin my Pinterest vision. We have the color spectrum

on one wall and the black-and-white gradient on the other side. This is the shelf for the books you're reading and they can be any color. That way, you actually keep track of what you're reading."

He blows a raspberry on his palms, but keeps on sorting.

When we're finished, we both survey the room.

"Are those all the boxes?" he asks.

We framed the pictures from his family and placed them around the wall. There's still a spot over the mantel, but I've got a surprise painting that I haven't shown him yet.

"That's all. Congratulations on your new home, Mr. Donatello." I get on my toes and stare into his jade-green eyes.

"Thank you, Lena."

"Oh, your manners are so sexy," I tease.

Just then, Ari texts me.

"How's she doing?" Patrick asks.

"She says she's super stressed about tests and wants to run away."

Patrick breaks down the empty boxes, and frowns. "Should we be worried?"

I like that he says "we."

"She'd run away here, so maybe."

He shrugs, not looking at me as he cuts and folds. "We have plenty of rooms. I'm sure there's one we haven't fucked in."

I want to laugh, but she sends me a sad-faced selfie in her room. I stand in front of the rainbow bookshelves and smile. I send her that photo. Patrick comes around me from behind and kisses my left cheek while I look into the camera. I snap the photo.

"I think this is our first photo together," I say.

"Let me see."

He takes a deep breath as we look at it. We are perfect. The hundreds of pearly scars are like the tail end of a shooting star on his cheek.

"Send that one to me," he murmurs on my skin.

When he kisses me, I get spinning, dizzying lust that clouds my thoughts.

I send it, and then hook my fingers around his waistband. "I have a surprise for you."

"Really?"

I lead him down the hall to my studio. "Ready?"

"Ready."

My studio is all cleaned up. My paintings are wrapped in brown paper so I can take them to class next week. The one that's of Patrick is covered in a white bedsheet. I want his approval before I pack it up.

When I unveil the painting, I watch his facial expression. At first, it is frozen, like he's too stunned to move. Then, his smile creeps up slowly, baring his teeth. His eyes roam the canvas from top to bottom, my own excitement building with his silence.

"*Well*, what do you think?" I ask tentatively.

He takes my hands in his. "It's incredible, and I'm not just saying that because I'm the subject matter."

"You know this has to be up in the gallery for a week, right? My teachers and classmates and the student body will see it."

He presses his forehead against me. "You've told me a dozen times, Lena."

"I just want to make sure you're okay."

"I think I am. I'm terrified about what people will say when they see me. I've spent so much of my professional life caring about this one thing. But I feel like I'm letting the world see this version of me. I get to choose it. You're helping me control that."

"So, you're telling me you like it."

"I love it, Lena." He lifts my chin with his finger. He takes a deep breath, and a part of me knows what he's going to say. Has hoped he'd say it, because if he doesn't, I will. "I—I love you."

I slip my hands under his shirt and feel the speed of his heart. There is no turning back for me once I say this. "I love you, too, Pat."

18
Breakup in a Small Town

PAT

I can't sleep that night. I know all of the things I told Lena, and I meant them. Mostly. The biggest one being that I love her. I've never loved anything or anyone the way I love her, with the exception of my family, and that's a different kind of love. I want Lena to be my family. I want her to be my everything.

And yet, I can't shake the thoughts of what will happen when she takes that painting to school. I shoot Chris a text. I haven't talked to him since Thanksgiving because I've felt better than ever. It was a little bit of a surprise seeing him there, but I can understand why Kayli had suggested him in the first place. I also send Jack a text message asking him for an update about whether or not he'll be home for Christmas.

By dawn, I realize I'm not getting any more than the couple of hours of fitful sleep I managed. It's strange that this is the first time since truly knowing Lena that I am this restless. While Lena's still knocked out, I decide I want to surprise her. I get into my truck, buckle up, and for the first time in nearly a year, I drive.

There is no one on the snow-covered roads but me. For the first half hour, I clutch the wheel hard, my shoulders tense. When I was a kid, our parents used to drive to the Christmas-tree lot nearby. Ronan and Jack and I would wander around the rows of giant pines and pretend we were in the North Pole. I wasn't going to decorate for Christmas since Lena was going to be gone and Jack and I haven't done that since our parents passed. But things are different now. I'm different.

Aren't I?

When I get to the lot, they aren't even open yet, but the guy on the grounds makes an exception because I pay in cash. He stares at my face the entire time, the scent of coffee and cigarettes clinging to his thick jacket. I am an oddity to him. I will be an oddity to anyone who sees me.

"Do I know you from somewhere?" he asks.

I shrug. "Did you go to Bozeman High?"

He shakes his head.

"Then I don't think so."

I carry the giant pine tree over my shoulder with one long-held breath, then drop it in the bed of my truck. As I drive home, my phone starts blowing up. I don't check it because I don't want to be distracted. Call me paranoid, but even though the road is empty, I don't want to take the chance. Worry takes over. I realize I didn't leave a note for Lena before I left. I thought I'd have more time.

I pull over and flip through the notifications. Scarlett. Chris. Miriam called me three times. Jack. Fallon and Aiden even. People I haven't talked to in years. Daisy. A wave of heat crashes over me as my heart races. I don't read any of the messages, but I know enough that something *just* happened.

Lena's name is the only one I care about. I try to call but it goes to voicemail. I have a single bar, but her latest text comes through.

Where are you? she texts.

Me: *I went out.*

Me: *What happened, are you okay?*

Lena: *I'm fine. Don't come home. Go to Scarlett's.*

I don't like the sound of that one bit, so I hit the gas and turn on the road leading home. My heart beats like a war drum the entire way there, and I understand why she wanted me to stay away.

As I crest the hill, I see her in our living room pacing back and forth through the glass. There's someone with a camera standing at my front door. I don't know why it takes me so long to see the others. Because I wasn't looking for them, I was looking for Lena. Half a dozen more men and women pour out of a white van and surround my truck.

The paparazzi have finally descended on me. The question is, why now?

I click on the voicemail from my agent.

"Hey, babe, it's Miriam. Why didn't you *tell* me you were out and about? We could've done something really big with this. Don't worry, there are still opportunities. *People*'s offer is still good as long as it's an exclusive. They want an interview with you and the girl. Call me back when you get this."

Me and the girl?

My heart feels like it's shot straight out of my body and a sick, twisting feeling returns, slick and twisted and all too familiar. I kill the engine and grip the steering wheel. I consider getting out of the car. I consider hitting reverse and running. But as the swarm of reporters encroach, a shotgun blast rings from the tree line.

Scarlett's black Jeep is zooming in our direction. The photographers race back into the van.

Why are they here?

I should go inside to get the answer, but I am frozen inside my truck. I clutch my phone in hand and search the internet for my face. For the photo I know I'm going to find.

Lena grinning into the camera, and me kissing her cheek, right there for the world to see.

LENA

I wake to the incessant buzz of my phone.

"Pat, is that you?" I ask, and roll over to find an empty bed and an eerie silence. I unlock my phone and scroll through a dozen text messages from Ariana.

I'm sorry.

She took my phone and gave it to her boyfriend.

I'm so, so sorry, Lena.

Please tell Pat I didn't know what she was going to do.

Panic shakes me from head to toe when I don't find Patrick in the house. Did he see the photo posted online? Did he decide to leave instead of confront me? I realize the picture's been up for hours, the traction building now that it's morning. But Ari's messages are from midnight, after we went to sleep. I didn't feel Patrick wake up. I wouldn't know when he left.

I rake my fingers through my hair and try to figure out what to do. Mostly, I pace around the house in panic.

The caption on the XYZ Instagram page reads: *Sources from the Martels have shared a photo of* American Speed *actor and his new lady love. Could the disgraced star be ready for a second chance? This is the first photo that's surfaced of Patrick Halloran since the accident that ended his career and nearly claimed his brother's life. Does everyone deserve a second chance? Stay tuned for our coverage leading up to the anniversary of the scandalous film.*

I call Ariana but she doesn't pick up. I call my stepmother and leave her a voicemail that I hope my dead parents forgive me for. When a white van crests the hill with out-of-state plates, I call Scarlett. She tries to calm me down, but how can I calm down when there are photographers with cameras all over the place?

I text and call and scream for Patrick. He can't come home to this. But he hasn't answered. All I can do is resort to pacing until his truck finally appears, soon followed by Scarlett's Jeep. The boom of a shotgun causes the strangers and trespassers to scatter. My mind is whirling, my heart twisting with fear.

I hear his heavy boot tread on the stairs before I see him.

"How could you?" he shouts.

He thinks I did this. *The Martels . . .*

His face is enraged. He smells like pine and the sky just before it snows. His eyes are full of resentment. Hurt. This is not my Patrick.

"Pat—"

"Don't—don't say my name. You did this. You used me. You—"

Scarlett and Ricky race up behind him, their faces green with fear and adrenaline. Ricky makes like he's going to pull Patrick back, to stop him from saying the cruel things that are coming out of his mouth.

I put my hand up. Whatever Patrick needs to say should be let out.

"You conned me. Is this what you were working toward all along? Waiting until I let my guard down so what—? How could you?"

I have already cried all the tears I ever will for Patrick Halloran, so it is easy to look into his eyes and not shed a single more tear. His words cut like a rusty knife, but I don't flinch. I don't defend myself. I don't have to.

I listen. I watch the *moment* he realizes he might be wrong, that he's too angry. That my love, our love, can't heal him.

You take in too many strays.

The words echo in my head because I know I do. I am too soft, too broken. I give and give until there is nothing left of me.

"If you really think any of what you said is true," I say, my voice wobbly like someone plucked a wrong chord. "Then you never knew me at all."

He remains quiet.

After everything that's happened between us, Patrick chooses to turn and stomp back down that hallway, into his bedroom. He slams the door and shuts the world out again.

"Lena—" Scarlett starts to say.

"You guys should go home." I stare out the glass window. Everything inside me feels numb. "I'll be in touch, I promise."

But the moment they leave, I go to the pool house and make an emergency phone call. "Hey, I'm sorry to bother you. Can you give me a ride?"

19
Moscas En La Casa

PAT

By the time I reemerge from my room, it is dark outside, and Lena is gone.

She didn't take any of the clothes she kept in my room, but she must have had a backup in the pool house.

I sit in front of the library fireplace, covered in pine needles, by myself when Scarlett and Ricky return. I'm surprised he's still here, but now's not the time to ask the circumstances.

"She was always planning on leaving," I tell Scarlett.

I don't know what possessed me to bring that fucking pine tree from the back of my truck into the house at a time like this, but I just needed something to do. Locking myself in the gym didn't feel right. Hitting the punching bags makes me think of her. Hell, everything in this house makes me think of her because this is her house. But the pine tree—that is for my brothers, my parents. It's so tall it fills out the room, even though the branches haven't dropped yet.

"Don't start that," Scarlett says, her arms folded over her chest. Her hair is loose and wind tossed, probably from the Jeep ride. Ricky always loved long hair. I don't have time to process how weird it is that they're together and that he's still here after Thanksgiving, but due to the situation, none of us address it.

"You know damn well that Lena wouldn't sell those photos to the *fucking paparazzi,* Patrick," Scarlett keeps talking. "I swear, you take one step forward and a hundred back. This time you went too far."

I raise my voice. "The caption said—"

"It doesn't *matter* what it said. You've never trusted them before, why would you trust them now?"

I shake my head. Why do I want to believe this? Why do I want to believe the worst of someone I professed my love to last night? "She took the picture."

"You don't know what happened," Ricky says solemnly. "You didn't let her explain."

"Don't you start with me," I tell him. "You get sick once and all of a sudden you start giving people second chances and throwing around your newfound wisdom?"

"I've given you more than second chances, kid. You know I have. Fuck me, Patrick, you're right back where you started. Don't you see?" He takes my face into his hands. He shakes me, like it'll snap me out of *this* wretchedness. I am not a good man. "You keep pushing us away. You said it yourself."

I relive that moment, yelling at her. When I was finished, I knew I was wrong. I knew I was wrong and I couldn't take it back.

If you really think any of what you said is true, then you never knew me at all.

I lie on the floor, the weight of today bearing into me. Anger makes my voice hard. "Then who was it?" I can't imagine Ariana doing this.

"Her stepmom," Scarlett says, walking to the bar cart and pouring herself and Ricky two fingers of whiskey. "On Thanksgiving, Lena told me she's been sending her money for months even though she stole Lena's identity."

"Wait, what?"

Scarlett sighs, and I know this is the most disappointed she's ever been in me. She won't even look into my eyes. She tells me about why Lena came to work for us this summer. I always thought it was because she needed the tuition money, but I had no idea that Lena's stepmother put her in real, terrible debt. On top of taking care of her sister, of me. On top of everything.

"She didn't tell me," I say.

Scarlett sighs and shrugs, not having an answer.

"I've fucked up."

"Yeah, you have, Patrick," Scarlett says.

I told Lena that she brought me back to life, but it wasn't her job to keep me breathing. It was mine. Why didn't I stop to think? Why didn't—

"Where is she?" I ask.

She shakes her head. Drains her glass and leaves it on the bar cart. "I don't know. And I'm not sure I'd even tell you if I did."

Scarlett leaves, but Ricky stays with me.

We watch the fire, Ricky in my favorite chair and me cross-legged on the floor. No matter how long I sit in front of this fire, I can't thaw out, I can't stop shivering. After a while, I turn to him and ask, "What do I do?"

He sips his drink.

I realize, I've never seen him in a T-shirt and jeans. I wonder, is this what it's like looking at Clark Kent?

"You make amends, kid," he says. "And hope to high heaven you're not too late."

But when I don't hear from Lena the next night, or the next, I know that I am.

LENA

I arrive in New York City with fewer things than I left with. When anyone returns home, they usually come back having gained something—wealth, success, *things*. But what do I have? A bloody heart, the single painting I could pass off as a carry-on, and the backpack I used to keep in case there was a family emergency and I had to race home. When River picked me up, I grabbed my purse hanging in the kitchen, and I didn't let myself look back.

River didn't ask questions, and I didn't offer any answers. I did tell her that I needed to go home, and she said she understood. That she'd been there. Out of everyone I've met, even Mari, she knew I made the right call.

I booked the next flight that would get me to LaGuardia Airport, but I had to spend the night in the Seattle terminal and make a connection in Boston. It took two days, but I drowned my sorrows in the cheapest beer each airport had to offer and kept myself distracted by sketching in a tattered old notebook I found in a pocket of my backpack. I turned my phone off and put it away. I should have told Ariana that I was coming home, but I didn't want Sonia to know. Has Patrick called me? Did he snap out of that anger?

I shake my head. I tell myself it doesn't matter. He never knew me at all. There are only so many times you can forgive someone for the same mistake. And despite it all—I haven't cried. Maybe that means something.

Maybe I've used up all my tears. Maybe I only cry during animated movies and when superheroes fail because they're dependable. Maybe I cry when something is truly terrible and a part of me knows that Patrick and me were never going to work out. What's the point of crying when I knew the outcome?

Maybe I don't care. As I take the M60, the hissing of the bus's door opening and closing at every stop, I try to convince myself of that. I feel numb, empty in a way I haven't since I accepted my dad wasn't going to get better.

But I know, if I *didn't* care, I wouldn't have flown halfway across the country to outrun my feelings. Maybe if I can keep moving, I can stop the heartbreak from settling in.

Sometimes retracing your steps helps with remembering something you lost. I get off at the same subway station the way I did days and nights when I lived here. I walk down the same three streets and pass the same delis and restaurants, the familiar scent of seared meat from the kabab stands and coffee from the Colombian spot on the corner. This is the part of home I love.

I walk up the clean, tiled steps of the building. The super decorated to the nines right after Thanksgiving. The halls smell like pine and cinnamon. Most of the doors have Christmas wreathes hanging from their front doors, but us? We have an eviction notice.

The ground feels like it's become wet concrete and I'm sinking into it.

"Dammit, Ari, why didn't you tell me?"

I crush the eviction notice in my fist and let myself in. At least the key still works.

The house, to put it delicately, is a fucking mess. Dirty dishes are stacked sky high and when I take a step, there's something sticky on the floor. The garbage hasn't been thrown out in what looks like weeks. The living room is littered in beer bottles and the scent of cigarettes is more powerful than the garbage.

This is not the pristine apartment I grew up in. The vase in the living room that my mom and I always kept full of flowers, is full of cords and used batteries. There are jackets and shoes all over the place. The only clean part is Ariana's bedroom. I don't even try to open Sonia's room.

It's nine in the morning and neither of them are home. I dump my bag on Ari's bed. This used to be my room. There's still one of my Backstreet Boys posters in the corner, which I glued so well that it will only come off when they wreck the wall apart. My mother chose this color, even though the rest of the house is white, she let me paint it. We picked it out together at the Home Depot, a pale pink orange. Coral. Salmon.

Ari's little touches are here, though. She's not into posters, but she has pictures of her friends at the movies, school halls, posing in the park. Was I really going to disrupt her life and take her away from everything that ties her here? If I had to make the decision over the summer, I would have. It would have been so I could have the best of both worlds.

I stare at my tired reflection in the closet mirror and say, "Enough."

I want to sleep and shower, but not in that bathroom. So, I clean.

I slip on rubber gloves to clean out the shower mold. I think of how my stepmom never even lifted a broom to clean when I was growing up. Was it my job to teach Ari? Was it my job to stay? I cycle through those kinds of questions, sweating as I move from the tub to the sink to the floors. I rip out the shower curtain and throw it out. I keep a supply of clear plastic ones in the hallway closet, and to no one's surprise, they're still there. I crush up newspaper and clean the glass like my mom taught me.

I move on to the living room. In an empty box, I throw everything that doesn't have a place. The shoes and cables and batteries and empty bottles of nail polish. I work my way across the floors, sweeping, then swiffering, then wetjetting. I wash the dishes and throw out the truly terrible ones that even I don't want to touch.

I do the best job I can, and then five hours later, I'm ready for a shower. I even get in an hour of sleep before I wake up to the sound of the front door opening.

"Ari?" Sonia's voice rings out.

I climb out of my old bed, my body is still wired. I step into the hallway. By the look of surprise on her face, I'm the last person she thought she'd see.

"What are you doing here?" Sonia asks.

Her arms droop from the weight of her shopping bags.

"Good to see you, too," I say. "I love what you've done with the place."

She sniffs and averts her gaze as she makes a right to the living room. She dumps her things and takes off her jacket and gloves. Her long brown hair is freshly blown out, and her eyebrows and nails are manicured.

"Bloomingdale's," I say, venom in my voice. "You couldn't start with paying the *rent* after selling the photo?"

"You don't know it was me." She narrows her eyes at me, but then lets go of the farce. How does she have the nerve to act like she didn't do anything wrong? "Someone was going to do it. You're stupid for sitting on that for so long, Maggie."

"Don't fucking call me that."

"God, sorry, *Lena*. You were always an uppity little girl."

"And you were always a selfish bitch. It wasn't enough that you had to bring down my dad during the end of his life? You had to put Ari in danger?"

She points a glittering nail at me. "Don't talk about things you know nothing about. You don't know how hard my life has been. You think because you give your sister an allowance that you know what it's like to be a single parent?"

"I'm not trying to be her mom," I say, my voice calm despite the barrage. I'm tired of people yelling and accusing me of things I'm not responsible for doing. "Ariana should come first. Your *family* should come first."

"Exactly! That's why I did it."

"No, you did it for yourself! I sent you money *every* week even though I should have put you in jail for what you did to me."

She raises her eyebrows and gasps. "What *I* did to you? A little loan was the least you could do after I spent my life's savings on your father's hospital bills. And even then, they're still coming! It was just a few credit cards. But Little Lena is always thinking about herself."

I blow a slow breath despite my heart slamming against my rib cage. You can't fight with someone who is this delusional. "It's not over, you know. I still have the paperwork."

"And what? You're going to put your sister's *mother* in jail?" She's practically gloating.

You take in too many strays.

"I used to think that Ari would never forgive me, but you know what? I'm okay if she's angry with me for the rest of my life just to make sure you get what's coming to you."

For the first time, there's real fear in her eyes. Unlike the other times, I am done backing down. She's taken my dad's happiness, and years from mine. She's taken Patrick's safety. She's taken the work I did on that last semester because I'm going to miss the presentation next week. But she'll take Ariana's future over my dead fucking body.

"Do you even care if you get turned out on the street? Was the eviction notice not high enough on the door for you to see? What's supposed to happen to Ari?"

"God, Lena! That's not going to happen because you would pay it!"

"I already did!" I yell, my eyes wild. "How? How am I supposed to work and go to school?"

She's flustered and her voice is high-pitched. "What do you want me to do?"

"Do you even care what happens to your kid?" I breathe fast, tears finally trying to surface. "No, you know what, I was supposed to be your *daughter,* too. I was eleven when you moved in. You never even gave me so much as a hug. Do you know how hard Ari is working to get through the day?"

She rubs her temples, pacing around the living room in her heeled boots. I'm running a knife at the seams of her life and I'm not even sorry.

"Then take her! Take Ariana and leave me alone. Does anyone care about how I was the one who got set up with two kids I didn't ask for? I thought your father was going to take care of me, but he *didn't*. He died. Who was going to take care of *me,* Lena?"

At the sight of Sonia's tears, mine dry up. Some people just aren't built to handle certain kinds of pressure. It doesn't make it okay for the way she's treating me. But I know that I can't expect her to be the mother I lost.

In that moment, Ari steps out from the kitchen hall. When did she come in? She must have been here before her mother because she's in her school uniform. I know she's heard it all from the tears running down her face.

"You said everything would be better!" Ari shouts, then runs into her room and slams the door. The thing is, I can't tell if she's talking to her mother or me.

"You see what you did?" Sonia asks, slapping her hands against her thighs before taking her bounty to her room.

I feel like I'm trying to stop myself from coming undone, but now everything is out in the open. The only thing I can do is stitch myself back up.

I make a cup of coffee and sit at the kitchen table. My mom used to sit here every morning, making her café con leche before the rest of us woke up. It was her meditation, her moment to think and write down the things she needed to get done. I use one of Ari's notebooks and do the same.

For the first time since I left Montana, I turn on my phone. First, I need a place to stay and find one on Airbnb I can check into later tonight. I have dozens of notifications, and my heart gives a painful squeeze when I see Patrick's name. But he's not the one I need right now.

I call my teachers and counselors at school, and finally Kayli.

"Hey," I say. "Remember when you said you knew lawyers? I'm finally ready to cash in that favor."

20
Te Duele

PAT

Christmas Eve

I wake up to half a dozen men in my bedroom, which is not a fantasy I'd ever thought I'd have but I roll with it. I must be dreaming because the guys of Mayhem City are gathered around. I know exactly what's going to happen when Aiden and Vin glance at each other and smile.

"What the fuck?" I yell as Aiden and Vin launch themselves on my bed. One of them hits my ribs with his elbow like we're in the ring of an MMA fight. I work my way out of the tangle of my comforter. "What are you guys doing here?"

Fallon pushes himself up from leaning on the wall. His blue-green eyes lock on mine, and for a moment, I relive that terrible two-day ride. He doesn't approach me, giving me space. But I decide to nut-up and hug my brother.

"We got an SOS from Ricky," he says, and slaps my back.

Vin makes an "aww" sound from the bed, and Aiden chucks a pillow at his head.

"You should really start locking your doors," says Gary, a smirk on his clean-shaven face. His brown hair is longer, but still not as long as mine. "Anyone could walk in."

Something wells up in my chest as I greet all of them. Even Lucky Kris and Greg are here, and I haven't seen them since before Vegas. They're all here. I wonder how many times I'm allowed to apologize before my words stop meaning anything. But I have to start somewhere.

"Guys, I'm sorry. For everything. That night, I was a dick to each and every one of you." I look around the room. *Make amends,* Ricky had said. "I can't believe you're here after some of the things I did. Aiden—"

Aiden sits up against my headboard. He combs fingers through his black hair away from his eyes, a beard cropping up. "We would have come sooner if you'd called."

"I guess, part of me didn't want to test that theory."

Wonderboy wags a finger to draw attention to himself. The only reason I can tell him apart from his twin brother, Vin, is the new beard. Did everyone grow a fucking beard in the last year?

"I want to point out," Wonderboy says, "I wasn't even invited to the premiere. But I'm not bitter."

They all laugh, and some of the weight on my chest the last week alleviates. "Come, I'll make breakfast."

"Yo, you can cook?" Lucky Kris asks, genuinely confused.

We go downstairs to the kitchen. Vin plugs in his music and the rest of the boys disperse to have a good look around. Aiden stays to help me get things out of the kitchen.

"Spit it out," Aiden says. "You have this look like you want to ask me something."

The last time I saw him, he was getting ready to propose to his girl and I told him not to do it. "How's Faith?"

Aiden rips open the packet of breakfast sausages, a wide smile on his face. "She's good. Engaged. To me, in case you were wondering."

"Good, I'm happy for you, really." I crack eggs into a silver bowl next to the counter. "When's the wedding?"

Aiden smiles, and when he does, he still looks so young. He reminds me of Jack. Jack who isn't coming home, either. He opens the cabinet and has a look around. "Next year. We're taking things slow. Holy shit, where did you get this?"

He brings out a bottle of seasoning. It's the stuff Lena puts in everything. I frown, but his laugh is contagious and in moments,

I'm spilling my guts to him. Everything I can say out loud about Lena, I do. The other guys come in and listen to me go over the highlights. This *thing* I've been missing feels like it's starting to piece back together as I talk about her. Everything Lena did and said that shook me awake out of a long sleep. Everything I did to ruin it.

Aiden takes over the cooking and Greg brings out the beer in the fridge. This is the first time I've had people in the house this way. They're a little invasion, opening drawers and closets, but that's family. That's my family.

We eat standing around the counter, piling eggs and sausages drenched in ketchup. Vin fills his orange juice with the expensive champagne I was saving for New Year's.

"Look, we've all fucked up," Aiden says.

Gary huffs and puffs. "Speak for yourself, I'm a prince."

"Fine, most of us have fucked up," Aiden continues. There's something changed about him. Easy. Confident. Grown. "Which means we're experts on groveling."

"Ricky's girl says you need help with a romantic gesture," Greg says.

"But you have to mean it," Fallon says, and for the first time, I see the ring on his wedding finger. Fallon got married and I wasn't there.

"I mean it," I say, knowing that this is my last chance. "I love her. I love her more than my own life. But Scarlett already told me Lena's unenrolled from Bozeman. She's not coming back."

"Leave it to us," Vin says, with a wink.

"You've never made a romantic gesture in your life," Wonderboy says.

"Listen, Tweedledee and Tweedledum, go get the shit out of the car," Fallon says, sighing like a—well—dad. I don't tell him as much, though.

"What stuff?" I ask.

"Decorations, bro," Greg says, making a face. "Christmas is in a week and this place looks like a ghost town."

"Don't worry," Aiden says, which is exactly what makes me worry. "We have a plan."

"Come on," Fallon says, slapping my shoulder. "We brought presents."

LENA

The Airbnb I rented through New Year's is right by Central Park. Despite it being in a prime neighborhood, it was super inexpensive. Within a week of coming home, I've managed to get my paperwork together to file transfer papers from Montana State to Hunter College, as well as adoption papers for Ariana.

As much as it irritates me that Patrick never cashed my rent checks since September, at least I have some extra money I can show in my bank statement. My stepmom is making it easier by giving me legal guardianship in the meantime. It's the holidays, and offices have come to a halt, so I know it's going to take time. I don't think I'll be able to breathe properly until everything is signed. Not to mention, we have to find somewhere to live.

"Are you sure you're okay?" I ask Ari.

She's brushing her hair at the window with a view of the snowy Central Park. A carriage rides down the avenue and shoppers bundled in winter clothes trudge through the snow. She shrugs. "I don't know yet."

"Talk to me." I take my coffee mug across the room and sit on the wide window ledge beside her. Her hair is long and curly at the ends. She's got her mom's features, but we share our dad's long lashes and lips.

"I'm still mad at my mom, and I want to hate her. But when she calls me, it's a little bit better, I guess. I don't know why you keep ignoring Patrick's calls if you love him."

I brush her hair away. I could say something about how her mother is family, but Patrick is family, too. Or he was. "Things don't always work out."

"I know, but you were so happy. Besides, couldn't we just explain that the picture thing was my fault?"

I shake my head and drink my coffee. "It doesn't matter anymore."

But I still feel the ache of him. I had to shut down the Instagram and Snapchat accounts I only kept to stay up to date in Ari's life. I've gotten thousands of people searching for information about me and leaving me emails and comments. I've even had an offer of representation to be a *media personality,* whatever that is. The attention will die down, and I can only hope that my feelings for Pat do, too.

"Merry Christmas Eve, I *guess,*" she mutters. "At least you came home."

When Dad was with us, we would have a small party and invite the neighbors. We'd roast a slab of pork and dad would butcher my mother's empanada recipe, but we would still eat them after we broke off the burned corners. We drank Bacardi in hot apple cider and Ariana would be in charge of putting the baby Jesus in the nativity scene at midnight.

This year, we don't have decorations, but we have Chinese takeout and each other.

"Can I ask you a favor?" Ari's eyes are wide and full of mischief.

"Depends on what it is."

"Well, my friend, uh, Sarah, told me about this artist. She's so dope and amazing and she's having a show in the Lower East Side on New Year's Eve. Can we please, please, *please* go?"

I think of all the paintings I left behind in my studio. Patrick's house. After all that work, I had to call Professor Meneses and drop out. Again. I could call Kayli or Scarlett to go and get them back and ship them to me in the new year. Hell, River offered to break in in the middle of the night and load them up. She was chuckling in that serious, dark way of hers, but I knew she meant it. Maybe they belong there, away from me, marking a time in my life I can't get back.

I don't want it back, I think.

Yes, you do want him back.

I don't know if I can be around another person's work the

night before the year starts. But this year is about to be hard to Ari, being away from her mom and all. Of course, I say yes.

Then, I get a call from a number I don't recognize. Part of me is nervous that it's Patrick because the area code is 406, but after it goes to voicemail, I lock myself in the bathroom and hit play. His voice strikes a chord in my belly because he sounds just like his brother.

"Hey, Lena? This is Jack. I'm still in New York and a mutual writer friend of ours says you are, too. I know it's not my place, but I wanted to reach out and say hi, since I won't be going home any time soon. Don't feel obligated, though. Merry Christmas. Bye."

"Ari?" I shout from the bathroom.

"What?" she shouts back.

"Get dressed, we've got one present to deliver."

PAT

"Hey, stranger," I say as I knock on the door.

Jack looks up from his bed. There are crutches leaning against the door and a stack of what must be recent presents on a chair beside him. He's grown a beard, his hazel eyes bright under dark eyebrows.

"Pat," he says, like he can't believe it. Like he expected literally anyone else to come through that door but me. He scrambles out of his bed. He isn't grabbing for his crutches, but I grab him before he starts to fall. I hold my little brother and I don't let go until we both stop shaking.

"What are you doing here?" he asks.

"It's Christmas." I touch the left side of my face. It's become a habit, like I'm trying to make sure the scars are still there. "I'm on my apology tour."

I pull up a seat just as a nurse comes to check on Jack. She fusses over him, making sure he's taken his medication, that he's feeling all right, and he's eaten. She winks at me on the way out, which is a strange feeling. Even stranger, is sitting in this room.

But the day has been filled with moments like this. There was the moment in the cab, the driver's eyes going to the rearview mirror over and over again. Before that, the flight over direct to JFK. The stewardess who did a double take before schooling her face from shock and into that practiced calm, and then real kindness. No matter what the reaction has been, especially since the XYZ post, I keep moving. I get from place A to place B, like Chris said.

Some of the boys made the trip with me. But seeing Jack? I knew I had to do that myself.

"You didn't come home," I say. "I talked to your doctor. You were cleared as long as you kept up with your PT and all."

"I wanted to." He nods, but I recognize the shame in his eye. "I don't know. I've been here for so long. I'm—I'm scared of what's waiting for me. What am I supposed to do?"

"You'll figure it out. We can do it together. Even if you want to stay in the city for a while longer. We can rent something. We can even take a train home."

He shakes his head, but laughs. "There's no train home."

"Buses, then," I say. "I should have been here sooner, and I wasn't. You're my brother and I was supposed to be there for you."

"We would have been no good together," he says. "I wasn't in a good place and neither were you."

I think of our calls when he was cheerful and laughing. He always sounded like he was steps ahead of me. "You always sounded like you were fine."

He shrugs, and in this moment, I remember the boy who ran away from home and I had to find. "I wanted to put on a brave face for you."

"You don't have to do that anymore. Come home."

"Okay, Pat," Jack says, finally. "You got a place here?"

"I'm staying with the guys. Just until New Year's Day. Depending on how Aiden's plan works out."

"Aiden?" He looks surprised. "They're playing a show? Wait, are you in the show?"

I shake my head. "Definitely not. It's safe to say, my professional dancing days are over. But, there will be a different kind of show—"

Another nurse comes in, highly disappointed that Jack is going to be leaving right away. She says she'll bring boxes for his presents.

That's when I see the painting sticking out behind the boxes of sweaters, books, and DVDs. It can't be here. And yet, I recognize our faces right away. The painting is of me and Jack and Ronan. Three little boys running around on a hill. It's her color palette, her brush strokes. I know shit about art, but it has to be hers. I know her.

"Lena," I say her name. I turn to Jack, unable to ask every question running through my mind. Lena was here? Lena spoke to Jack?

He grins. "She was here yesterday and came to see me. We talked about home, about being here."

Did she talk about me? I want to ask but I don't. Everything inside me hurts. I beg every single god and spirit in the universe that I'm not too late, and this gives me a little bit of hope.

"Do I still have a shot?" I ask.

"Depends. Tell me more about Aiden's plan."

21
Waiting for Tonight

LENA

New Year's Eve

The gallery Ariana drags me to is tucked between a ramen place and a sneaker shop. Ari is in a pretty blue and green sequin dress that makes her look like a mermaid who wanted to ice skate. I was going to go with jeans and a T-shirt because that's the mood I felt. But Ari would have none of it. She marched me a couple of train stops to the mall and picked out a sleek black dress with gold accents, since my fifteen-year-old sister insisted that I needed some bling for the new year.

It has been two weeks since I've spoken to anyone from back home—back in Montana—with the exception of Kayli. On a night like tonight, I find myself missing Mari's laugher. I want to know how her finals went and if Scarlett turned in her book on time and if River picked out a wedding dress yet.

As we weave through the throngs of partygoers and news vans covering the partying all over town, I feel the kinetic energy that I've only ever been able to find in New York. There are girls in fur coats and glittering mini dresses waiting in long lines to get into clubs and parties. What would we be doing if we were in Montana? I remember the champagne we bought in preparation. I was also going to get grapes, a New Year's midnight tradition that both of my parents shared with me. I even picked out new underwear. You're supposed to pick the color of the thing you want to manifest for the new year. There's green for wealth, yellow for luck, red for love. I stick with a lace yellow because, though it might be an unsexy color, you can't have too much luck. Plus, no one is going to see it.

"Let me make sure you don't have lipstick on your teeth," Ari says, tugging my arm.

"No one will care if I do," I say.

"What if you meet a super-fly guy, Lena? What if—"

I cheese if only to get her to stop theorizing. "What's the name of this artist anyway?"

But when we step into the gallery, I am blindsided with a flash. If I wasn't wearing eyeliner, I would rub my eyes because I'm seeing things. I have to.

"Scarlett?" I ask.

She grins so hard her eyes are narrow slits crinkled by laugh lines. Her hair is brushed back in pretty auburn waves, and she's in a simple blue velvet dress. I hug her and she pats my back, smoothing it, because of course I'm crying.

"What are you doing here?"

"No tears yet," she whispers. "The night has only just started."

Clearly. The room is full of new and familiar faces. But the most arresting part is that the long, narrow gallery is full of my paintings. *My paintings.* How did they get here? I turn to Ariana, who is cheesing and giggling behind her gloved hands.

"What is this?"

"Surprise!" my little sister says, barely containing her enthusiasm.

I look back at the walls. These were all in Patrick's house. I search for him in the crowd but he isn't here.

A high-pitched squeal comes from around the corner and Mari comes running in her sharp heels. "She's here! Bring the champagne!"

There's a hot waiter dressed in all black right behind her, carrying a bottle of champagne and two glasses.

"You're early!" Mari says, her lush brown curls bouncing in a halo around her. Her minidress is gold covered in thousands of dazzling beads. "Okay, everything is perfect. Can you believe this is my first exhibit? I mean, yours, too. I always knew we would do this, but I thought it would be later. Like, way later. When he called, I wasn't sure what to do, but it came together seamlessly, really."

Her words fade away as I stare at my work from this semester. The closest is the one I gave Jack. Jack, who is standing right beside it, supported by his crutches! Seeing him blurs my sight with tears. I embrace him gently, before I'm surrounded by hugs and kisses and well wishes.

My old friends from when I worked at the Met, former classmates, cousins that only Ariana could have invited, including some of her friends and their parents. They stare at my work, especially the one of my mom and dad. Others point at a particular painting covered by a black cloth. It's the only one that isn't out in the open. My stomach twists with nerves because I know what's under there.

"Oh God," I say when I walk farther into the gallery and see the massive canvas. Pinks and greens and blues. Watercolors that were spilled when Patrick and I were rolling around it. Heat burns my cheeks to a blush as I see Professor Meneses walk up beside me.

"Tell me, Lena," she says in that very serious way of hers, tapping the gold wire of her glasses. "What medium did you use for this piece? It's frantic, almost sensual in the way you used the brush strokes."

How do you tell your art teacher that the six-foot-long canvas is a mix of acrylic, gesso, and sex juices? "I—what are you doing here?"

"I admit, this is a bit unorthodox, but when Mr. Halloran told me about your family emergency that prompted your *immediate* departure from school, he offered me a ticket to come here and give you a second chance."

I shake my head. Mr. Halloran. Patrick. I can't breathe. I can't. And somehow, I find a way to ask. "But I unenrolled—how?"

"My dear," she says, resting her slender hand on my shoulder. "I never submitted your paperwork. See you next semester. Consider yourself a B student."

As she leaves me for the cute waiter holding a tray of champagne, I go, "Wait, what do you mean a B?"

"That seems pretty fair," River says, sidling up next to me.

I nearly scream. They're all here. Hutch and Kayli. They wish me luck and tell me how much they've missed me. Kayli seems to be having her own moment as she sits beside Jack.

Bodies keep walking into the gallery, the narrow hall feels too cramped and tight, but no one seems bothered. Music pumps from the speakers and drinks and hors d'oeuvres flow.

He isn't here, I keep thinking.

I excuse myself to the bathroom once to fix my eyeliner, and Ariana follows me to help.

"How did you do this?" I ask.

She makes a zipper motion across her lips. "You'll know everything soon enough. Are you mad?"

I shake my head. "Overwhelmed. But I'm happy."

"Good. I can drink champagne, right?"

She leaves as I shout, "No!"

I give my reflection a final once-over to make sure I'm presentable. I'm at my very own art show with people here to look at my work. I can do this.

The minute I walk out, River drags me over to meet her friends. "Lena, meet my New York crew. This is Sky Lopez and her cousin, Leti, and this is Lucky Pierce and James Murphy."

They all take my hands. James winks at River. "She's Lucky Pierce Murphy now."

Lucky elbows him playfully, but I can see the love there. I search the room, a bud of hope that Patrick's face is here. But he isn't.

"Thank you all for coming," I tell them. What are the things that you're supposed to say at your own gallery when you're not prepared? Am I supposed to give a speech later? Isn't someone supposed to introduce me? I suppose that will be Mari's job later on.

"Oh, for sure," Leti says. She's a full-figured girl with brown skin and dark curly hair. "River's told us all about you."

River does her best attempt at looking abashed. "Lucky and James did the catering."

Lucky's sexy alto voice takes me by surprise. "*He* cooked. I just make sure we know where we're getting on time."

The tattooed chef keeps an arm around her waist and pulls her into a kiss. An ache rises in my throat but there is no room for that now. I get to be happy surrounded by my work and my loved ones and new friends.

"I really like this one," Sky says, pointing a pink nail at the same painting my professor favored. "Is there a story behind it?"

I need to come up with a story. River sees my deer-in-headlights expression, and steps in. But she doesn't have to create a distraction when Rick Rocket struts in with a horde of *men*.

"Holy shit," Leti says, eyeing the men dressed in fine suits. She reaches for Sky to steady herself, like she's about to faint.

River arcs a dark brow. "And here I thought *I* brought an entourage."

Each and every one of the guys is more beautiful than the other. A dark-skinned guy with a flash of white smile kisses my cheek. A guy who looks like Maluma hugs me tightly and thanks me without explanation. A bearded white guy with piercing blue-green eyes introduces himself as Fallon. Twin brothers try to pick me up, but Ricky clears his throat, and they behave.

"Someone is going to have to start explaining things soon," I tell Scarlett. Ricky is at her side. I glance back and forth at their smug faces.

"Oh, this?" Ricky says, nonchalantly pointing between him and Scarlett. "She couldn't resist my charm."

"I mean *this*," I tell Ricky. "Where is he?"

Scarlett and Ricky share a long look. It's the kind of stare you can only give the person who can read your mind because you've shared so much together.

In all the time I spent with Patrick, did I even really know him? I knew he was broken. I knew he was lost. I knew he matched my own feelings in a way I wasn't ready for. When he looked at me, I felt complete. When he held me, I felt home.

"He's making amends," Ricky says, and winks.

Why do they all keep winking at me? I mean, it's cute, but damn.

Mari does a loop around me and refills my champagne. "People are having a good time, Lena."

There's music coming from the speaker, and more people filling the room. A woman with curly brown hair and a nerdy, retro-chic look waltzes in like she owns the room.

"You're the girl," she tells me, her voice husky, and she laughs for some reason I'm not sure I understand. A drink seemingly materializes in her hand from a waitress.

"I'm *a* girl, sure," I say.

"I'm Miriam. Okay, here's my deal with Patrick." She points to the front door, her hands poised like they're holding a cigarette. "You say nothing to the press until I've made my rounds."

"Press?"

Her eyes dart to our left where River, Leti, and Sky are huddled. "Who are those girls? Do they have representation?"

Miriam leaves me, utterly befuddled, as Ariana bounces back over to me with a horde of her high school friends.

"I can't believe this is our lives," one of them says. They freak out and go try to sneak champagne on the other side of the room.

Though it's my party, I don't feel like I'm in it yet. I am a chess piece waiting to be moved while everything else happens around me. And yet, it's almost the best time of my life because my worlds have come together. There is music and food and dancing. There is my art on the walls. I turn to the black veiled painting that hushed voices speculate over. I reach for the bottom of the fabric, intent on pulling it, but Mari's hand stops me.

"Just a second," she says, her green eyes darting to the door.

The press arrives, sending everything into an excited discord. I can't do this. I am not press ready. Why didn't anyone give me a heads-up? I look around the room and no one seems to notice that I'm a ball of anxiety waiting to burst.

Then, the cameras flash and the hair on my spine prickles.

I turn around to find Patrick walking through the doors and my wretched heart revolts with desire and want.

He's in a pitch-black suit, the button-down open at the collar to reveal the scar that snakes across his collarbone and neck. His hair is cut short and styled back. He's trimmed his beard down. He is the picture of confidence, but when he takes a step to my side, I notice the tremble in his hand.

"Friends," he says, turning around, his voice powerful. Every eye in the room is on him. He shoves that trembling hand in his pocket. "For those of you who aren't here because a romance author shot blanks at a bunch of reporters outside of my house—" Scarlett gives a little curtsey. "Allow me to explain. My name is Patrick Halloran. They call me Hollywood's Fallen Star. There are other names, worse names. I deserve each and every one of them. For the last eleven months, I've been hiding from the world. Then, this artist, this force, ripped through my life. She filled my world with color, my food with far too many chilies, and she forced light where there was only darkness." He turns to me, and I know that I'm dreaming. I know that this can't be real.

Patrick traces the scars on the left side of his face, a movement that the cameras capture, a movement I've grown accustomed to in the privacy of our own little universe.

"Lena," he says. "You brought me back to life."

Instead of taking my hand, he takes the cloth over the painting and pulls. It falls in a ripple, unveiling the rendering of him— stark naked, perfect, flanked by a forest of saturated green and radiant flowers. His lip quirks as people start shouting and asking us questions faster than I can hear them all.

Mari steps in, the epitome of #bosslady. "All the paintings will be for sale except for this piece. Ms. Martel will be available for interviews in the new year."

Patrick holds out a hand, an offering I hesitate to take. When our eyes meet, I can see his remorse, his guilt about the way things went down.

It's not enough, a part of me says.

But the rest of me begs, reaches for him because I have missed his touch.

"Lena," he finally says. "Can we talk?"

I nod and Mari takes us into the manager's office in the back for some privacy. A desk is shoved into a corner with a swiveling chair. The door to the bathroom is open, the lightbulb inside flickering. I sit on the edge of the desk and Patrick stands in front of me. There is so much that I want to say to him. I want to yell and cry and tell him that I still love him. But all I say is, "You let me go."

"I'm sorry."

"You're always sorry, Patrick."

Here, alone, the bravado from outside becomes slack. He's just Patrick—the flawed, beautiful, angry, sorrowful, loving man I've gotten to know.

"I don't deserve you," he tells me. "I never did. I pushed you away and I regret every second of it."

"Then why did you do this?"

He looks up, one strand of hair too short so it flops over the scar on his left eyebrow. I take a step to him, my body heating up as I brush the irreverent hair back.

"Because I love you. Because I meant every word I just said. You brought me back to life. You, Lena, are the cure for everything."

"I don't want to be someone's cure. I don't want you to use me to fix yourself and then throw me away." But I'm spreading my hands against his chest, roaming the planes of his shoulders, strong and solid and *here*.

"What do you want, then?"

My heart is unsteady. I shouldn't be making these decisions when I am feeling too much of everything. But for the first time in so long, I am sure of this one thing. "I want you."

I said those words before and I still mean them. Now, in this cramped office stacked with papers and prints, I grip him by the collar and kiss him. I press myself against him, letting my hands explore him after our long absence.

Kissing Patrick is different this time. There are no walls between us. In a way, we were both hiding away in that house. We were so enveloped in the security of each other. His mistake was not trusting me, and I want to believe that we can work on this because I love this man in ways that have changed me from within.

"I love you, Lena," he says.

He rakes fingernails up my thighs, and I work nervous fingers on the snap of his pants. I free his erection and guide it, pushing aside my underwear. Thank goodness I chose to wear a dress. He lifts me up and pins me to the wall, nestling his face in the crook of my neck. He's fast and hungry and I know that I can't let go of this love any more than I can stop breathing.

As we both come, I kiss his face, his beautiful face. "I love you, too."

When we're finished, I clean up in the office bathroom, and make sure my makeup and hair don't scream "I just had makeup sex."

He chuckles and zips up, a pink blush on his face. "I'll go out first."

"I'm sure everyone will guess what we've been doing."

"We can always keep them guessing." With a wink, he's gone.

I stay in here a little bit longer, going through the orders Mari has taken. Lucky and her husband have bought the sex canvas, and I realize I should give it a name. Two of my paintings, landscapes of the area around the house at midnight, have been bought as well.

When I'm ready, I fold back into the party, grabbing another glass from a waiter.

"Lena! Is this piece still available?" my teacher asks. "I think you should consider taking it back to the art department for show. What's it called?"

"Actually, it's just been bought by a couple," I say. Mari darts by and puts a little red sticker on the wall beside it. I look at the painting, think of everything that led Patrick out of his dark torture chamber and me into painting again. "It's called *The Salmon Run*."

Moments before midnight, everyone gathers outside on the

street. Ari dances on the sidewalk with her friends, music out-pouring from everywhere all at once. A couple of guys are handing out sparklers, the scent of embers drifts through the air. I sink into Patrick's embrace. We are surrounded by the people we love and we've made it through the night. He presses his forehead against mine and we share a sigh of relief.

I love this city with all my heart, but I can't wait to go home.

"Lena?"

"Pat?"

"Will you kiss me at midnight?"

I can't think of another way I want to start the new year. The breath between us is a puff of warm clouds, and as I bring my lips to his, I ask, "Why wait?"

EPILOGUE:
Vivir Mi Vida

LENA

February

"Don't give Kayli a hard time," I tell Ari over the phone. "Don't move things around my studio. Don't forget to do your homework. And—"

"Oh, my gosh, Lena, *relax,*" Ari sighs, clearly annoyed with me. I haven't found a balance between guardian/sister/friend yet, but I'm sure we will. "You're only going to be gone for a weekend. Thanks for bringing me by the way."

"It's an adults-only resort," I remind her.

"That sounds gross."

"It just means there are no children clogging up the pools," I say, and can practically hear her eyes rolling to the back of her skull. "Seriously, don't burn the place down. We love you."

"Bye, Pat," Ari shouts, without a single acknowledgment to me.

Patrick grins, and takes my phone from me. We're in the resort in Playa del Carmen for the wedding. "Okay, no more cell phones. If there's an emergency, Kayli has all of the numbers to have the front desk get ahold of us. You deserve this weekend off, too."

I know he's right. January was a long month for all of us. We moved both of our siblings from New York to Montana. I've been pronounced legal guardian of Ari while we sort out the adoption papers. I had my first successful show, but then I got right back to work. Professor Meneses is already talking about being my advisor should I want to go to the grad school program. It's been a whirlwind for Patrick, too. He did one appearance on a late-night show and spoke about the accident for the first time in a year. He has the support of the director and his co-star. Though he keeps saying he doesn't want to act again. He's still finding his way.

This weekend is about rest and relaxation and celebrating our friends getting married. River and Hutch will get the low-key wedding they've always wanted.

That evening, we join everyone for the joint bachelor and bachelorette party by the pool. The guys from Mayhem City, River's New York Crew, and plus ones are all in attendance.

"What exactly happens at a joint hen-stag night?" Ricky asks, his arm slung over Scarlett's shoulder.

"Well, Hutch wouldn't let me have cigars and poker," River says with a wink at her groom. He gives a playful shake of his head.

"So, we're settling for cigars and an open bar," Hutch says.

A round of drinks appears, and Patrick picks one up. "Wait, I thought River brought us all here to dance for her?"

Hutch blanks, but then Aiden tackles Patrick into the pool. They're like this for hours. I join River and her girlfriends under the cabana.

"I don't know about you lot, but I'm going to catch up on my reading," Scarlett says, and takes the book she bought at the airport to a hammock nearby. Ricky joins her, and pretty soon, they seem to fall asleep that way. So much for reading.

"How do you smoke these?" I ask, grimacing.

River takes a slender one from the box brought over by the concierge, a gift from Ricky, and cuts off the tip. "I had this manager who used to dip the end of cigar in sambuca and then smoke it. I took a liking to it."

"One of my uncles did that," Faith, says as she slathers sunscreen on her brown skin. She's Aiden's fiancée. "Don't tell Aiden, but I'm really loving these piña coladas."

I breathe in the cigar and let myself sink into the Mexican sea and sun. Sky and a girl I haven't met join us.

"Hi, I'm Robyn," she says, and settles in.

"Okay, who's my wingwoman tonight?" Leti asks.

"I thought you and Sky were each other's wingwomen," River says, lounging in a way that made her curls look like a golden halo.

"I call dibs on Jack," Mari says, glancing over to check and see if Patrick's brother is looking at her. He is.

I laugh out loud. "Oh, is *that* why you've spent the last three weeks surprise visiting me? I see how it is."

"The heart wants what it wants," Sky says. "Shoot your shot."

"What about you, Sky?"

"I just broke off an engagement," she says. There's a round of apology and sympathy, but she gives us a smile. "It's good, really. I'm perfectly happy to help, but I'm not looking for anything. It's River's weekend!"

"River is already getting married," River says, and we all laugh. "This is just the formal part. Do me a favor. Have fun."

Lucky stands, her red bikini already leaving tan lines on her shoulders. "This is my new challenge."

"Luck!" Sky shouts, but the girl is already heading to the pool.

She stands there, and there's a back and forth between Lucky and the guys. When she returns, she's got a smirk on her face.

"What just happened?" Faith asks.

"I just arranged a water volleyball competition for your hand in marriage," Lucky says.

River cackles as Sky nearly chokes on her beer. Before she can get more riled up, Lucky comes clean.

"I'm kidding, jeez. We're all playing. Losers have to streak down the beach."

We all glance toward River. She takes a puff of her cigar and considers this. "Then we'd better not lose, ladies."

And we don't. Leti is our ringer, crushing them at the very end of the game.

At sunset, as we're all full of food and drinks and joy, the guys run across the beach stark naked while we hold their clothes and cheer. I keep my eye on the shamrock tattoo on Patrick's ass until he returns and we have to hand back their clothes.

Hutch walks back over to River and takes her back to the room to get ready for dinner.

The guys all stop and lie down on the sand in weird poses. Mari seems to know what's going on because she snorts behind her hand.

"Hey Lena," Vinny says, brushing his hair back.

"What?" I ask, waiting for the prank.

"Paint me like one of your French girls," Aiden says in a high-pitched voice.

Patrick growls. "I hate all of you."

The two of us linger on the beach after the others have gone. The sunset bleeds pinks and purples on the horizon.

"I love you, Lena," Patrick whispers in my ear. "I never want you to doubt that. I will love you as long as you let me."

When Patrick kisses me, his lips are salty and soft. When I tell him that I love him, I feel complete, certain that our story might have started in an empty house, but we made it home.

I pull back and say, "Forever, then."

Acknowledgments

As always, this novel is possible because of Natalie Horbachevsky and Sarah Elizabeth Younger. Your insights and wine-infused outlining has been pivotal for this series. I don't know what I'd do without your guidance and faith.

To my editor Norma Perez-Hernandez for championing these characters and their stories, and for believing in me. Thank you to the wonderful Kensington team, who work so hard turning my words into real-life books, Paula Reedy and the production team, the sweetest publicity squad: Jane Nutter, James Akinaka, Lauren Jernigan, Alexandra Nicolajsen, and Vida Engstrand.

To the romance community, especially Rebekah Weatherspoon, Sierra Simone, Sarah MacLean, the wonderful organizers at Lady Jane Salon, and Romance Twitter, who stands up for what they believe in. You inspire me. Here's to a brighter day and HEAs for all.

Finally, my love goes out to romance readers, especially those of you who have come back for Pat & Lena's story. I've never known such passionate readers. Never let anyone shame you for what you love. It is important and it is worth it. Thank you for keeping romance alive.

Connect with Us

Visit us online at
KensingtonBooks.com
to read more from your favorite authors, see books
by series, view reading group guides, and more.

Join us on social media

for sneak peeks, chances to win books and prize packs,
and to share your thoughts with other readers.

facebook.com/kensingtonpublishing
twitter.com/kensingtonbooks

Tell us what you think!

To share your thoughts, submit a review,
or sign up for our eNewsletters, please visit:
KensingtonBooks.com/TellUs.